A Wedding *at the* Orange Blossom Inn

BY SHELLEY SHEPARD GRAY

SISTERS OF THE HEART SERIES
Hidden • *Wanted*
Forgiven • *Grace*

SEASONS OF SUGARCREEK SERIES
Winter's Awakening • *Spring's Renewal*
Autumn's Promise • *Christmas in Sugarcreek*

FAMILIES OF HONOR SERIES
The Caregiver • *The Protector*
The Survivor • *A Christmas for Katie* (novella)

THE SECRETS OF CRITTENDEN COUNTY SERIES
Missing • *The Search*
Found • *Peace*

THE DAYS OF REDEMPTION SERIES
Daybreak • *Ray of Light*
Eventide • *Snowfall*

RETURN TO SUGARCREEK SERIES
Hopeful • *Thankful* • *Joyful*

AMISH BRIDES OF PINECRAFT SERIES
The Promise of Palm Grove
The Proposal at Siesta Key

OTHER BOOKS
Redemption

A Wedding *at the* Orange Blossom Inn

AMISH BRIDES OF PINECRAFT,
BOOK THREE

Shelley Shepard Gray

AVON
INSPIRE

An Imprint of HarperCollins*Publishers*

FIRST EDITION

Designed by Diahann Sturge

Illustrated map copyright © by Laura Hartman Maestro
Photographs courtesy of Katie Troyer, Sarasota, Florida

Library of Congress Cataloging-in-Publication Data has been applied for.

ISBN 978-0-06-233774-0

15 16 17 18 19   OV/RRD   10 9 8 7 6 5 4 3 2 1

In loving memory of
Phoebe, our beagle.
She loved napping,
kids, and pizza.
Because of that,
we loved her, too.

Your word is a lamp to guide my feet and light for my path.

PSALM 119:105

It takes both sunshine and rain to make a rainbow.

AMISH PROVERB

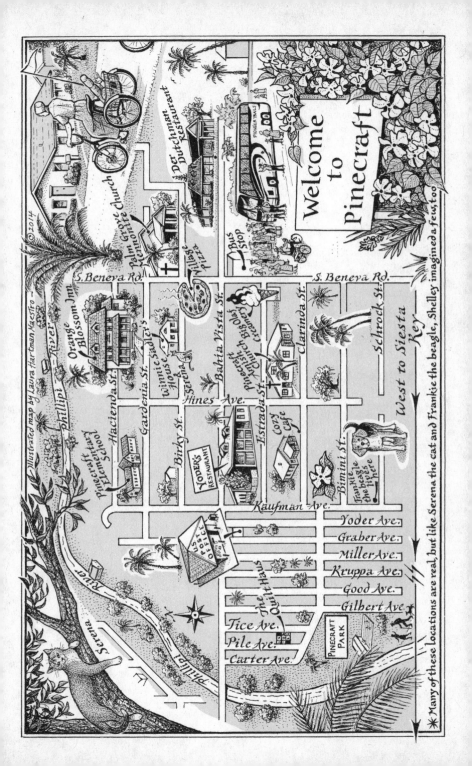

Welcome to Pinecraft

© 2014

— Illustrated map by Laura Hartman Maestro —

Der Dutchman Restaurant

PIONEER TRAILS

Bus Stop

S. Beneva Rd.

S. Beneva Rd.

Palm Grove Church Mennonite

Village Pizza

Orange Blossom Inn

Phillipi River

Winnie Sadley's House

Serena

Pinecraft Amish Church

Big Olaf Creamery

Clarinda St.

Schrock St.

West to Siesta Key

S. Beneva Rd.

Hacienda St.

Gardenia St.

Bahia Vista St.

Estrada St.

Hines Ave.

Pinecraft Elementary School

Birky St.

Yoder's Restaurant

Cozy Café

Bimini St.

Frankie the beagle lives here

Kaufman Ave.

Yoder Ave.

U.S. POST OFFICE

Graber Ave.

Miller Ave.

Kruppa Ave.

Good Ave.

Gilbert Ave.

Phillipi River

Serena

Phillipi

The Quilt Haus

Tice Ave.

Pile Ave.

Carter Ave.

Pinecraft Park

✳ Many of these locations are real, but like Serena the cat and Frankie the beagle, Shelley imagined a few, too.

Chapter 1

*F*rankie was on the loose. Again.

"Mandy, dear, are you sure you didn't see where he went off to?" Emma Keim asked her six-year-old daughter.

Mandy shook her head, the long white ties of her *kapp* swinging with the movement. "I was talking to Frankie about my daisies, but I guess he weren't too interested in them."

"I fear his actions have less to do with your daisies and more to do with the scent of pizza," Emma said around a frown. "He's never smelled a pizza he didn't want."

"I'm sorry, Mommy. I thought the gate was closed."

Walking to the freshly painted white fence that surrounded their house like pretty icing on a cake, Emma examined the gate. The latch was in place. Then she noticed the beagle-sized hole underneath it.

"Looks like Frankie dug his way out this morning."

"Oh, brother." Mandy blew out an exasperated lungful of air. "Frankie can sure be a bad beagle."

"Indeed." Ever since Frankie had been a puppy, he'd had an inordinate fondness for pizza. But now that he'd reached the ripe of age of ten, he seemed to have developed a real problem of wandering off in search of his favorite snack. Honestly, one would think he was too old for such nonsense.

Emma knew *she* was. She had three girls to take care of by herself, as well as her home and a part-time job baking treats for several local inns in the area. She had no time to track down wayward beagles.

"One day I'm going to have had enough of his foolishness," she muttered.

"Frankie don't mean to be bad, Mommy," Mandy protested as she grabbed Emma's arm. "Don't be mad. He's simply a really hungry beagle." Her middle child brightened. "Like the caterpillar in that picture book!"

"I know, child." Gently, she rubbed her thumb over the little line that had formed between Mandy's brows. "You know I would never do anything to hurt Frankie. Go get your sisters, and hurry, please. We're going to have to look for him."

While Mandy ran back inside, Emma put her hands on her hips and glanced around the neighborhood, valiantly hoping that Frankie would suddenly appear trotting down the street toward them.

But that was unlikely to happen. If her silly dog had managed to sneak a snack, he wouldn't still be wandering the streets of Pinecraft, Florida. Instead, he would be looking for a shady place to take a nap. And because he was a very deep sleeper, he would likely not even hear the four of them calling his name.

Behind her, the screen door squeaked open with a sprinkle of giggles. Looking at her three angels, Emma did a quick inspection. All were dressed for the warm summer day: three dresses in different shades of violet neatly in place, rubber flipflops on clean feet, and white *kapps* on just so.

Her daughters were her heart, for sure and for certain. After Sanford had passed away three years ago, Emma had wondered if she'd ever smile again. But then she'd looked into her sweet girls' faces and known that the Lord was good, indeed. He might have taken Emma's husband away far too early but He'd also given her three *wonderful-gut* reasons to live.

All she needed now was for Frankie to stop escaping and her life would be fine. Well, as fine as it could be as a widow.

"Where do you think Frankie went this time, Momma?" little Annie asked.

"Wherever he smelled pizza." Feeling a bit silly, she sniffed the air. "Do you girls happen to smell pizza?"

"We never do," Lena said. At eight, her eldest daughter had an answer for everything lately. "But I think we should head to the right when we start looking today."

"How come?" Mandy asked. "The Kaufmanns live to the left and they are always eating pizza."

Lena shrugged. "Frankie went left last time. Plus, it's kind of early for them to be eating pizza. Usually, no one's ever at their house until closer to dark."

That was as good a reason as any. Holding out her hands for Mandy and Annie, Emma turned right and let Lena lead the way.

"Frankie? Frankie!" Lena called out as they made their way past their neighbors' houses. "Frankie, you silly beagle. Where are ya?"

"Frankie, come home! You . . . you hound!" Emma yelled in her best no-nonsense "mom" voice.

"I don't think Frankie likes being called a hound, Mamm," Mandy said.

"Let's just hope he comes when one of us calls."

Taking that as an invitation to bellow, Lena took a deep breath. "Frankie!"

Emma winced as an elderly couple reading books on their front porch looked up in alarm. "Lena, not quite so loud."

"But if he's sleeping he won't wake up if I call quietly."

"I know, but still . . ."

As they approached the Orange Blossom Inn, a boy sitting on the front steps said, "Who's Frankie?" He looked to be a year or so older than Lena and was dressed in long trousers, a light blue short-sleeved shirt, suspenders, and a wicker hat. He was surely Amish, but his attitude told Emma all she needed to know; he, like Lena, was blessed with know-it-all syndrome.

Never one to be shy, Lena marched right up to him. "Frankie is our beagle. Have you seen him?"

"Nope. Why's he called Frankie?"

" 'Cause that's his name, that's why."

"Well, I wouldn't come if I was a dog named Frankie. That's a silly name for a dog."

Lena planted her hands on her hips. "Frankie likes his name. A lot."

He smirked. "Then why doesn't he come when you call?"

"He likes pizza," Annie said, scampering over to him. "Do you?"

Emma braced herself to step in. Surely this boy was about to say something snarky. Lena would then get mad and blurt something inappropriate, or Annie would start crying.

But instead, the young man stared at little Annie for a moment, then stood up and smiled like he had all the time in the world for little blond five-year-olds. "Did you say he likes pizza?"

"Oh, *jah*. He loves it!"

"My family does, too. And they just happen to be eating it out on the back patio. Come on."

Next thing Emma knew, all three of her girls were following the boy into the inn. Though Emma wasn't afraid for them—she'd known Beverly Overholt, the proprietor, for several years now—Emma wasn't especially certain that Beverly would want little girls traipsing through her inn.

But since they were already inside, she followed, looking for Beverly as she stepped into the lovely entryway. When Emma saw her standing by the stairs, her arms folded across her chest and grinning, she grimaced. "Sorry about the interruption. I'm afraid we're searching for Frankie again."

Beverly's green eyes lit up. "When I heard you calling for him down the street, I thought that might be the case," she replied. Pointing toward the kitchen, she said, "They went that way."

"*Danke.*" Emma hurried on. There would be plenty of time to apologize further later. For now, she had to keep track of her busy girls before they managed to get into as much trouble as one missing beagle.

The moment she passed through the swinging kitchen door, a pretty blond girl about eighteen or nineteen smiled at her. "They just went out the back door."

"*Danke.*"

But when she finally stepped out onto the cement patio, six—no, seven—pairs of eyes turned her way. Three belonged to her girls, the other four to three boys and one man—one very handsome man with dark blond hair, a neatly trimmed beard, and very light blue eyes.

"Hi," she said.

"Hi," he said right back, sounding perplexed. "William told me you're looking for Frankie the beagle?"

She nodded. She was embarrassed, but this was no time to wish for better behaved beagles or less trusting little girls. "He wandered off." Feeling more than a bit foolish, she asked, "Have you seen him, by any chance? He's tricolored and has white feet and a white-tipped tail."

"Just as if he stepped in paint and got his tail dirty, too!" Mandy supplied. "He really likes pizza."

"I think we just met a dog with that very description," the man murmured almost a little too mildly.

Just then, Emma noticed that he was staring at his pizza box. Then she noticed that the paper plates next to the box were still in a neat stack.

And a slow, sinking feeling settled over her.

"Did, um, Frankie find *your* pizza?"

"He certainly did." When he opened the lid, Emma groaned. At least half the pizza was gone. And the slices that remained were decorated with paw prints.

Frankie had struck again.

"I'm so sorry. I'll go buy you a fresh pizza."

His lips twitched. "I'd take you up on it if I didn't feel so sorry for you."

"Why?"

That's when the boy they'd been talking to out front silently pointed to a clump of boxwoods just beyond the edge of the patio.

Both Emma and her girls glanced over to see what he was pointing to. Sure enough, there was Frankie, lying on his side with his stomach distended and his eyes closed. He was breathing deeply and kind of snoring, too. Orange pizza sauce dotted the white patch of fur on his chest and, from what she could see, two of his paws. It was obvious that Frankie was going to have a pizza hangover for most of the day.

While the girls groaned, Emma fought against taking a seat at the table and silently hoping for some stranger to come along and take over her life for the next four hours. If they attempted to move him, he was liable to throw up. Unfortunately, she knew this from experience.

The man looked like he was trying hard not to laugh. "I'm starting to get the sense that he's done this before."

"All the time," Lena whispered, obviously trying not to wake up Frankie. "He can't help himself, though. Pizza is his weakness."

"I really am sorry," Emma said, looking at each of the boys and the man. "I don't know what to say."

"Why don't you tell me your name instead?" he asked.

Suddenly, a whole other feeling came over her as she noticed again just how attractive he was.

"My name is Emma. Emma Keim. And these, here, are my daughters Lena, Mandy, and Annie."

"Where do you live?" the eldest boy, who wasn't actually a boy, asked. No, he was more a young man, at least seventeen or eighteen.

"Just down the way," she said evasively.

"We have a white house and lots and lots of orange and cherry trees," Mandy said.

"We're living here at the inn while my *daed* gets our new *haus* fixed up," another boy added.

"Oh?"

"I'm Jay," the handsome man said, "and these are my sons Ben, Mark, and William." Pointing to the youngest, he said, "I believe you and William already met."

She smiled at them and couldn't help but notice that all three had their father's light blue eyes and muscular, lanky build. In fact, the only big difference, besides their ages, was their varying shades of blond hair. Ben's was dark blond, Mark's matched his father's, and William's was by far the lightest. "Pleased to meet you. I am sorry about the pizza. If you could wait a minute, I'll run home and get my purse and give you some money to pay for a new one."

"That's not necessary."

"But I'm sure your wife won't like your boys missing a meal." The moment she said it, Emma wished she could take back every single intrusive word.

All four males looked mighty uncomfortable.

"We don't got a *mamm*," William said quietly. "She's up in *Himmel*."

"I am mighty sorry to hear she's in heaven," Emma said. "It's hard to lose a parent."

William looked at her curiously. "How do you know? Is your *mamm* up in *Himmel*, too?"

"No, but, um, my husband is."

A new awareness crackled in the air. The man—Jay—lost his smile but he seemed to be examining her more closely. "I'm sorry for your loss, too."

"Daed, how about me and Tricia take William and Mark to Village Pizza?" Ben, the eldest boy, asked.

"Tricia?"

"She's the girl who works here, remember? You met her yesterday."

"Oh. Well . . ."

"They need to eat, Daed."

After giving him a long look, he nodded. *"Jah*, sure. Go ahead."

"Can the girls come, too?"

"Nee. We don't really know them," Jay said before Emma could say the same thing.

Ben looked tempted to argue, then shrugged. "Let's go," he said to his brothers.

"Ben. Manners."

"What? Oh, sorry. Nice to meet you," he mumbled before shuttling his brothers back inside the inn.

Emma noticed all three of her girls staring at the boys' retreating backs. She wondered if it was because they were new, because they'd been rather nice, or because they were boys.

She stood up. "Well, um, I think it's time to grab my beagle and be on our way."

"How will you get him home?"

"I'll carry Frankie," she said. Though there was a fairly good chance he might get sick, she certainly didn't want him messing up Beverly's pretty patio, either.

Jay looked extremely doubtful. "Is it far?"

"Nee, just a couple of houses down."

Mandy lifted two hands and showed off eight fingers. "Eight of 'em."

"That's too far for you to carry a heavy dog," Jay said. "I'll carry Frankie for you."

"I couldn't let you do that."

But before she could protest any further, he bent down and, with a grunt, lifted the snoring beagle into his arms. Emma had to believe that any man who would carry a dog so gently must be a good person.

And with that, she decided to go ahead and let him carry Frankie home.

Feeling good about her decision, Emma led him through the inn's back gate and up the side yard to the street.

"He's a pretty hefty *hund*. Ain't so?"

"He's chubby. Sometimes I think he needs to go on these pizza hunts," she joked, "since they seem to be the only exercise he likes. In fact, he went fairly far today."

"We'll need to change that, I think."

"We?" she asked as they walked down the street, her girls scampering in front of them.

Looking down at her, he smiled. "I have a feeling that between your three girls, my three boys, and one beagle with a penchant for pizza, we're going to be seeing a lot more of each other."

She thought that was a pretty cheeky thing to say. But, since he was carrying Frankie, she supposed he had that right. "We do have a lot in common, I suppose."

"Yep. Not too many folks our age who have lost their spouses," he said as they passed yet another home.

That had never been a club she would have imagined she'd belong to. "It'll be nice to have more friends for the girls. That is, if you're intending to stay in Pinecraft."

"I bought the old Borntrager Organic Farm, just east of Sarasota."

"You're a farmer."

He nodded. "Farmed all my life in Ohio. Now I'm looking forward to enjoying the Florida sunshine all year-round." Turning, he gazed at her over Frankie's head. "We're here for good. And until this very moment, I wasn't sure why the Lord had called us to move."

"But now?"

He smiled at her before looking straight ahead again. "Now

I'm coming to see that yet again, the Lord works in mysterious ways."

He seemed to be thinking something he wasn't ready to share and so she had no idea how to respond. Therefore, she decided to say nothing at all.

Chapter 2

The inn was dark and silent. Peaceful. Everywhere except in the attic room where Jay had been tossing and turning for the last thirty minutes. When he determined that sleep wasn't going to come anytime soon, he went back downstairs to wait for Ben.

Being eighteen, Ben was certainly too old to ever attempt to keep tabs on. Why, when Jay had been Ben's age, he'd been courting Evelyn in earnest. Looking back, he was thankful that both his and her parents had been so trusting. Though remembering what they'd done after they'd become engaged but before they'd actually said their vows, Jay was starting to think maybe they'd been a little *too* trusting. He'd certainly have something to say to Ben if he ever acted that way.

Of course, Jay realized, Ben's life was currently far different than his own had been. He and Evelyn had been tightly nestled in Charm, Ohio, and surrounded by most of their family and friends. He'd grown up in the house both his parents and grandparents had lived in, farming land that earlier generations had cared for and prospered from.

From the time he'd been ten or eleven, Evelyn had been a part of his life, too. Because she'd been fragile and delicate, he'd looked out for her on the playground, in the classroom, and during Sunday singings. In return, she'd always gazed at him like he was the strongest, best man in the world.

With her, he had been.

After he and Evelyn had married, they'd had Ben right away, then set about living much the same life of their parents.

Well, almost. His mother had raised five *kinner* by being bossy and rather outspoken. Evelyn had needed Jay's help disciplining the boys and managing the chickens and pigs. She'd had asthma and allergies and was often exhausted.

When she'd started complaining about pressure in her chest, they'd taken her in for an x-ray and discovered that she didn't simply have pneumonia—but lung cancer.

One year later, she'd gone up to heaven.

That had been eighteen months ago, soon after his fortieth birthday. Jay had cried and grieved, tried to make sense of something that made no sense.

The only thing that gave him any semblance of peace was remembering his promises to her. Over and over he'd reassured her that they would still be married even when she was in heaven. That had comforted her. It had almost seemed as if she'd needed to know that he was going to be by her side in the afterlife.

His throat tightened.

He shook his head to clear it. It had become his habit of late to push the past from his mind because it was too painful to deal with. It was far better to concentrate on the here and now and their new life in Florida.

Six months after Evelyn's death, he'd begun thinking about making a change. Everything on their farm had reminded him of Evelyn. Their friends and family couldn't seem to talk about anything but his loss and how sorry they felt for the boys.

Little by little Jay had watched Ben, Mark, and even William raise their guards. Instead of being their usual open and chatty selves, they'd become withdrawn and wary. Instinctively, Jay had known that they weren't simply grieving for their mother. Like him, they were becoming exhausted by attempting to move forward when practically everyone around them was determined to keep them in the past.

So, one night over supper, he threw out his idea about moving to Florida, just to see how the boys would react. For the first time since Evelyn had been diagnosed with cancer, new life had appeared in their eyes.

After that, Jay had begun making plans in earnest.

Now, in just a few days' time, they'd be moving into their new house, connected to three acres of prime farmland. It was a small place, both the house and the land—he'd farmed almost sixty acres at home—but he had modest goals now. He wasn't hoping to sustain everything his forefathers had built—Ben or Mark or even William could move back to Charm to do that.

Instead, Jay was merely hoping to occupy himself while William was in school. Maybe make a little money to add to his sizable savings. And, if by chance, his hard work enabled him to fall into an exhausted slumber before one or two in the morning? He would be grateful for that benefit as well.

Feeling restless, he walked outside, glad Beverly had mentioned that he should feel free to use the patio anytime he wished.

It was still warm out, most likely seventy degrees. However, the humidity had increased, and the scent of Beverly's citrus trees filled the air. He sat down in one of the chairs and stretched his legs.

And tried to relax.

"Hey, Daed?"

Jay started, unsure of how much time had passed. He looked across the darkened patio, lit only by some dimly glowing solar lights and a citronella candle burning in the center of the table, and saw his eldest. "Hi, Ben. I didn't expect you home so early this evening."

Ben walked to the wrought-iron chair beside him and flopped down with a grunt. "I was about to go upstairs, but I noticed you sitting out here."

"And you thought you'd see how I was doing?"

"Maybe." He cracked a grin. "You'd do the same thing for me."

Jay couldn't help but return the smile. "Indeed, I would. So, what did you do tonight?"

"I went to Pinecraft Park."

"And how was that?" Jay knew most of the Amish in the area spent at least an hour or two there a day and often several hours there after suppertime. The park had everything from shuffleboard to basketball courts to a pavilion under which community members attended auctions, shared simple meals, or even listened to groups like the famous Knoxx Family speak.

"It was fine."

"You don't sound too enthused."

"I was hoping to see someone there but I didn't."

"Tricia, perhaps?"

Even in the dim light, Jay could see that Ben looked a little self-conscious. *"Jah."* He shrugged. "I guess that was obvious," he said with a grin. "I mean, there's not too many girls here that I know."

"That will change, son." Ben was a handsome, strapping boy who had helped farm fields for most of his life. He was also friendly and patient with other people. It would be only natural for the young girls to want to get to know him.

"*Jah.* Maybe."

Jay knew a man liked his privacy, so he refrained from asking about Tricia though he was curious as to how their time at the pizza parlor had gone. Neither Mark nor Will had had much to say about Tricia, preferring instead to talk about their newfound love for pepperoni pizza with mushrooms and peppers.

So Jay just leaned back and enjoyed the warm evening air. Back in Charm, it was still too cold to spend much time outside at night.

"Hey, Daed?"

"Hmm?"

"When you were courting Mamm, did you know she was the one?"

"I did when I married her."

"Well, of course you knew then. What about before then? What about when you talked with her for the first couple of times?"

Jay tried to recall a time when he hadn't known Evelyn. "Things were easy for us because our parents—your grandparents—were friends. And we had been in school together, too. I knew her for most of my life. Eventually, people assumed we would become a couple."

"Is that why you married her, 'cause everyone wanted you to?"

Jay had to think about that. "Um, I don't think so. No one was pushing us at each other or anything, but we both knew that a relationship would make everyone mighty happy. I guess in some ways we fell in love because it would make so many people we loved happy."

A line formed between Ben's brows. "That's it? You started seeing Mamm because it was convenient?"

"I wouldn't put it that way," he retorted. "I'm trying to answer you as honestly as possible. Like a man."

"Sorry."

"I understand, son. Believe me, I do." He glanced over at Ben to gauge his reaction, but found himself gazing into nothing but memories. He recalled the way Evelyn had looked when he used to walk her to school and how she'd tilt her head a certain way when she was listening hard or concentrating on a problem. The way she'd looked the summer she'd turned sixteen and he'd suddenly realized that his feelings for her had moved beyond mere friendship, and that he'd never wanted to look at another girl for the rest of his life.

Perhaps that was it?

"I think I knew Evelyn was the one when I realized no other girl mattered to me," he said simply. "I think that was when your mother was sixteen or so."

"That's when you knew you were in love?"

Jay hated to categorize the complexities of a relationship into one simple moment. Though he'd heard of love at first sight, he'd always thought it was a bit too fanciful for his tastes. "That was when I knew I *wanted* to be in love with her," he allowed. "Falling in love is a complicated thing."

"Sounds like it." Ben shifted, allowing Jay to get a real good look at his scowl. "Daed, you're not helping much."

Only by biting the inside of his cheek could Jay keep a straight face. "I'm sorry about that. Like I said, it's hard to compare my relationship with your mother with the way most people meet and date. We had been friends for years. Why don't you tell me what has you thinking about love tonight?"

"Nothing."

"Ah." He'd learned over time not to push his eldest.

"Okay. Even though I have only known Tricia a week, I think there's something between her and me."

"A week isn't very long."

"Don't forget that I did meet her two months ago. I talked to her quite a bit when we came out to look at the farm."

"Ah." Jay refrained from pointing out that that still wasn't much time.

Ben sighed. "But maybe I simply think she's pretty."

Jay thought of a dozen reasons for Ben not to do anything he might regret but he elected not to say a word. Evelyn would've said something, of course. Though she hadn't been especially forceful in nature, she was thoughtful and very sweet. She'd doted on her boys and they'd loved her attention.

But that was part of the problem. She wasn't there.

With an impatient grunt, Ben said, "Daed, aren't ya going to say anything? Aren't ya going to offer me any advice?"

"Not tonight," he said as he got to his feet. He still wasn't exactly tired but he was feeling particularly old. "If you still are interested in Tricia in two weeks, we'll talk then."

"Why do I have to wait two weeks?"

"Because then you'll know whether it's her pretty face or her pretty mind that has caught your attention."

"Pretty mind?"

"I'm a farmer, son, not a poet. If you want better words you're going to have to seek them someplace else." With a wink, he added, "I heard Michael Knoxx moved here. Since he's used to giving speeches the whole world over, I'm sure he will know what to tell you. Next time you see him, ask away."

"Good to know," Ben said sarcastically. Shoving his hands in his pockets, he said, "Hey, Daed?"

"*Jah?*"

"You going to be able to sleep tonight?"

"I don't know. See you in the morning, Ben."

"*Gut naught*, Daed." Ben's voice was filled with disappointment and worry.

Jay was sorry for that, but he knew he simply wasn't able to pretend to be okay in front of Mark or Ben anymore. With William, he would put up a front, but not his two oldest.

When Jay entered their attic room, he tried to be thankful for the comfortable linens on the twin bed, tried to concentrate on the soft snores coming from his youngest. But all he could really think about was how much he missed his king-sized bed, with all its room to spread out and stretch.

And how much more he missed the person he used to share it with.

BEVERLY OVERHOLT KEPT TO the shadows of the kitchen while Ben Hilty gazed out into the foliage for a few more minutes after his father left, before at last heading upstairs.

Then, and only then, did she carefully close the kitchen window, which had been cracked open just enough to allow her to hear every bit of the men's private conversation.

When Jay had been sitting alone outside, she'd left the window open, feeling there was no need to disrupt him and every need to enjoy the fresh breeze wafting inside. When Ben had arrived, she'd had every intention of closing the window, but then she'd heard Ben ask about his mother and she'd sensed that even the slightest disruption would be reason enough to end the conversation.

From the time they'd arrived, Beverly had had a feeling that the Hiltys were a group of four lonely souls adrift without their anchor. It was apparent in the way William ate only cornflakes for breakfast because that was what his mother had served him, and in the way that Mark smiled a little too quickly, acted a little too easygoing, as if he was afraid to cause more pain to his already pained family. She'd noticed Ben's restlessness and Jay's determination to pretend that all was well, too.

And it all broke her heart.

But now she knew just a little too much about one of her guests' love life . . . and it just so happened to have a whole lot to do with her own niece. If Tricia had merely been visiting with her family, Beverly would have been tempted to sneak over to her room and tell her that she'd made quite an impression on Ben! But now that Tricia was more or less under her care and working at the inn, Beverly decided that it would be much better to simply let things happen between the two of them as they would.

As long as Tricia remembered to guard her heart.

Beverly knew from experience that trusting a man too quickly could lead to heartache. After all, three years ago she'd learned that her fiancé, Marvin, had been cheating on her with her best friend. If two people she'd known so well could betray her so easily, there was no telling what could happen to Tricia if she let down her guard too fast.

She was just about to consider the best way to counsel Tricia when she remembered what had happened the last time she'd stuck her nose into another couple's romance.

It wasn't that long ago that Michael Knoxx had been her

guest for a few weeks while he'd been recovering from surgery. During this time, he'd developed a relationship with Penny, one of Beverly's employees. When Beverly had seen the two of them holding hands, she'd overreacted and had made quite a mess of things. Eric, the actual owner of the inn, had given her a stern talking-to, as had Michael. And because she'd known that both men were right and she'd made an error in judgment, Beverly had promptly apologized.

She'd also chosen to use that experience as a learning opportunity.

Which meant that she really shouldn't stick her nose into something that wasn't her business. Yet. But all bets were off if she became aware of Tricia being in danger of getting her feelings hurt. If that happened? Well, she would do whatever it took to make sure Tricia didn't make the same mistakes she had.

Chapter 3

*E*mma, how is it that you have three girls and a part-time job but you still manage to get everywhere ten minutes early?" Dorrie Beachy asked as she slipped into their booth at Yoder's Restaurant.

"I don't know," Emma said with a tight smile, though actually she was pretty sure she did. Dorrie had a loving husband who liked to spend time with her. Emma knew if Sanford was still in her life, she'd likely be running late a lot more often. "Don't worry about it, though. I haven't been waiting long."

After looking at her a bit more closely, Dorrie turned her mug right-side-up when the server headed their way, signaling her need for coffee. "Have you ordered pie yet?"

"Not yet. I was waiting for you. Do you know what kind you want today?"

"Key lime," Dorrie said, smiling at the server as she poured coffee into her cup. "What about you, Emma?"

"Chocolate."

After the server left, Dorrie narrowed her eyes. "You want chocolate? Now I know something is wrong. Start talking."

"Dorrie, this fascination you have about matching pies to moods needs to stop."

"Why should it? It always rings true. When you're happy, you choose coconut cream. When you're sad, you pick a berry pie. And when you're especially troubled, you ask for chocolate."

"I don't do that."

"Oh, yes you do. Every single time." After tasting her coffee, carefully adding another bit of cream, then stirring with the same kind of care Emma figured gourmet chefs put into fancy dishes, Dorrie leaned forward. "What's wrong? Are you worried about Frankie?"

"My beagle? *Nee.*"

"You sure? I heard he got loose again two days ago."

"He did. But he's home safe. And none the worse for the wear."

"So what is it?"

"Dorrie, we are meeting to plan what to make for our booth for the school fund-raiser. We did not meet to discuss my life."

"Ah. So you're troubled by your life. I know the girls are good. And Frankie is *gut*, too. So that only leaves you. What's wrong, Emma? Are you finally lonely?"

Finally lonely?

There was no "finally." She'd been lonely for years now, which was quite an accomplishment considering she was never in a room by herself.

Immediately, tears sprang to her eyes. She blinked at them

furiously and told herself that she was simply frustrated by Dorrie's rudeness. *Not* that her longtime girlfriend might have hit the nail on the head. "Oh, for heaven's sake, Dorrie. Stop pestering me."

"I won't stop," she said quietly as their server placed their pie in front of them, each heaped high with freshly whipped cream. "Someone has to be completely honest with you."

She was wrong, though. The trouble was that her two sisters, their spouses, her parents, and even Sanford's parents were completely honest with her, too. They didn't have the slightest bit of trouble letting her know that they expected her to always, always, *always* miss Sanford. And while she was grateful for their love and concern—and for the fact that they all lived nearby—she wasn't as grateful about their constant need to give her advice, or their unwillingness to let her move forward. After all, it had been three years since Sanford had died of congestive heart failure.

Three long years.

"I canna speak about this now. And certainly not here, in the middle of Yoder's."

Dorrie shrugged. "The Lord picks the right time, dear."

"He did not pick this time. You did." And because she was so irritated, Emma shoved a too-big bite of chocolate pie in her mouth. As the decadent mixture of dark chocolate and whipped cream hit her taste buds, she slowly began to feel a little measure of calm.

"So, are you lonely?" Dorrie asked in her blunt way.

And just like that, her little bit of calm vanished. "I've *been* lonely. But that is what happens when a woman loses her husband."

"You've been mourning. I think there's a difference."

"I didn't know you were such an expert."

"I'm not. But I am an expert on my best friend. What has happened recently that put you in this mood?"

"I'm not sure." But of course she was. It was that long walk to her house by Jay's side. That long walk where she'd chatted with a man and laughed. It was only after she'd gotten home that she realized she hadn't compared him to Sanford. Instead, she'd been thinking that she liked his smile and had been glad he was carrying Frankie.

She'd also been thinking how nice it was to be around someone who understood what it was like to promise to love someone until death parted them . . . and then feel betrayed because death had come far too soon.

Looking at Dorrie, with her wide-eyed expression and her cherubic cheeks, Emma realized that she was probably right. She did need to talk to someone, and it needed to be someone she could trust. She'd known Dorrie since they were children, having grown up next door to each other in Pinecraft.

Perhaps the Lord had put them together today for this very reason.

Her friend was patiently sipping coffee, waiting for Emma to unburden herself.

"When Frankie ran away, the girls and I discovered him in the back of the Orange Blossom Inn. One of the guests had picked up a pizza and he and his boys were eating it on the back patio." Remembering the pizza paw prints, she grimaced. "I mean, they'd been *attempting* to eat their pizza. But then Frankie had shown up."

Dorrie's lips twitched. "Frankie struck again." Setting down her mug, she said, "How bad was it?"

"Frankie's behavior?" Emma shrugged. "About the same as always. Though he didn't throw up, so it could have been worse."

"Indeed."

"Um, anyway, the man at the inn with the pizza? He is a widower."

"And he has *kinner*, too?"

"*Jah*, he does. Three boys."

"Same ages as yours?"

"*Nee*. The oldest is almost twenty, I'd say. The youngest is about Lena's age, give or take a year or two."

"Where are they visiting from?"

"Charm, Ohio," Emma replied. "But they did not come to Sarasota simply to visit. They are moving here."

"Is that right?" Dorrie took another bite of pie.

"*Jah*. He said they were moving in another couple of days." Her voice drifted off. So far, she hadn't said anything of note or anything to warrant chocolate pie, but Emma knew Dorrie was used to her reticent ways. In the give-and-take of a relationship forged over decades, Dorrie merely continued her rapid-fire questions.

"Where is he moving to? Did he say?"

"He's going to take over the old Borntrager Organic Farm."

Dorrie smiled. "He is a farmer."

"*Jah*." She tried to remember everything he'd said. "I think he is looking forward to farming in the sunshine."

"Oh, to be sure. Well, the farm isn't next door, but it is nice and close. Just a SCAT stop or two away. Convenient."

Emma hadn't thought of that, but Dorrie was right. The Sarasota County Area Transit shuttle would make it easy for Jay and his family to get to the heart of Pinecraft in no time at all.

And, she supposed, it would make it easy for her to do some shopping out there. If she ever had a need to do that.

Around another bite of pie, Emma said, "Don't act like it

means anything. But, um, I think meeting him made me realize that maybe I'm not the only person in the world to suffer such a great loss." Taking a deep breath, she forced herself to say the rest of what she'd been thinking. "I think I would like to get to know him better. You know, because he is someone who I have so much in common with."

"To be sure. I've met other widows and widowers, but not too many who are so young. Or who have three *kinner*."

"He seemed nice." She reached up and rubbed the back of her neck. "He was so nice, he even carried Frankie all the way home. And Frankie let him!"

"If he's carrying that dog around, he would have to be nice. Frankie is one hefty beagle."

Dorrie had a point. Emma smiled at that . . . just before she remembered what her family would say. "I don't want a new husband, Dorrie. I don't mean to sound like I do." She winced as she imagined Patty's and Mercy's reactions. "I'm afraid my sisters won't understand that I only want a new friend."

"Of course," Dorrie soothed. "But making a new friend is a good thing. And just think, I bet this man— What's his name?"

"Jay."

"I bet this man Jay is feeling mighty blessed indeed to have met you. I bet he's been feeling alone, too."

"*Jah.*" Her stomach churned. "A new friend is always a blessing. I, um, just wish I knew what I was supposed to do now."

Dorrie pointedly looked over to the window where folks could simply walk in and buy pie. "When he moves in, you should bring him a pie."

Emma weighed the pros and cons of that idea. She knew where the Borntrager farm was, most everyone did. After the girls went to school one day, she could hop on the SCAT, deliver her pie, and officially welcome him to Pinecraft. She could go as his friend. Why, there was nothing untoward about that. Everyone needed a new friend.

But just the thought of bringing Jay a pie . . . Emma worried what would happen when not only her family, but Sanford's parents heard that she'd done such a thing. They wouldn't want to hear how innocent her gesture was, nor would they say how thoughtful it was to bring a widower with three boys such a simple gift. They would ask her questions and chide her for behaving in an immodest way. In no time at all, her simple gesture would reach mammoth proportions.

Even thinking about the fuss they would raise made Emma shake her head. "That would be too forward."

Dorrie scoffed. "It might be too forward if you wanted something in return, but you don't. And it's especially not forward for a single man moving in with three boys," she added in her matter-of-fact way. "Boys eat a lot, you know. Besides, everyone likes pie."

"That is true."

Once again she contemplated the pros and cons, and—to her dismay—began running through the choices of pie. If Dorrie's theories were true, it seemed that, along with delicious flavors, pie could be filled with certain hidden meanings. "Now I'm even more confused! What kind of pie should I bring? I don't want to give the wrong impression."

Dorrie laughed. "Take cherry."

"Cherry?"

"Cherry pie is cheery."

Emma winced at the play on words. "Oh, brother."

Dorrie chuckled. "I know that sounded silly, but I am a pie

connoisseur, you know. You should remember that and listen to me."

"You are more of a pie soothsayer," Emma teased. For sure and for certain, her best friend never failed to make her laugh.

"Whatever I am, I always know the best pie for the occasion. It really is a shame I can't bake too good."

"You can't bake at all. Or sew."

"I can raise four *kinner*, clean my *haus*, and take care of all the bookkeeping for my husband's job. That is enough."

"You are also a *gut* friend."

She smiled. "Does that mean what I think it does? Are you going to listen?"

Making a decision, Emma nodded. "All right. I'm going to do it. I'm going to wait a couple of days, and then I'm going to take Jay and his boys a cherry pie."

"Wunderbaar!"

"But if everything falls apart and my family makes me feel like a Jezebel, I'm going to blame you."

"Nothing is going to fall apart." Reaching out, Dorrie grasped her hand. "See how *gut* our Lord is? He gave you a new friend this week. A friend who knows only too well the burdens and pain you have been facing. This is a blessing."

"You are such a blessing to me, Dorrie. I walked in here feeling completely confused. And now I feel like everything is going to be all right again."

Dorrie looked delighted. "Glad I could help." Then, in her usual efficient manner, she pulled out her notebook. "Now, let's get our real reason for being here taken care of. What should we make for our booth?"

"I was thinking socks."

"Socks?"

"Socks are something you can make easily. You might not be able to bake an edible batch of cookies but you can knit as well as anyone."

"This is true."

"You and I can each knit a pair of socks in two days. If we get some other women involved, we'll have a couple of dozen socks to sell, and the money will go to a good cause."

"Socks it is."

"You're not going to argue?"

"Nope. You might trust me where pie is concerned, but you are the one with the best ideas for the fund-raiser."

"We're a good pair, Dorrie. *Danke* for today."

"Anytime, dear. Anytime at all."

Chapter 4

*F*or some reason, even though they'd spent the entire day to-gether, Tricia was pretty sure that Ben was still trying to think of ways to delay their return to the Orange Blossom Inn. First, he'd insisted they go for an extra long walk on the beach at Siesta Key. Then he'd taken her to a charming restaurant for fried shrimp instead of merely grabbing a quick bite at one of the many shacks offering snacks and hot dogs. Now, as they were walking back to the inn, he'd slowed their pace even more. She didn't mind since she wasn't in any hurry to return, either.

But she was becoming a little curious as to why he was practi-cally jumping at any chance to delay their walk back.

"Would you like to go get an ice cream?" He pointed over at Olaf's.

Tricia hugged her stomach and frowned. "I can't eat another thing."

"Oh."

"It was a *gut* idea, though." Smiling, she tilted her head up to meet his gaze. "I'd say yes if I hadn't already had a hot fudge sundae today. And a plate of fried shrimp."

"Those shrimp were good."

"They were great," she corrected. Suddenly concerned that she hadn't conveyed just how much she'd enjoyed their time together, she reached out and squeezed his forearm. "Everything today has been *wonderful-gut*, Ben. I promise."

"*Jah*, it was." He smiled back at her, but she noticed that it didn't quite reach his eyes.

"Would you like to walk around Pinecraft?" she asked. "There's a couple of benches over in front of the Palm Grove church."

"You don't mind?"

"Not at all. I'm not ready to go back yet."

"I'm not, either. I don't want today to end."

"Me, neither," she said and pointed to a group of little Amish girls, all four of them holding hands as they skipped behind their mothers. "Look, Ben. Aren't they cute?"

He chuckled. "*Jah*. They remind me of Emma and her trio of little ones."

Tricia sighed contentedly. Their conversation came so easily, it was just the kind of thing she'd always wished and dreamed she would have. It was nice to relax and talk about nothing in particular.

As they crossed the street, dodging a man on a bright red bicycle, Ben added, "I'm really looking forward to having my own room once we move into our new house, but it's going to be hard to not see you all the time."

"I was just thinking that I was going to miss seeing you around the inn. I was going to mention it earlier, but I didn't want to sound too forward," she admitted as they continued their journey down Bahia Vista before turning right on Orchard.

"You shouldn't worry. I'm not going to think you are too forward. I like your honesty."

"I'm glad." She pressed her lips together so she wouldn't start telling him how most people found her to be a bit too blunt and outspoken.

Now that they were off the main street and the area was far quieter, Ben began walking a little closer to her side. Tricia felt her stomach flutter. Suddenly, it felt as if they were very alone, and she realized that this was the first time they'd been that way. It made her giddy and nervous, all at the same time. She didn't want to do or say the wrong thing. She clasped her hands tightly together so she wouldn't accidentally grab hold of his arm.

Ben noticed. "Hey, you're looking a little tense. Are you all right?"

"Oh, *jah*. I am fine." After all, what else could she say?

"You sure?" After a pause, he blurted, "Am I pushing you too much? I haven't been serious about a girl before. I don't really know what I'm doing."

"You're not pushing too much."

"Then what is it?"

She didn't know how to admit how insecure she felt. And because of that, she took a step away. "Here's the church," she announced, her voice just a little bit too bright. "It's pretty, isn't it?"

Ben looked around. Shrugged. "It's nice," he said at last.

She walked over and sat down on one of the benches. Then, knowing that she had to take a chance and admit her feelings, too, she added, "Ben, I don't know what I'm doing, either."

He didn't bother to hide his relief. "That's *gut* news."

"Every time I think I know what you're going to say, you say the unexpected. I'm starting to learn that you are good at taking me by surprise." She chuckled. "You are definitely keeping me on my toes."

He sat down on the edge of the next bench, so he was angled toward her. "I don't mean to," he said with a wry look. "Like I said, I don't have much experience with relationships."

"I don't, either." After all, her only experience had involved writing notes about a boy she'd had a crush on then having some so-called friends show them to everyone. "But I think we're doing all right."

"You know what? I think we are, too."

"We're certainly sharing a lot with each other." Tricia smiled.

But Ben didn't look so confident. "Actually, I think we've talked a lot about me. About how I felt losing my mother, and how hard it's been to step in and try to be there for my brothers."

"I'm glad you shared your feelings, Ben."

He continued, just as if he hadn't heard her. "I think I spent an hour telling you about how we all decided to move here from Ohio." He rolled his eyes. "I think I repeated every conversation that took place at our kitchen table."

Because he looked so apprehensive, she said, "We can talk about it more, if you'd like."

"No, that's not what I'm getting at."

"Then, what?"

"I want to talk about you for a change."

She started. "I told you that there wasn't anything all that interesting about me. I needed a change and so I moved down here to be with my aunt."

"I think there was more to it." He gazed at her steadily. "Actually, I know there was."

"Okay, there was, but it's not important."

"Tricia, I'm going to be honest. I like you. I like you a whole lot. But I'm starting to feel like you are holding something back."

His words were painful to hear. They were also true. But still, she hedged. "I don't know what you want me to say."

"Just talk to me. Why do you insist on keeping your past a secret? Tricia, why did you move?"

Before she could begin her explanation, he added, "It's okay if you have had relationships before. You are a few years older than me, after all. Did you get in a fight with your boyfriend or something?"

"Ben, I *was* telling you the truth. I really don't have a lot of experience dating. I didn't leave Ohio because of a boy. Not directly, anyway."

"Then, why? Did you not get along with your *mamm*? I'm pulling at straws here."

"I got along with her fine." She chewed on her bottom lip. "We're not real close, but that doesn't mean we're not close at all. Or we don't get along."

When he stared at her long and hard, Tricia knew she had to swallow her pride and tell him the whole truth. "Ben, the truth is I did something dumb and everyone found out about it."

"That's it?" He looked disappointed.

"Jah." Of course, the way she'd been dancing around the topic had to have made him think she was harboring some dark, terrible secret. Pushing herself a bit, she continued. "I wrote something dumb about a guy I liked. Something I never should have put to paper. Something I never should have shown anyone else. Have you ever done anything dumb like that?" she

asked hesitantly. "Have you ever made a stupid decision that you regretted almost the instant it happened?"

"I have two younger brothers. Of course I've done and said stupid stuff." He smiled. "My mother used to say that *kinner* make mistakes all the time and that's why they live with their parents for years and years."

"My stupid notes caught the attention of a couple of mean girls who made things worse. No matter where I went I was teased." Her voice cracked. "A lot. It happened for a long time. Months." She winced, hating to remember all the unkind words her girlfriends had said to her and how one of her friends had completely lied about the things she'd done.

He blinked as he finally understood. "You were bullied."

She nodded. "Most people think bullying only happens between boys with their fists, but it happens between girls, too, with rumors and gossip. It was horrible." Swiping her cheek, she continued to pour out her heart. "I got depressed. Really depressed. I knew I had to get away."

"And so you came down here."

"Yep. I took all the money I'd saved, even borrowed some of my mother's grocery money, and got on a Pioneer Trails bus without telling anyone." She blew out a ragged sigh. "Well, now you know my secret. Aren't you glad you asked?"

He got to his feet. "I am."

"You are?" She didn't even try to hide her surprise.

He reached down, grasped her hand, and pulled her to her feet. "Uh-huh." When she was standing, he reached for her other hand, then linked their fingers together.

"What should we do now?"

"Well, I have an idea. But it's a little scary," he teased. "You can always say no if you want."

She stared at him, wide-eyed. "What do you want to do?"

He tugged on her hands, pulling her closer. "Give you a hug."

"What?"

"I want to hold you for a minute, Tricia. Is that okay with you?"

They were standing so close to each other that her dress was brushing against his shirt and trousers. Close enough that Tricia knew Ben could lean down and brush his lips against hers. If he wanted.

So close that she could see the small flecks of brown dotting the blue of his eyes. Saw the faint scar on the corner of his lip.

"You can hold me, Ben. I you want to."

He didn't delay another second. Ben wrapped his arms around Tricia and held her close.

After a few seconds, she relaxed against him. After surviving so many very dark days over the last year, God, at last, had given her a blindingly bright one.

It was the best day ever.

Chapter 5

*M*oving was far more taxing than Jay remembered.

The moving van had been late—five hours late. Then, the exact moment the truck parked in the driveway of his new home, the heavens burst open. Luckily, that didn't prevent the movers from doing their jobs. They simply ignored the downpour, carefully unloaded all of Jay's worldly goods, carried them up the house's front porch, and at last placed everything inside their new, sprawling, two-story farmhouse. They worked without a bit of complaint . . . but without any urgency, either: cardboard boxes got completely soaked, shoes brought in mud, and tabletops arrived dripping.

By the time the men closed the truck and pulled away, Jay's money deep in their pockets, his new home smelled like rain and grass and wet cardboard. As he and the boys moved and rearranged furniture—finding out belatedly that some rooms were smaller than the ones back in Ohio, while others were far more spacious—Jay realized he had never missed Evelyn more.

She'd had a true sense about what went where. He had none of that. Neither did his boys. Therefore, they unpacked and rearranged in a hit-and-miss kind of way. It was time-consuming and frustrating, and his back was starting to hurt a bit, too.

"Mark, watch the corners," he warned for at least the fourth time. "You are going to scratch the table."

"I'm being careful," he grunted. "And the table was already scratched." Setting the small table down and wiping his hands on the front of his pants, he added, "And wet."

"How scratched is it?" Jay really needed to begin a list of damages that the movers were responsible for.

"It ain't from the movers, Daed. The mark is from William, when he was three."

"Oh."

"I don't remember hurting that table," William groused. "Or making the stain on the coffee table, neither."

"That's because Mamm let you get away with everything," Mark announced with a glare. "You *always* got away with everything."

"That's not true."

Knowing from experience that the blame game could go on for hours, Jay redirected things. "Mark, go back to work on your room. Ben, go find my toolbox and help me put together William's bed."

"Any idea where that is?"

"In one of the boxes in the garage."

Grinning, Ben nodded. "All right. I think there's only about eight of them."

"It's getting kind of late, so we'd best hurry if we can."

"Sure, Daed."

Sitting back on his haunches, Jay clenched his teeth as he heard Ben chatting with Tricia, who had shown up about an hour ago. Ben had invited her over, saying she would be a lot of help.

Jay imagined she might have been helpful, too. If she had known what their furniture looked like, knew their house better, and hadn't been so besotted with his eldest boy. Of course, he knew the attraction was mutual for Ben. Ever since he'd met Tricia, nothing seemed to matter but that fresh-faced girl. Part of him was glad that Tricia was making his son's move so pleasant. But honestly, the boy could use a lesson or two about managing his time better.

After sending William to his room to unpack his boxes, Jay grumbled to himself, "We'll never get this done."

"Oh, I think you will," Emma Keim said with a cheery smile as she came in through the kitchen, three little girls following behind her like a trio of ducklings. "You men look as busy as a hive of bees."

Climbing to his feet, he managed to hide a moan as his back protested. "Emma, hello." Seeing her daughters' sweet, clean faces staring back at him, he smiled. "And hello to you, too, Lena, Mandy, and Annie. You three look pretty in blue today. What brings you here?"

"The girls and I brought you boys some supper."

"You did?" His heart softened as he saw little Annie peek at him from behind her mother. She was clutching Emma's dark blue dress like it was her lifeline to the rest of the world. But she also looked intrigued by their visit. "Did you help, too, Annie?"

Annie bit her bottom lip and nodded shyly. "I helped with the cookies."

Mark entered the room, William behind him. "Hi, Mrs. Keim. Hey, Lena, Mandy, and Annie."

Emma's eyes twinkled. "Hello, Mark and William."

"Did you really make us cookies?"

"We made you a whole supper," Lena said. "Pulled-pork barbecue sandwiches, potato salad, deviled eggs, cookies, and a cherry pie."

William's eyes turned as big as saucers. "You brought us pie *and* cookies?"

"I had a little bit of time, so I made you a cherry pie. Then the girls pointed out that not everyone likes cherry pie. So I made some cookies, too."

Jay felt extremely humbled. "I can't believe you spent so much time on our meal. *Danke.*"

"It was no trouble, especially since Frankie ate your pizza. We enjoyed making it," Emma said. "Didn't we, girls?"

Three little heads nodded just as Ben and Tricia entered the room, Jay's smallest toolbox in his hand. "I found it, Daed."

"*Gut.* Is there a wrench and a hammer inside? Did you check?"

"Yep. I checked." Turning to Emma, he smiled brightly. "Hi."

"Mrs. Keim brought supper," Mark announced.

"You boys should simply call me Emma," she said.

William looked pleased. "Can I, Daed?"

"I suppose that would be all right."

After making sure Tricia and Emma and her girls all said hello, Jay said, "If you wouldn't mind putting everything down on the kitchen counter, we'll eat in a little while."

Instead of going directly to the kitchen, Emma turned to Mark and said, "Have you boys unpacked the kitchen yet?"

"Not really."

"I wanted to get their rooms set up first," Jay explained.

"That makes perfect sense. Tricia, would you like to help me in the kitchen? I bet the two of us could get a lot done in no time. That is, if you don't mind me organizing your kitchen, Jay?"

Ben grinned. "Daed is *gut* at growing things that belong in the kitchen, not organizing it."

"That is true," Jay admitted. "Thank you, Emma, for your help."

After giving Ben a sweet smile, Tricia followed Emma and her three daughters into the kitchen. Jay did his best not to roll his eyes at the way Ben gazed after his girl.

When they disappeared from view, Mark whistled softly. "Wow. Emma sure has a lot of energy."

"That she does," Jay said as he picked up his toolbox.

Lowering his voice, Mark asked, "Ben, do you remember Mamm ever being like that?"

"*Nee*, but Mamm was sick. Remember? She was sick for a long time."

Mark slumped. "*Jah*. I kept hoping she'd get better but she never did."

William froze, then rushed to his room.

Mark frowned. "What's wrong with Will?"

Jay had a pretty good idea but he didn't want to risk hurting his middle boy's feelings. "I'm not sure, but I'll check on him in a minute." Holding up his toolbox, he said, "I've got a bed to put together anyway."

"I'll go with you, Daed," Ben said.

"What about me?" Mark asked. "What should I do?"

Ben folded his arms over his chest. "If you can't figure out something to do right now, you're hopeless."

"Hey!" Mark sputtered.

Jay grinned at his eldest as they walked into William's room. "You should try to have more patience with your *bruder*."

"He needs to stop saying dumb things," Ben said as they stepped over two folded cardboard boxes.

"Looks like you're making good progress, Will," Jay said. "You've got a lot put away already."

"And I like the color of your walls. I thought it might be too bright, but it's a *gut* color," Ben added.

William didn't answer, simply shrugged.

Sharing a concerned look with Ben, Jay grabbed two of the metal bed frames and started fastening the bolts into place. "So, Will . . . You okay?"

"*Jah.*"

"Sure? Mark didn't mean to upset you, you know. He always simply says what is on his mind."

"I know."

Though it was obvious Will was still upset, Jay decided not to prod any further. Each of his boys responded better when they had some time to think about things. Instead, he concentrated on the task at hand. "Grab a side, wouldja Ben?"

"Sure, Daed," Ben replied and knelt on the floor to help. Less than thirty minutes later, the frame was fastened securely and the mattresses were placed on it.

After sending Ben to go help Mark with his bed frame, Jay picked up the sheets and motioned his youngest over. "Take a side, Will." Together, they slipped on the bottom sheet. Next, Jay pulled on the top sheet.

"Hey, Daed?" William mumbled as he tucked one side of his sheets underneath the mattress.

"*Jah?*"

"Can I ask ya something?"

"Of course."

"Um . . . what did Mark mean about Emma being so different

from Mamm? He weren't just talking about when she was sick, was he?"

Though it would have been easier to pretend that Mark and Ben had only been referring to Evelyn's illness, Jay couldn't bring himself to lie. "Mark simply meant that all women do things differently. Just as each of us are different, different mothers have favorite ways of doing things, too." The conversation was making Jay uncomfortable. It brought up things that he hadn't wanted to admit, even to himself. Emma *was* different from Evelyn. And once again, Jay had noticed that in no time at all.

William shook his head. "I don't think that's what he meant. Ben agreed with him."

"They didn't mean anything. No one wanted to hurt your feelings, either."

William glared. "Daed, I know Mark meant something other than Mamm being sick."

Jay didn't want to talk about Evelyn. But, he supposed, the Lord and Will had decided it needed to happen whether he was ready for it or not. Now that he had the blue, white, and yellow building-block quilt over William's sheets and blankets, Jay figured there was no time like the present. He patted the mattress. "Let's sit down."

After Will was settled next to him, Jay said, "Your mother was a wonderful woman. She was a wonderful mother and I loved her." He sighed, navigating his way through the conversation with as much care as he could. He didn't want to upset Evelyn's memory for Will or accidentally be disrespectful to the woman currently organizing his kitchen, either. "But Mamm wasn't the type of woman to be so forthright or, um, capable."

"What does that mean?"

"It means your mother wasn't much of a self-starter."

"But didn't she cook?"

"She did. Of course she did. But she wasn't necessarily the type of woman to cook for other people, bring it by, and then offer to organize their kitchen. All Mark did was point that out."

"Do you wish she had been like that?"

Secretly, he wished for a lot of things. But those would always remain his secrets. "I loved your mother for who she was. We're all special in our own ways, William. Your *mamm* was so very sweet and had a giving heart, too. She was special."

"Even when she was sick, she read me stories," William said quietly.

The lump that had been lodged in Jay's throat the whole time Evelyn had been dying from cancer returned suddenly. It took some effort to say the words his youngest needed to hear. "She loved to read to you. She loved books."

"Was Mark being mean?"

"No. He's just being Mark. You know how he always says what's on his mind the moment he thinks it." Giving into the impulse, Jay wrapped his arms around William and squeezed. "It will be okay, Will. And you can always ask about Mamm. Always."

Pulling away, William nodded. "Can we eat now?"

"I hope so. Why don't you go find out how the kitchen is going and I'll check on your brothers." Jay was glad when William walked out of the room without another word. He needed a moment to think about everything he'd said—and how he felt about it, too.

Closing his eyes, he forced himself to relax and reflect on the things he'd told William about Evelyn. After a few seconds, he realized that he had, indeed, spoken the truth. Evelyn had been very sweet and had loved all of them dearly. Just as they had loved her.

But she had also gone to heaven and now existed only in their hearts and memories.

"Supper!" William called out.

Jay opened his eyes and grinned. His Evelyn was gone, but life had also moved on. They were now in a new home in a new state and supper was ready.

"Everyone wash up first," Jay called out.

After a pause, he saw Mark run into the bathroom. "I'm so hungry, Daed," he said with a smile.

"Me, too." He joined him at the sink, then headed to the kitchen, trying to remember the last time he'd had homemade cherry pie.

Emma's girls were setting out plates, forks, and napkins when he entered the kitchen. Tricia was putting away a couple of pots and pans. On the floor next to the back door was a stack of neatly folded cardboard boxes. "You girls have been busy."

"We are nowhere near done, but at least you'll be able to eat your supper," Emma proclaimed.

"It was mighty kind of you to think of us. *Danke*."

She beamed but looked a bit embarrassed, too. "It's just sandwiches and such, Jay."

It wasn't "just" that. It was more. With a sigh, he said, "I was hoping to get further along but I guess I need to let the boys enjoy their supper."

"I think so. I mean, I hope so. It's been my experience that *kinner* get more done when their stomachs are filled."

"I think you might be right about that." Of course, his boys' bellies were rarely completely full. Jay stood by her side and helped organize the meal.

"We should probably leave now."

"Of course not. You need to stay with us and help us eat all the food."

"We made it for you."

"We'd rather you stay." He looked toward his boys, who already had their plates piled high. "Right, boys?"

"Right!" Mark said with a smile.

Jay hid a grin. That was Mark's way. He was naturally easygoing and loved nothing better than a full house or a large gathering. It was obvious Ben cared about little at the moment except for Tricia, but even William looked as if he'd shaken off his doubts.

"Please stay."

"We'd be happy to, if you'd like for us to."

In no time, Jay, Tricia, Emma, and the girls were lining up and helping themselves to the wonderful-looking meal. As soon as plates were filled, each headed out to the back porch. The rain had gone, leaving the air thick with humidity.

Once everyone was gathered together, he said simply, "Let us remember the Lord."

All of them, even little Annie, bowed their heads. Then, one by one, they started eating. After a bit, Jay told Emma all about the truck and the rain and the soggy boxes. The boys added their two cents, and soon the most frustrating day became a good story.

Emma smiled at it all, laughing at all the appropriate times. It made Jay realize again how much he liked the ease of feminine company.

Little by little, he began sharing more about himself, too. Ben told a story about a box of toads he'd collected at their old house, much to Tricia's dismay. Soon Annie's laughter rang through the air as Mark described how long it had taken them to gather all the frogs—they'd kept hopping out of their box.

Through it all, Jay found himself meeting Emma's eyes and sharing a knowing look. It was the kind of meal that he'd always wanted to share with his boys and their mother—but something that had never actually happened. It was the kind of meal he knew he'd be thinking about when he closed his eyes that night. Some moments were simply too sweet to forget.

Chapter 6

You didn't have to see me home, Ben," Tricia said as they hopped off the shuttle and started walking down Kaufmann Avenue. "The SCAT stops very close to the Orange Blossom Inn. I couldn't get lost if I tried." Gesturing with her hand, she said, "Plus, it's very safe here. I never worry about walking alone around Pinecraft."

"I know where the SCAT stops."

When Ben didn't expand on that, she peeked up at his face. "So, you must realize that I am perfectly capable of getting on and off a shuttle by myself."

"I know you are perfectly capable of doing just about anything you want to do." The corners of his lips turned up. "After all, you're the girl who traveled all the way to Sarasota, Florida, without telling your aunt you were coming."

Tricia was beginning to regret ever telling him that. Ben was so responsible he couldn't seem to wrap his head around the idea that she would do something so impulsive. Still, she kept their conversation on target. "So . . ."

"So, I like seeing you home."

Deliberately, she kept her gaze forward. No way did she want him to see how much his words affected her.

"Besides, Tricia, I wanted to get out of there."

"You did?"

"Oh, *jah*. You saw how crazy my *haus* was." He shivered, making her grin. "All those little girls running around? William going crazy? Furniture and boxes and my *daed* acting like it was gonna be perfectly possible to organize it all in about six hours? I needed a break."

She giggled. "Your *daed* did act like he was going to have everything organized in no time."

Ben nodded. "That's his way." He shook his head in exasperation. "He's not a big fan of sitting around. Sometimes I think he resents having to sleep."

"Perhaps I should point out that we were just sitting outside eating sandwiches for the last hour. I thought it was a lot of fun."

"That was fun. That was great. Thank goodness for Emma Keim. If she hadn't come along with her girls and that picnic basket I don't think my *daed* would have let us stop yet."

"Emma is really nice. And boy, can she cook. Almost as good as my aunt Beverly, and that is saying a lot."

"Especially those deviled eggs. I could have eaten five of them," he said as he pressed a hand on her waist to guide her around a pair of tourists taking pictures of some flowering orange-blossom trees.

When they got back on track, the delicious fragrance of the blossoms permeating the air, and warmth from his touch still fresh in her mind, Tricia glanced up at him again. "Emma's girls are cute, too," she added, hoping to keep her focus on their conversation and not on just how happy she was to be spending more time alone with him. From the moment she'd practically run into him in the hall outside his room at the inn, there had been a connection between them that was special. It seemed as if they always had things to tell each other.

She was so glad God had brought them together.

He chuckled. "*Jah*. They were girly and busy and squealed a lot. I've never really been around little girls that much and I don't think I could handle being around them all the time, but I thought they were mighty cute. Especially little Annie. She was a lot of fun."

"She liked you. She kept edging closer to ya."

"I was glad. She's funny, telling me about her beagle, Frankie."

As they passed a large family with six or seven *kinner,* Tricia noticed how both parents looked kind of exhausted, like they were counting the minutes until bedtime. Which got her thinking. "Why do you think Emma and her girls came over?"

Ben looked down at her. "What do you mean?"

"I mean Emma went to a lot of trouble."

"They were simply being neighborly."

"*Jah*, but your family is not in her neighborhood. Your farm is a ten-minute SCAT ride away. She had to load up all the food and keep track of three little girls all the way to your *haus*."

As they turned down Burky Street and began to pass house after house framed by bright flower beds, Ben seemed to consider her words. Then he shrugged. "I think you're overthinking things, Tricia. Emma brought us a welcome meal. I bet she brings lots of families food all the time. Plus, you know, her dog ate our pizza the other day."

"Well, I've lived here in Pinecraft a few months now and I've never seen her do too much besides be with her girls. And chase Frankie, of course."

Ben didn't even smile at her mention of Frankie. "I'm sure Emma was only being nice."

"Of course," Tricia said quickly, though she didn't really believe that. She'd seen how Emma kept glancing at Ben's *daed*. And how Jay's eyes had softened when Emma smiled, and then how hard he'd tried to hide it. "I'm sure they're simply glad to meet each other because they have a lot in common."

Ben stopped right in front of Winnie Sadler's house. Mrs. Sadler's cat, Serena, looked up from her nap on the front porch, then flipped onto her side. "Wait a minute. Are you saying you think they like each other?"

"Maybe," she hedged. Though she thought the idea of Jay and Emma liking each other was rather sweet, it was now obvious that Ben didn't care for the idea. At all.

"Tricia, my father is a widower," he said.

"I know." She shrugged. "I only meant that I think it's nice that they met each other, since Emma is a widow and all." She bit her lip. Had that come out completely wrong? Had she just made it sound as if she thought it was good that Jay and Emma had lost their spouses?

"You know, my *mamm* only passed away a year and a half ago." Ben looked so appalled and his voice so pained, that Tricia wished she could navigate a conversation as well as she could the shuttle stops.

Feeling worse than terrible, she backtracked quickly. "Ben, I'm so sorry. I've been really insensitive," she said in a rush. Here she'd been so thankful for their connection and the way they were able to converse about most anything, and she'd ruined it by saying too much. "Please forgive me. And forget I said anything, too. Actually, let's forget *everything* I said."

Reaching out, he pressed his palm to the center of her back. "Hush, Trish," he said gently. "You don't need to apologize. I'm sorry for snapping at you. You were only speaking your mind."

She sighed in relief as she realized that he wasn't mad at her. She hadn't messed everything up.

"*Nee,* I was being silly. Again, I'm really sorry. I'm sure your *daed* and Emma are just friends. And there's nothing wrong with that. Actually, there's *everything* good about that." Ack! She was talking too much. She had to stop herself from blabbering on about things she knew little about.

Ben sighed. "You're right. There isn't anything wrong with my father making a friend. I mean, look at us."

Tricia forced herself to smile brightly. After all, she had practically brought this on. "*Jah,* look at us! We hit it off right away."

She ached to tell him just how glad she was that they were friends, but she didn't want to scare him off. Then, of course, there was the fact that she didn't want to simply be *friends* with Ben Hilty. She already knew for a fact that she liked him a lot.

"We did—well, we *ran into each other* right away."

"Hey, I had a whole lot of towels stacked in my arms. I could hardly see where I was going."

"But that didn't stop you from walking down the hall like your feet were on fire." He chuckled. "The moment we collided, they all fell in a heap at your feet."

"And you helped me pick them all up . . . and place them in the linen closet."

"I was using any excuse to be around you a little longer."

"And I was glad you did," she admitted. She'd relived those first few moments between them a hundred times. It had been like she'd known something momentous had just taken place.

Ben pressed his hand to her waist again as they turned left toward the inn, passing right by the Palm Grove Mennonite Church with the beautiful flowering tree gracing its front yard. "I'm glad we met, Tricia."

"Me, too."

"My *grandmommi* always used to tell me that the Lord shines on us even when we aren't looking for his rays of light. I guess that's what happened when we met. I wasn't looking for anything special but there you were, at our inn."

"The Lord does know everything we need," she said with a smile.

"You know, I never thought about my *daed* being lonely, but maybe he does get lonely every now and then," he said slowly. After a pause, he continued, sounding more reflective. "Mark and me, well, we don't spend a lot of time with him. Not anymore."

"At least he has William."

Ben shook his head. "William is a handful. Managing him takes the patience of a saint. If I were my father, I would want a break from my little *bruder* every now and then."

"I'm sure your father misses your *mamm*."

"I'm sure he does. My mother . . . she was great." He looked at her again. "Let's not talk about my parents anymore."

"What do you want to talk about?"

When he looked down at her this time, there was a new, mischievous look in his eyes. "How about we talk about when I'm going to get to see you again."

She bit her lip before deciding not to play any games. "I want to see you whenever you have time to see me."

"It's as easy as that?"

"Well, as easy as a SCAT ride," she teased. "And, as long as I am not working."

"I'll see if I can pick up William from school sometimes in the afternoon."

"If you do that, stop by the inn and say hello. Or maybe I'll see you at church? Here in Pinecraft, because of all the tourists, we all go to the Amish church instead of worshipping in other people's homes. Maybe we could meet there one Sunday? I mean, if you'd like to meet there."

"I'd like that," he said as they stopped in front of the inn. "I'll be seeing you, Tricia. Count on it."

She smiled at him before walking up the steps. "I already am," she murmured to herself.

FOR THE REST OF the night, Tricia replayed their conversation over and over, reflecting on how fast things between her and Ben were happening . . . and how she didn't want it to be any other way.

Chapter 7

The inn was half empty.

As Beverly Overholt scooped up the last of the Hilty boys'
sheets, she knew that she should be breathing a huge sigh of relief. The boys had been well-behaved and mannerly, but they'd
still been boys stuck on the top floor of a bed-and-breakfast.
The youngest, especially, had been growing rather restless. He
needed room to run and play.

But now they were at their new farm and the inn was far quieter. Yet instead of feeling a renewed sense of peace, Beverly felt
the same as she had when Leona, Mattie, and Sarah had left the
attic room four months ago . . . a little blue.

She had no reason to be, either.

Business at the Orange Blossom Inn couldn't have been better. It was a rare day when they had one room vacant, let alone
several. Rarer still when she wasn't booking reservations, baking

scones and cakes for afternoon tea, or feeling the need to weed her front flower garden.

But today was one of those days. With half of her guests checked out and the remaining having informed her that they wouldn't be back until dark, Beverly had been able to forego her usual afternoon tea service. And since she'd given Tricia most of the day off so she could spend it with Penny Knoxx, Beverly had unexpected time on her hands.

After depositing the sheets in her washing machine and turning it on, Beverly poured herself a Mason jar full of iced tea and went outside to her front porch. She ignored the inviting trio of white rocking chairs and simply sat on the stoop, content to smell the lingering scent of orange blossoms on the trees and watch the occasional bicyclist pedal by.

As the minutes passed, Beverly knew that she needed to face the facts. She wasn't fretting about the Hilty boys leaving or simply relaxing after a busy couple of days.

She was missing Eric Wagler.

A good portion of her brain was shouting that such a thing simply didn't make sense. Eric had first appeared in her life earlier this year to inform her that he rightfully owned the inn she'd thought belonged to her after her aunt, the previous owner, had passed away. In the beginning, she'd resented him something awful. Beverly had arrived at the inn during a time of need and for years it had been her haven. When he'd told her about his plans for the inn, she'd been angry. Why, she'd even called her lawyer to straighten things out!

But eventually, she'd discovered that her aunt Patty had merely been leasing the inn. Beverly still had no idea why Patty had never told her. Maybe it had slipped her mind. Maybe, after running it for so many years, Patty had actually thought of the

Orange Blossom Inn as hers, and when she'd known she was about to pass on into heaven she hadn't thought to explain to Beverly how things really were.

Whatever the reason, Eric's news had stung.

Eric, too, had been surprised by things. At first he wasn't sure he even wanted to run an inn in Florida. But after spending some time at the inn a few months ago, he had decided to move from Pennsylvania to Florida.

They'd also come to an agreement about running it: She was going to manage the day-to-day operations while he would handle the finances. She'd been so relieved to know that she was going to keep her job.

But she'd been even happier to realize that, as time passed, Eric had become a good friend.

Now, however, he was a distant one. He'd returned to Pennsylvania in order to put his house on the market. His plan had been to sell it quickly and then move to Sarasota, but the Lord hadn't seen fit for that to happen yet. His house hadn't sold and he was still in Pennsylvania.

And she'd come to truly miss him.

They'd taken to calling each other on occasion, presumably for work reasons. But usually, after dwelling on inn business for a few minutes, they would simply chat. It was funny, but their distance seemed only to bring them closer than ever.

Noticing that her Mason jar was empty, Beverly took it to the kitchen and filled it again. Then she finally did what she'd been wanting to do for the last hour. She picked up the phone and dialed his number.

As it rang, Beverly tried to tell herself that it would be a good thing if he didn't answer. She could leave a message and do something productive instead. There were always chores to do around the inn. Why, she could clean out the pantry!

"Hello?"

"Hi, Eric," she said quickly, so very happy that she wouldn't have to tackle that pantry anytime soon. "It's Beverly."

"Hey. What's going on? Is there a problem?"

"Not a single one." He didn't sound all that happy to hear from her and now she felt foolish. "I, uh, was simply wondering how your house sale was going today." She frowned, realizing how she sounded: awkward!

"It's the same. Which means my house is still on the market and hasn't received an offer."

"Oh, dear. I am sorry."

"I am, too, but I haven't given up yet. My real estate agent promised that things usually pick up this time of year. I guess a lot of families move around the end of summer."

Thinking of the Hiltys, she said, "We recently had a family stay here for that very reason. Well, actually a widower and his three sons. He is going to take over an organic farm on the outskirts of Sarasota."

"Poor guy. I can't imagine raising three children by myself." His voice sounded warmer now, his words easier, as if he'd settled into their conversation.

"I did feel sorry for him, though I never heard him complain about his situation. Oh! Guess what?" she added.

"What?"

"Tricia has a beau. His name is Ben and he's one of that man's sons."

Eric's chuckle on the other end of the line eased her, and for the first time all day, she felt like herself again. "Bev, don't keep me in suspense! Tell me all about him. Do you like him? Do you think it's serious?"

"Well, I think I like him. He's mannerly."

"Mannerly? That's it?"

"*Nee*. Let's see, he's rather handsome. And strapping."

"*Strapping?*" Eric laughed. "Bev, I do love your descriptors."

She supposed she was sounding rather old-fashioned. "Let's see, he seems mighty strong. Full of muscles. And he's tall, too. Plus, he has blond hair and blue eyes. It seems he grew up on a farm in Charm, Ohio. He also seems quite taken with Tricia."

"He sounds like quite the catch."

"To be sure." Smiling, she said, "Tricia noticed him immediately." Sitting alone in the kitchen, Beverly rolled her eyes. Who wouldn't have noticed Ben immediately?

"Are you worried about him breaking her heart?"

"A little, though I'm sure it's just a little crush. You know how kids are." Though, of course, neither Ben nor Tricia were actually kids . . .

When Eric chuckled and asked about Beverly's best friend, Sadie, Beverly twirled the telephone cord around her finger and chatted some more.

She also decided that she was going to write him a letter that week. There was nothing wrong with having a friend to write to and talk with occasionally. Nothing wrong with that at all. After all, they needed to get to know each other better, since he *was* technically her boss now. Yes, getting to know each other better was a mighty good idea. And an important step in their friendship.

She simply needed to keep reminding herself that she and Eric were destined to be friends and friends only. Only a foolish woman would ever dream of becoming more than that with her boss.

Only a very foolish woman indeed.

AFTER WALKING HER GIRLS to Pinecraft Elementary, Emma decided to work on their new dresses when she got back home.

Thankful to have some quiet time to herself, she carefully cleared off the kitchen table and wiped down the surface with a rag. Most of the time, she merely handed down Lena's dresses to Mandy and Mandy's dresses to Annie—it made the most sense—but every couple of months she took the time to sew each of them a new one.

She'd ordered some beautiful fabric in shades of yellow for their new dresses. Emma loved outfitting them in coordinating colors, loved seeing how the three of them looked as they walked together, their similar frames and brown hair making them look almost like triplets. She imagined one day soon Lena would have enough of that and protest that it was time she decided what to wear. And Emma knew that when that day came, she wouldn't blame her. But until then, she mused as she bent over the table and traced her pattern with a thick pencil, her three girls were going to match as much as possible.

A brief knock sounded at her back door, followed by the creak of it opening. "Emma, where are you?" her mother called out.

"Standing by the kitchen table," she answered just as Frankie got to his feet and padded toward the kitchen. After hearing her mother greet Frankie, Emma grinned.

"Oh, no, Frankie. You stay out of my basket," another voice chimed in. Rachel, Emma's mother-in-law.

Rachel and her mother had been friends for years. Their

friendship had grown after Emma married Sanford and had cemented in the years since. Now they were true blessings in Emma's life. No two women could care for Emma and her girls more.

But this addition to her mother's visit changed things. She loved her mother. She loved Rachel, too. But she found them to be exhausting when they paid a call on her together.

As Frankie trotted back in, circled Emma, then lay down to sleep under the card table, Emma mentally prepared herself to face them both. When they walked into the room, she noticed that they were both wearing gray. "Have you two decided to start wearing matching dresses like your granddaughters?" she teased.

Rachel chuckled. "*Nee*. We didn't plan this at all. I was pretty surprised to see Mary Beth wearing gray like me."

"You both look nice. Rather somber for a Tuesday, but nice."

Her mother took a seat in one of the wicker chairs. "I'm not somber. Merely busy. Mighty busy."

Rachel sat down in another chair. "I've been mighty busy, too. Joseph is courting!"

Joseph was Sanford's youngest brother. "That's *wonderful-gut* news. Who is he interested in?"

"Katie Byler."

"I don't know her."

"You'd know her if you saw her. She's a lively thing. She and Joseph are a *gut* match, I think. I hope he doesn't mess things up."

Emma knew better than to touch that comment. Rachel had a definite opinion on how most things should happen, whether it was making a bed, frosting a cake, or properly courting. "Ah. Well, as you can see, I thought I'd spend the day making some new dresses for the girls."

Both of her visitors exchanged looks. "Any special reason you're making them something new to wear?" her mother asked.

"*Nee*. None other than that they need some new dresses. They are growing tall." Emma waited for the usual comments about how they had inherited Sanford's height, but when nothing came, she straightened, set down her pencil, and pulled up a chair. "I'm starting to get the feeling that you two didn't come over simply to say hello."

"The truth is that we heard that you took Lena, Mandy, and Annie to another man's home," Rachel said, in a deceptively off-hand way.

Which Emma knew wasn't offhand at all.

Because she'd known that news traveled around their small community faster than lightning bugs in the woods, Emma had been mentally preparing herself for this since her visit to the Hilty farm. It was time to tread carefully. "Please don't worry, Rachel. The girls and I delivered a meal to a new neighbor's house. That's all."

"But that wasn't all, was it?" her mother interjected.

"Pardon?"

Looking at her intently, her mother said, "We heard you ate with them."

"That is true." Looking from her mother to Rachel to her mother again, Emma attempted to allay their concerns—and, with any luck, change the topic. "Tricia Overholt from the Orange Blossom Inn was there, too. Tricia is seeing the man's eldest boy. His name is Ben, and I have to tell you that they are smitten. It's so sweet to see."

Mamm leaned forward. "Ah, Emma, I'm sure you didn't think about this, seeing how your heart still belongs to Sanford and all, but your visit could have been misconstrued by others."

"I realize that, but I did nothing wrong. It was a simple, neighborly visit. That's all."

"That man is a widower, yes?"

"He is."

"Some people in our community might think you are attempting to form a romantic attachment if you spend too much time with his family."

"Who is worried?"

"I wouldn't want to spread any gossip, Emma," Rachel said. "We merely wanted you to hear what people might start thinking."

Emma knew the easiest thing to do was nod politely and follow their advice. The women meant well, and people did gossip, but she wasn't ready to give up her new friends. "I hope I can count on the two of you to set everyone's doubts to rest," she countered.

"I'll do what I can, but you know how it is, dear. We mothers need to hold ourselves to the highest standards."

"I think you're both making mountains out of molehills. Nothing untoward is going on. Jay and I simply found that we enjoy each other's company."

"Does this mean you will see him again?"

"Well, I'm not going to avoid making a friend because I'm suddenly worried about gossip. The Hiltys have just moved here and they need to feel welcome. We're going to be their friends."

"All right. But just make sure you let that man know that your heart belongs to your husband."

That stung. And to her surprise and dismay, the pain settled in and grew. Her mother was right. Her heart would always belong to Sanford. Ever since he'd died, she'd been doing her best to honor his memory.

But she couldn't help feeling that she'd been a little forgotten in the effort to preserve Sanford's memory. What about how *she* felt? What about *her* pain? Her loneliness? Sometimes it felt as though her in-laws and parents would never see her as anything more than Sanford's widow.

Didn't she matter anymore?

"I don't need reminders about what is in my heart," she blurted.

"Of course not."

"I'm the one who lost a husband. I don't need you reminding me about that."

"I'm sorry if you thought I was inferring."

"You were. I also know *what* you were inferring. For some reason, you both came over here to make sure I did nothing to ruin Sanford's place in my life."

Rachel's eyes filled with tears. "I'm not sure why you are reacting like this."

"Rachel, I know you care about me, and I am mighty grateful for that. But it isn't fair for you and Mamm to think you need to remind me about how I should be feeling. Or what I have lost. If I want to befriend a man who I have much in common with, you need to let me do that. Both of you do."

Her mother looked on the verge of arguing, but to Emma's surprise, Rachel cut her off. "You are right, dear," she said in her sweet way. "I'm so sorry if you thought we came over here to judge. I didn't mean to. You have every right to keep making friends. You have every right to be yourself. I promise, both your mother and I only want you to be happy."

"Is that true, Mamm?" Emma asked.

"Of course, Emma. Rachel is right. We might have overstepped ourselves today. Maybe."

But Emma knew that her mother was only backing down because Rachel looked on the verge of pulling her out of the room if she didn't.

It was time to make amends. The three of them had been through too much together to dwell on disagreements. "Would you two ladies like to have some tea or *kaffi* and help me make three little girls dresses?"

Rachel opened her purse and pulled out her glasses. "You cut, I'll pin."

"And I'll sew on your treadle," her mother announced. "Why, with our help, I bet you can have them done by the time the girls come home from school."

"That would be *wunderbaar*, Mamm," Emma said quietly. When her mother's expression softened, she knew that her mother understood that she was talking about so much more than just the sewing project.

Emma hoped they'd feel the same way tomorrow, too.

Chapter 8

$\mathcal{A}$re you sure Emma won't mind if we stop by today?" Jay asked William as they walked up the steps to the Keims' front door.

"She ain't going to mind at all. When I saw Miss Emma at school yesterday morning, she said I could stop by anytime. This is anytime, ain't so?"

It was comments like that that made Jay think the Lord had a sense of humor. Headstrong, eternally optimistic, and constantly in motion, his youngest was as different from his two older brothers as could be. He wasn't sure how he would have gotten through each day without William's quips and comments. "Perhaps, but sometimes people say things they don't mean," he cautioned.

"Oh, she meant what she said, I'm sure of it. Lena said her *mamm* loves visitors."

"All right. I guess we'll see if she likes *unannounced* visitors." Rapping his knuckles on the door, he said, "Don't forget your manners, Will."

"I won't. But Daed, you don't have to have *gut* manners with Lena's *mamm*. You just have to be yourself."

"That may be true, but still, I'd like you to be your *best* self," he said just as Lena opened the door with a smile.

"Hi, Mr. Jay," she chirped as she bounded out onto the porch. Her pink dress was a little on the short side, showing off her tan lower calves and bare feet. "Frankie and I were watching you out the window."

She looked so proud of that fact, Jay realized she was expecting a response. "You were? I didn't see you there."

"I was there. We didn't know if you were ever gonna knock. I wanted to open the door right away but Mamm said I had to wait until you knocked before opening it up. What took you so long?"

Before Jay could fashion a reply, Will walked right inside. "There was no reason. My father was being a worrywart."

After bending down to greet Frankie, Jay said, "Is your mother around?"

"Oh, *jah*. She's sewing me a new dress." Pointing to her ankles, Lena added, "I'm growing."

"Actually, I'm right here," Emma said as she joined them at the door. Smiling brightly, she said, "Come on in."

Jay shut the door behind him just as William edged closer to Lena and whispered something in her ear.

The little girl grinned. "Mamm, can William and I go in the backyard with Mandy and Annie?"

"Sure, that is fine. Don't forget to look after Annie, Lena."

"I won't."

After the children disappeared, Emma clasped her hands in front of her waist. "How are you, Jay? Seeing you here is a nice surprise."

"I'm fine." Feeling more awkward by the second, he added, "Um, I hope you don't mind that we came by without an invitation."

"You now are officially invited to come over anytime you would like. Would you like to sit down?"

"Oh, sure. And since we're here anyway, I was hoping to talk to you about something. If you have time, that is."

"Of course I have time." She walked over and perched on the edge of a beautiful cherrywood rocking chair. After she smoothed a wrinkle in her violet dress, she smiled.

Jay sat down on her couch, liking the thick white canvas cover on it. He couldn't help but wonder, however, how in the world she kept a white couch clean with three little girls and one busy beagle.

Realizing she was patiently waiting for him to speak, he said, "It's about school and William."

"Yes?"

He wasn't sure how to begin. "I thought about sending William to the elementary school near the farm, but there aren't many Amish kids who go there. Mark and Ben are done with their schooling, so I decided to ride with William on the SCAT every morning and take him to Pinecraft Elementary."

"Since it's an Amish school, I can see why you would make that decision. I saw William yesterday when I dropped off the girls. He seemed happy enough." Looking at him closely, a new concern entered her expression. "Or are you not happy with it?"

"I'm plenty happy with the school. I think it's going to be fine. Miss Meyer seems to be competent."

"I think she does a *gut* job. There are almost thirty *kinner* in the classroom and she handles everyone from first to fifth grade well." She paused. "Does William not care for Miss Meyer? Some *kinner* don't do as well in a one-room school, you know. Around here, many Amish children simply go to the regular elementary schools, if that's what you're worried about. All of the English *kinner* are accepting of them. He'll make friends in no time."

"*Nee*, he seems to like Miss Meyer and the school, too. It just looks like he's a little bit behind in his reading and math. Miss Meyer thinks that he'll get caught up in no time, but he's going to need some help." Stumbling forward, he finally broached the idea that had been floating around in his head. "I wondered if you knew of someone I could talk to about helping him with his homework. Sometimes he needs a little extra help or explanation."

"That doesn't seem like too much to ask."

Now he was embarrassed. Emma was probably thinking he was the worst sort of father, a man who was not even willing to take the time to help his child when he needed it. "Here's the thing. I've got my hands full with the farm and the house and the produce stand. In order for us to start making a profit, I need to plant some fresh crops and see if there's a way to salvage some of the berry bushes and citrus trees that are already bearing fruit. All this takes time, you see."

"To be sure."

"I can do all that and help William, but I can't help him right after school, which is when it would be best for him. He gets tired after supper, and I know from experience that trying to get him to do homework that late is a recipe for disaster."

"That sounds like my Mandy. When she gets tired, we all try to stay away from her until she falls asleep."

He sighed in relief. "So you can understand why I'm asking?"

"Yes and no."

"What don't you understand?"

"Jay, why don't you simply ask me for help?"

He was confused. "I did. I'm asking you for names of tutors."

"Ask me to look after William after school. I'm home and I don't mind."

"I couldn't ask that of you."

"Why not? I'll be picking up Mandy and Lena anyway. And we always do homework in the early afternoons, after the girls have some time to play and a snack. William will fit right in."

"But I couldn't ask it of you."

"I offered. But I don't know why you wouldn't want to ask it of me anyway. We are two people in much the same situation. It's hard to do everything on one's own, I think. Even with my family nearby, it, well . . ."

"It isn't the same," he finished.

"Exactly," she said with a look of relief in her eyes. "Jay, I think we should be helping each other out as much as we can."

Everything she said made sense, but it was hard to come to terms with the idea that he would be asking so much of Emma when they hardly knew each other. In addition, he didn't know how he would be able to return the favor. "Will you let me pay you?"

"For helping William?" Hurt flashed in her eyes. "Definitely not."

He held up his hands. "I don't want to offend you, but I wouldn't have asked about getting help if I didn't intend to pay. I don't want to take advantage."

Looking slightly more mollified, she said, "You are not taking advantage."

Jay figured he should be coming up with a bunch of new reasons why he couldn't accept Emma's offer, but he really couldn't think of any. It was going to be an answer to his prayers. "Then, will you accept my thanks?"

"Of course."

"Thanks." He ran a hand through his hair, thinking yet again how challenging life had become since Evelyn's death. "Do you ever miss being married?" he asked suddenly.

She flinched. "What?"

"Sorry. I didn't mean to bring that up in such a clumsy way. It's just that while of course I miss Evelyn, there are times, like today, when I simply miss the ease of it. She took care of things like this." Thinking about all the years he'd pretty much only worried about the fields while she'd dealt with Ben's and Mark's issues at school, he added, "My *frau* did a lot of things around the house and with our family that I didn't even realize until she got sick."

"Tell me about her," Emma said.

"I wouldn't know where to start." Jay waited for the familiar pain that usually came from simply remembering Evelyn, but instead he only felt a curious emptiness.

"I can help you with that. What was she like?"

He blurted the first thing that came to mind. "Peaceful."

"How so?"

He felt his cheeks flush. "She was a *wonderful-gut* mother and wife. She would have had all of us far better organized if she'd been in charge of the move." Thinking about their relationship, he had to admit that in many ways he'd always felt like her protector. She'd needed him to help her find her way and he had gotten used to making her life easier. "She was quiet and a little shy. Kind of timid around strangers, too. But she was caring and helpful. She depended on me, but the boys also knew they could depend on her to give them her time. She loved to sit with them and hear about their days."

"She sounds like a wonderful woman."

"Evelyn was." Only now did he realize that he wasn't pining for her in the ways he used to. He missed *her*, of course, but often he found that he was really missing her tasks around the house and with the *kinner*. He missed her help.

What did that say about him?

"Jay, what's wrong? You look like you swallowed a cricket!"

"I'm sorry, I was just remembering something."

"Something bad?" Emma had such compassion in her eyes. In her blue eyes. Blue eyes that were framed by thick dark lashes and brows that swept up in a natural arc.

"Not at all." He knew he was stumbling but he suddenly felt like he was Ben's age and trying to get a pretty girl's attention. "Tell me about Sanford. What was he like?"

She pressed one of her hands to her chest. "Oh, goodness. Well, he was organized, too. And he liked things in order. He loved his little girls dearly, too. He was a *gut* man."

Jay noticed she didn't mention how much Sanford had loved her. He wondered if that was on purpose or if she simply thought it was understood. "I guess we both were blessed with good marriages."

"We were. I was blessed. Still, I can't believe Sanford left me so young. But then again, I guess since we grew up together the Lord decided that we'd already had lots of time together."

"I grew up with Evelyn, too. From the time I was twelve or thirteen, everyone assumed that we'd marry."

"That happened with Sanford and me, too." Looking back out at the front porch, she said, "We had a big wedding. Practically our whole church community was there."

"The same thing happened with Evelyn and me."

"It was nice." Her voice had turned wistful. A little melancholy.

He was feeling the same way. "*Jah*, it was," he agreed, though, "nice" didn't really cover the many emotions that had been running through him on their wedding day. He'd been glad to finally stop planning and worrying about everything going all right during the ceremony. He'd been eager to have Evelyn as his wife.

If he was being honest, he'd also been struggling with his emotions. Jay had begun to wonder if he and Evelyn had made the right decision, if their long friendship had really melded into a romance, or if they'd simply been too comfortable to want to shake up their lives.

Before he brought up any other topic that made him doubt how things had been between him and Evelyn, he got to his feet. "Well, I'd better collect William and get him home. Ben is no doubt waiting to ask me what time he can go see Tricia."

"They sure seemed smitten when I saw them together," she said as she walked to his side.

"I thought the same thing," he said as he stepped outside into her backyard. What he saw there made him smile. William was playing tag with Lena, and Frankie was barking at their heels. It was obvious that the beagle knew he was an important part of the family and loved "his" girls very much. William bent down and ruffled his velvety-soft ears. Frankie had just closed his eyes in what looked like extreme happiness when Annie's squeal lit the air.

"There's Serena!" she called out, pointing to a slim gray cat reclining on a tree branch just on the other side of the fence in the front yard. The cat was staring down into Emma's yard like she'd just discovered a very plump canary.

Emma tensed as she stared at the cat, as if she feared it was about to turn into a crazed mountain lion. "Oh, no."

"What's wrong?" Jay thought the cat looked rather harmless, and he really couldn't understand why Annie had taken off running.

"So many things," she muttered. More loudly, she said, "Serena is a roving cat. She doesn't seem to ever want to stay home. And Mrs. Sadler, her owner, bless her, never seems to keep track of her."

He shrugged as Frankie ran to the fence and let out a howl. "That little cat will be okay. We always had a couple of barn cats back in Ohio. They're smart creatures."

"Oh, Jay. That is not what I'm concerned about," she said as she gazed at Frankie worriedly. "Girls, one of you grab Frankie's collar, wouldja?"

Jay chuckled. "Dogs and cats don't always fight, Emma. Why, we had a shepherd once who was practically best friends with one of our barn cats."

"That ain't the case here." She looked around at the girls who were still playing. "Oh, those girls never listen when I need them to. Excuse me, Jay."

"Emma, can I help you?"

Before she could answer, somehow, some way, Frankie shoved himself under a very small gap under the fence, leaving only a cloud of dust. And Emma's groan.

"Uh-oh!" Annie cried. "Mommy, Frankie has found Serena!"

"He certainly has," Emma said under her breath.

As soon as Emma opened the gate, she and her three little girls scampered through, William on their heels. Jay followed as well. He was happy to help, though he wasn't sure how good he was going to be capturing a wayward cat or an excited beagle.

By the time he'd gotten through the gate, around the side of the house, and reached the middle of Emma's front yard, he didn't know whether to laugh or take charge of the situation.

Serena was about halfway up the tree and hissing angrily. Frankie had his front paws on the trunk, howling his displeasure. The girls were all calling for Frankie and Serena. And his boy? William was swinging from the bottom limb of the tree, on his way up.

"I'm gonna go save Serena, Daed!" he yelled. "I can climb trees real good, right?"

William also happened to be mighty good at falling out of trees. But before Jay could stop him, his son was on the next limb.

"Serena, come here!" his boy yelled again.

As William climbed, Frankie barked and howled. Serena taunted Frankie from her tree limb with a haughty flick of her tail, and Emma's little girls squealed, called for Serena, and egged William on—somehow all at the same time. Emma was standing a bit off to the side. Her arms were folded and she looked as if she'd been part of this scenario more than once or twice.

Jay couldn't help it, he started laughing.

To his pleasure, Emma began chuckling, too. "It seems that things have gotten out of hand yet again, *jah?*"

"*Jah.* Do you care if William is climbing your tree?"

"That's what they're there for. Ain't so?" she asked as she walked over and grabbed Frankie's collar. "Come here, you silly *hund*. Won't you ever learn that that cat lives to tease you?"

Frankie simply sat down and gazed at Emma with big, sad brown eyes.

"Oh, Frankie." She gave the dog a quick hug. "What am I going to do with you?" she murmured before walking him over to the girls.

Looking up at the tree, Jay called out to William. "Come on down, son. I'll get the cat."

"*Nee.* I got it, Daed," William said as he reached for Serena.

Serena meowed her protest, throwing in a hiss and a paw swipe for good measure. Looking alarmed, William jerked back. It seemed the cat thought she was a fierce lion or tiger instead of a plain gray house cat. Then Serena flicked her tail, gave him a superior feline sniff, and at last leapt from her branch to the ground. Seconds later, she was out of sight.

"She scratch you, son?" Jay called.

"*Nee*, but I lost her." William moaned.

Jay was just about to go offer him a hand out of the tree, but Emma got there first. "That cat is a wily one, William. She's confounded a great many people before you, I'm afraid. Can you get down all right?"

"Yep." Looking almost catlike himself, William swung down and landed on the ground. "That was fun. Daed, can we come again real soon?"

After sharing a smile with Emma, Jay asked, "What do you think about coming over here a couple of afternoons a week to do homework?"

"Really?"

"*Jah.* Emma said you can stay with her and the girls, then either Ben or I will come get you."

William looked up at Emma. "That's okay with you?"

Emma nodded. "It's more than okay," she said softly. "I'd like to spend time with you, William."

When William smiled and his eyes lit with something that looked a whole lot like hope, Jay knew that he'd reached a turning point with his youngest. William might not be done grieving for his mother—that might not happen for a very long time—

but it seemed as if he'd at last shed some of the sadness that he'd been wearing like an ill-fitting shirt.

The whole way home on the SCAT, as William told Jay about his day at school, the new friends he was making, and how much he wanted a dog just like Frankie, Jay smiled.

Well, until that very last part. "I don't think there's too many dogs like Frankie, son," he said through a chuckle. "Come to think of it, I think one Frankie in Pinecraft might just be all any of us can handle."

Chapter 9

$\mathcal{S}$ince Tuesday, Beverly had started making sure she was in the kitchen between ten and noon every day. That was the time Eric would phone, if he had time to give her a call.

In earlier conversations he'd explained that he usually took care of business in the mornings. It seemed he had all kinds of paperwork in his line of work. Lately, if he found that he needed a break around midmorning, he would pick up the phone just to check in.

It hadn't happened every day this week, but instead of feeling frustrated by the uncertainty of his calls, Beverly found herself enjoying the element of surprise. She actually kind of liked waking up in the morning and wondering if she was going to hear from Eric that day. After spending her first three years in Pinecraft making sure that everything was just so with the inn, she found herself enjoying the spontaneity of their relationship like few other things she'd known.

But as much as she looked forward to chatting with him, his phone calls didn't make or break her days. If he called and they talked for a while, it made her happy. If he didn't have time to call and she was forced to wait another day or two to hear his voice, she found that suited her, too.

Little by little, she'd stopped spending her late-morning hours preparing rooms and dusting. She did that first thing, or even had Tricia tend to the rooms when people checked out at eleven, as she was doing today. That suited Tricia fine because most of the guests tipped and Beverly allowed her to keep the tip money.

It also ensured that Beverly would have the kitchen to herself if Eric called.

In fact, Eric's calls were also why she had begun baking in the morning. Beverly had just rolled out the yeast dough for a fresh batch of caramel-pecan cinnamon rolls when the phone rang. After quickly wiping her hands with one of her favorite dishrags—one that was made from an old flour sack—she picked up the phone.

"Hello?"

"It took you three rings this morning," Eric teased. "You must have had your hands in soapy water."

She laughed. "My fingers were in something far better than that. Flour! I had to wipe them off so I wouldn't get dough all over the phone. That wouldn't do."

"Makes sense. What are you making today?"

She could practically hear the smile in his voice. "Caramel-pecan rolls."

"Oh, Bev," he said with a groan. "You're killing me. I haven't had anything that good to eat in days."

"Oh? What have you been eating?"

"Hmm. I had two slices of leftover pizza this morning."

He sounded so grumpy about it, she laughed. And because she knew him to be extremely capable, she said, "Eric, I hate to be the one to tell you this, but I do believe they have milk, fruit, toast, and eggs in Pennsylvania, too. You need to take advantage of your markets instead of just the pizza delivery service."

"Having a bowl of cereal and a banana while standing at the kitchen counter isn't the same as enjoying a plate of your caramel rolls, Beverly."

"This is true. But look on the bright side. If you ate homemade caramel rolls every morning you wouldn't think they were special anymore."

"I doubt that. Your baking is that good."

She smiled at his compliment. He wasn't the first person to compliment her baked goods, but for some reason, his enthusiasm for her cooking made her feel especially good inside. Like she could do something pretty special.

Feeling a little flustered about the direction of her thoughts, she moved the conversation forward. "It's your turn. Tell me how things are going. Have you had any showings this week?"

"Two."

He didn't sound very happy about that. "Two is *gut, jah?*"

"Well, two is better than none."

"Tell me what they said. Is anyone coming back?"

"Maybe one of them."

As Eric told her about the showings and then described the Realtor's reports, she tucked the phone under her chin, sprinkled the nut-and-cinnamon-sugar mixture on the dough, then easily rolled it into a loaf. It would rest for another forty minutes, then she'd slice it and place it into some prepared baking dishes.

She found conversation with Eric so easy. She liked how she

could do something simple while speaking to him on the phone. It seemed to make every task in her kitchen go faster.

"Do you have any more showings scheduled?"

"Not yet." He paused. When he spoke again, it was with a new thread of apprehension. "I wish I knew what was going to happen. I hate not being able to make plans. I hate not knowing when we're going to see each other again. Bev, I'm afraid it really is out of my hands."

"Of course it is. 'This God is our God forever and ever. He will guide us from now on,' " she quoted from Psalms.

"Those words are so true."

"Always," she said, looking around her cozy, bright kitchen that smelled of fresh bread and coffee and caramel. Who would have thought three years ago, when her heart had been broken from a failed engagement, that she was to have so many blessings in her life?

"I guess I need to keep remembering that my future is ultimately in the Lord's hands."

"It would be a good idea, I think." And just so he wouldn't think that she was too full of herself, she added, "Don't forget, I had to learn this lesson, too."

"I'll try my best. Though it is hard. I am really getting tired of waiting."

She walked to the window and looked out into the backyard, thinking how pretty the flowers and shrubs looked after she'd weeded and trimmed everything the afternoon before. She also couldn't help but remember how content Eric had looked when he'd sat next to those beds and read his paper in the early-morning hours.

And how much she'd enjoyed seeing him there.

After a short pause, Eric spoke again, his voice sounding slightly thick with emotion. "Now, tell me about Tricia. Is she still seeing that young man?"

"Boy, is she." Turning away from the window, Beverly quickly peeked through the kitchen's doorway. "I'm starting to worry about her."

"Why?" Sounding more agitated, he added, "What's wrong with the guy? I thought you said he seemed nice."

"Ben is nice. Well, so far, he has been. It's just that, well . . . this relationship of hers is moving kind of fast."

"I didn't think you saw anything wrong with that."

"I didn't . . . when I thought they weren't too serious. But the other day, I was sure I heard Tricia talking to a friend about marriage."

"Surely a lot of girls her age talk about getting married someday."

"I agree, but she didn't sound like she was dreaming about one day in the future. It sounded far more serious than that. Eric, I fear she's going to get hurt."

"I can see how you would feel like that," he said quietly. "Have you talked to her about it?"

His question soothed her because he was taking her seriously. She so appreciated that he wasn't making light of her concerns.

"Beverly, you there?" he prompted.

"*Nee*. I haven't talked to her." Thinking again, she amended her words. "I mean, not really."

"Why not?"

She thought the answer was rather obvious. "Because I'm not her mother, that's why. It's not my place."

"Bev."

By now she knew exactly what that one word meant coming

from Eric: It was both a reminder about her responsibility toward Tricia and a subtle hint that she had something important to offer. "I don't want to overstep my bounds."

"If she was worried about that, she would have never moved to Sarasota to live with you."

He did have a point. But, still . . . "What if I say the wrong thing?" she blurted.

"Then you'll say the wrong thing, apologize, and try to say the right thing. Tricia doesn't need you to be perfect and neither does God."

"I never thought about it that way. I think you are right."

"I know I am right," he said, his voice full of confidence. "Give it a try, Beverly."

"I will, but if I say the wrong words, you're going to hear about it," she warned.

He chuckled. "Promise me you'll pray about it first."

"For guidance."

"Yes, but also so that if you do say the wrong thing, I won't have to take all the blame for it. I'll share that burden with the Lord."

Beverly could just imagine Eric sitting at his desk, smiling, with his feet propped up on the corner of. It was obvious that he enjoyed their exchanges as much as she did. "You know I won't blame God, Eric," she teased. "Only you."

"Gee, thanks."

"Don't forget, I just reminded *you* to not forget that He guides us in all things."

"Fair enough." As the sound of voices floated across the line, she heard him shift. "I've got to go. I'll call you soon."

"Talk to you when I talk to you," she said and then hung up just as she saw Tricia peek in.

"Are you done with your phone call yet?" she asked with a knowing smile.

"Done? Oh, *jah*. I'm off the phone." Beverly hoped she sounded as nonchalant as she was trying to be.

"How was Mr. Eric today?"

"He was *gut*." Then something occurred to her. "How did you know I was speaking with Eric?" Oh, she hoped Tricia hadn't overheard her!

Looking like she had all the answers, Tricia grinned. "Aunt Beverly, I know you've been talking to Eric every couple of days. I've been trying to stay out of here when you take his calls."

"*Danke*, but there was no need. We simply enjoy catching up."

Tricia's smile softened as she looked down at her bare feet. "I'm sure you do."

Deciding there was no time like the present, Beverly said, "Come in here and sit with me, wouldja? I want to talk to you about something."

Immediately, a line formed between Tricia's brows. "Is anything wrong? Oh, no! Did that family from New York City complain about the noise again?"

"Noise? What noise?" Beverly couldn't imagine that their street sounded any noisier than the streets in New York.

"They are in Michael Knoxx's old room and that mother mockingbird has returned."

Relieved that the problem merely came from a pesky bird and not something worse, she said, "I guess we'd better tape some paper on the window."

"I tried to tell them that but they didn't believe it would work."

"No?"

Looking disgruntled, she added, "I don't think they believe I know what I'm talking about."

"I'll touch base with them and see if they have any concerns," she soothed. "Don't worry."

Tricia smiled but then looked expectantly once again. "So if it's not that couple, what's wrong?"

"Oh, nothing."

"You look kinda worried, Aunt Bev. You're gripping your coffee cup in the way you always do when something's on your mind."

Immediately, Beverly loosened her grip. Right then and there she knew she should have taken Eric's advice and prayed before saying a word to Tricia. Then again, since the Lord was always with her, she hoped He would feel compelled to simply jump in wherever He saw fit to do so. "I wanted to talk to you about Ben."

Tricia's light green eyes immediately turned wary. "What about Ben?"

"Um, well, you seem mighty happy with him."

"I am happy with him. He's a *gut* friend."

"Is that all he is to you?"

She leaned back, effectively putting up her guard. "What do you suspect him of being?"

"Tricia, I was not born yesterday. It's fairly obvious that you two are courting. Furthermore, as your aunt, I feel I should let you know that I'm starting to get worried about how serious things have gotten between you two."

"Aunt Beverly, I thought you liked Ben."

"I do. I like him *verra* much. But it, um, seems like you two are, um, progressing a little fast." There. She said it.

Tricia looked down at her hands, which were now folded in her lap. "I'm not doing anything wrong."

"I didn't say you were. Only that I am hoping to save you from getting hurt, Tricia."

"Ben isn't going to hurt me."

"You don't know that for sure." Of course, the moment she said that, Beverly wished she could take back her words. She sounded so judgmental. Almost like an old maid.

"You don't need to be concerned with this, Aunt Beverly. This is my personal business. Not yours."

That hurt. It also made her feel that she'd been correct when she'd told Eric she didn't have the right to offer Tricia advice. She wasn't the girl's mother. "I am not judging. I simply wanted to warn you. And tell you that I think it would be better for you in the long run if you slowed things down a bit."

"Slow things down?" Looking extremely annoyed, Tricia said, "Aunt Bev, what do you think we are doing?"

"Nothing bad, of course. I'm worried about your heart, that's all."

"My heart is fine."

Beverly got to her feet. It was obviously time to retreat. "All right, then . . ."

"You know, I got my heart broken at home. Not by a boy but by my friends."

"Anyone can be thoughtless," she said slowly. "That is why I want you to be more cautious."

"But Ben understands me."

"How can he understand you? He doesn't even know you." With a sigh, she added, "Tricia, all I'm saying is that a girl can sometimes get carried away by romance when she needs to keep a clear head."

"A clear head," she echoed, her voice flat.

"*Jah.*" Feeling a little defensive, Beverly lifted her chin. She was well aware that she hadn't just dispensed the greatest advice ever given, but she was doing her best. She didn't have much experience counseling younger women.

"Aunt Beverly, did you say all this to Penny when she fell in love a couple of months ago?"

"Of course not."

"Did you warn Michael to keep a clear head?"

"*Nee*, I did not." She'd learned her lesson about interfering when Michael was recuperating from surgery at the inn. When she'd tried to tell Penny to keep her distance because she was an employee, Michael had not been shy about telling Beverly what he thought about her becoming involved in their business. Now she did her best to stay out of her guests' lives.

"Hmm. Well, what about Zack Kaufmann and Leona? They just got married. From what I heard, their romance happened rather fast."

"That was different," she said quickly.

"Why?"

"Because *they* were different," she snapped, knowing she wasn't making a lick of sense. But what she really meant was that none of those people were Tricia.

"It sure sounds like you think they're more deserving of love and a good relationship than I am. Or do you just think I'm not deserving of love at all?"

"Of course I don't think that."

"It sure sounds like it to me. It sounds like you aren't taking me seriously at all," Tricia countered. Then, to Beverly's dismay, her bottom lip quivered. "I trusted you, Aunt Beverly. I can't believe you just said all that!" she exclaimed before running out of the room.

Sitting alone again, Beverly glared at the phone. Oh, that Eric. He'd been so right. She should have prayed before broaching this subject with her niece. And she should have waited. Yes, she really should have prayed a whole lot more and waited until the right time.

It seemed she still had much to learn about curbing her tongue and keeping her opinions to herself. Perhaps she should take some time to remember what she'd told Eric, as well. Tricia's future was in the Lord's hands. Not Tricia's.

And definitely not Beverly's.

Chapter 10

*H*i, Emma," Penny Knoxx called out from the front of the Quilting Haus as Emma rushed down the sidewalk lining Bahia Vista two weeks later. The Quilting Haus was one of Emma's favorite places to visit whenever she had an hour or two to spare, though today she only had twenty minutes before she needed to pick up William and her girls from Pinecraft Elementary.

"Hello, Penny." Penny Knoxx, formerly Penny Troyer, looked as pretty as a summer's day. A few of her blond curls had escaped the confines of their pins and framed her rosy cheeks, and her cornflower-blue dress made her eyes look even brighter than usual. "How are you? I haven't seen you out and about much lately."

Penny blushed prettily. "Michael and I have been pretty busy getting our house in order."

"How is it coming along?" Emma asked. "Do you need any help with curtains or such?"

"*Danke*, but I am hoping to do everything myself."

"You sure?"

"*Jah*. Michael hasn't had a real *haus* to live in for several years, you know. I think he is having fun watching me make our *haus* a real home."

"I can understand that." Emma remembered her newlywed days well. Every little thing she and Sanford had done had felt like an important task. She was about to comment about decorating when she noticed that Penny didn't simply look happy about her life—she looked like she was guarding an important secret. "You seem to be in an especially good mood today."

"I am." After a pause, she leaned in close. "Michael and I are expecting a *boppli*."

"Oh my goodness." Grasping one of Penny's hands, Emma gave it a little squeeze. "That is wonderful! Congratulations!"

"*Danke.*" A dimple appeared in her cheek as she blushed again, making her look even more adorable. "We are happy."

"Of course you are. What a blessing. How are you feeling?"

"Some days sick, some days not." She smiled. "I'm trying my best to concentrate on the baby and not on my queasy stomach."

"Take care of yourself. I was tired and suffered from morning sickness with all three of my girls."

"I have been tired, but it's nothing too bad. Michael keeps fussing over me, though. He suddenly seems to think I'm made of glass."

"Let him fuss over you, Penny. He just wants to help you."

"I know." She rolled her eyes. "I just sometimes wish he wasn't quite so attentive. He hardly let me leave the *haus* today by my-self."

"I'm sure he'll settle down soon. Please let me know if I can help in any way. The girls and I would be happy to bring you a meal. You don't have to try to do everything on your own."

"*Danke*. I'll remember that. My parents have been over a lot, as have the Kaufmanns, but I'll remember to ask you for help, too. I'm grateful for friends."

Until recently, hardly anyone had ever seen Penny. But now that she was none other than Michael Knoxx's wife, she was coming out of her shell a bit. "How is Michael adjusting to life in Florida?" Everyone in the area knew that after years of touring and speaking to crowds, he and Penny had quickly married and settled into their new house.

"He is *gut*. He's writing today."

"Is he finding it difficult to write about his life instead of talking about it?"

"Some days he says writing is far harder than touring ever was. Most days, however, he says it's the best job in the world." She shrugged. "I'm just glad he's happy."

"I'm glad you both are."

"Enough about me. How are you? How are the girls?"

"We are fine." Then, remembering the time, she took a step back. "Actually, I had better run off to the school. It's about to end for the day and I need to get them and William."

"William?"

"Oh! He's the son of a new family in the area. They took over Borntrager's Organic Farm."

"How many *kinner* do they have?"

"Three boys, but their father is a widower. William is the youngest."

"Oh, my. He's raising three children all on his own. Just as you are." Immediately, Penny covered her mouth with a hand. "Oh, forgive me, Emma. I didn't mean it like it sounded."

"There is nothing to forgive. It is the truth," she said with a shrug. Everyone in Pinecraft knew she was a widow. And no matter what, without fail, when they were reminded of her loss, they got that same look on their face—one of embarrassment and dismay. She appreciated their sympathy but she did get tired of always being reminded of her widowed state. "Though, Jay's boys are older than my three."

"Oh?" Pure relief flooded Penny's expression as she realized that Emma hadn't been hurt by her blunt comment.

"*Jah*. His boys are much older. The eldest, Ben, is almost all grown up, and Mark is in his teens, but *jah*, I know what you mean," Emma said with a small smile. "It's hard, but Jay and his boys seem to be doing well."

"Got is *gut*. Well, I had best get my fabric, and you have *kinner* to fetch."

Impulsively, Emma gave Penny a hug. "Take care of yourself. Don't forget to put your feet up when you can."

"Don't worry. Michael is constantly reminding me to rest. He's worse than a mother hen."

Penny's famous husband being described that way made Emma grin the whole way to the Amish school. As she stood outside the door and heard the children's teacher wish them a *gut* afternoon before dismissing them, Emma had to agree that Penny's statement about God being good was true. Though she was tempted from time to time to feel sorry for herself, all she had to do to lift her spirits was look at her precious girls and be reminded that He had not left her alone.

She stepped to one side as the *kinner* raced out the doors.

Some started walking home, while others grabbed their bikes. A few kids had parents there waiting for them as well.

At last, out came Lena, Mandy, and Annie. Shuffling behind them was William.

"Hi, Mamm!" Annie cried as she ran to Emma's side for a quick hug.

Emma gave her one before hugging Mandy, too. Lena and William simply smiled their greetings. After making sure everyone had all their books and papers and lunch boxes, the five of them started walking back to the house.

But when they were about halfway there, Emma began to realize that William wasn't simply being a little shy and quiet. He was upset about something. She kept an eye on him during the rest of their walk. She hoped he hadn't had an argument with Lena, though she knew children got upset with each other for all sorts of reasons. But when he seemed to be okay with Lena, and with Mandy and Annie, too, Emma grew a little more worried. Was he upset that his father wasn't there to pick him up? Was he missing his friends back home? Did he not want to be surrounded by a bunch of little girls for the next couple of hours?

Or was it even something more serious?

By the time they made it back home, she was determined to find out. Luckily, she'd prepared their snacks ahead of time and had orange slices, celery and carrots, and tiny frosted buttermilk cookies set out for them along the counter—too far back from the edge for Frankie to get to, no matter how hard he might try.

After supervising hand washing, Emma passed out paper towels and their snacks. As she'd expected, the girls grabbed oranges, a couple of pieces of celery and carrots, and several cookies before they raced out the back door with Frankie at their side.

William merely asked for something to drink.

After getting him a glass of lemonade, she said, "Wouldja like to sit down with me on the front stoop?"

He looked at her suspiciously. "Why do ya want to sit out there?"

"There's a pesky pair of blue jays with a nest nearby. I like to think if I sit out there from time to time they know they can't cause much mischief."

As she'd hoped, William smiled at her silly comment and followed her out to the front steps. After they sat, she showed him the blue jays' nest as well as the pair of hummingbirds near a feeder. William watched them but didn't say anything.

Trying a different tactic, Emma said, "I noticed that you seem a little quiet today. Do you feel all right?"

"*Jah.*"

"Are you tired? Or is there something that's bothering you?"

He shrugged.

"You don't have to talk to me, but if, by chance, you feel like telling me anything, I'd like to listen."

He turned his head and stared at her for a time. Then at last he said, "Our teacher was talking about families this afternoon. I was the only kid in class who didn't have a mother."

"My girls have shared that they feel sad when everyone talks about their fathers. It's hard, not having one of your parents."

William nodded. "I wish I had her still."

"I know." Scooting a little closer, she wrapped an arm around his shoulders. "I used to wonder what to say when people asked me where my husband was."

"How come?"

"Well, once I tell them that Sanford died three years ago, people begin to ask questions." She lowered her voice. "Sometimes silly questions, if you want to know the truth."

His eyes widened. "How were they silly?"

"Well, women used to ask me how it was, raising three daughters on my own." She sighed. "Between you and me, I hated that question."

"You did?"

"Oh, *jah*. I thought it was stupid because there was only one answer."

"What was that?"

"Raising my girls all alone was hard, of course," she said with a small smile. Remembering the burden of having to do everything herself and how lonely she was at the end of each day, she added, "It was all hard. However, when people asked me how I was doing, I never felt that they really wanted to know my feelings. Or if they did, they didn't want to help."

Suddenly, Emma felt a bit melancholy herself. Here she'd been trying to ease William's mind, but all she was doing was dredging up old memories best left forgotten.

But to her relief, he let out a breath of air, then blurted, "Sometimes kids ask me if I miss my *mamm*. I think that's a stupid question, too."

"Because of course you do. She was your mother and you loved her."

He nodded. "She was my *mamm* and I loved her. And then she got real sick and died." He swallowed. "The girls' *daed* died three years ago?"

"*Jah*. He did." She gave him another little squeeze before dropping her arm. "Some days it feels like a mighty long time ago. Others, it feels like it was just yesterday. But I promise, it does get easier. It might never be easier to understand why the Lord took him away from me so early, but each day, my heart feels a little lighter."

"My *daed* said the same thing."

Emma felt her stomach turn a little somersault at his mention of Jay. She didn't quite understand it, but knowing that Jay had gone through so many of the same things was comforting.

But she would tackle how she felt about that another day.

"Hungry yet?" When he nodded, she grinned. "*Gut.* Let's go get you a snack and you can play with Frankie and the girls. Then we'll get started on homework. Okay?"

"Okay."

Minutes later, as she watched him running with Frankie, Emma sighed. He was such a sweet little boy but had so many burdens. She hoped she could be a person in his life whom he could continue to share his worries with.

Of course, she was sure Jay and Ben and Mark tried their best, but experience had taught her that sometimes a child needed a mother's patience and understanding to completely let his guard down. Though she could never replace his mother, she hoped she could one day be his friend.

Two hours later, Ben came to pick up William, Tricia by his side. Of course, Emma sent Ben home with a container of cookies. She had just waved good-bye to them at the front door and was about to head back inside when she spied William looking back over his shoulder at her. After the briefest of pauses, he smiled.

It melted her heart.

She wasn't sure why the Lord had put the Hiltys into her life, but she was sure it wasn't a mistake. That little boy needed her. And she knew she needed him, too.

Chapter 11

Where did the time go? Jay wondered as he leaned against the chain-link fence at Pinecraft Park on Friday night. Watching Mark play basketball and William play tag in the nearby field, he felt a true sense of peace. Now that they had been in Florida for six weeks, he felt certain that moving here had been the right decision. It was almost starting to feel like home.

Not that it had been an easy adjustment. He, Ben, and Mark had their hands full, working outside in the Florida sun every day. The heat and humidity was hard to get used to, especially since it was September. By now, he was used to anticipating cooler weather and seeing miles of fall foliage. Instead, temperatures were in the eighties and he had months of being warm to look forward to. Before long, he was sure he and his boys would end up packing their winter gear and sending it north to his brothers' families.

All in all, the boys were doing all right.

Mark had had a couple of days when he'd been moody and sullen. Only after practically forcing him to sit down and really talk about his feelings had the boy revealed just how much he was missing his friends from home. Jay had encouraged him to write to his buddies and to take advantage of the phone shanty down the street to give them a call.

Now two of his best friends were planning to come to Pinecraft in November, after the fall harvest. Though November was still a couple of months away, those plans had been all Mark needed to perk up.

After a bit of a rocky start, William was finally settling into school. The only bit of concern Jay had about him was his new bond with Emma. Jay was worried about William trying to find a replacement for his *mamm*, but it was Ben of all people who'd given Jay the best advice.

"Emma is a nice lady, Daed. The best. You shouldn't worry about how she and William are getting along."

When Jay had pointed out that it wasn't Emma's kindness that worried him but rather William's growing dependence on her, Ben had given him even more thoughtful words of wisdom.

"I can't imagine that Got would give William a nice lady like that without a *gut* reason. You should stop doubting everything, Daed."

Perhaps *that* was the reason he was so worried, Jay reflected as he looked over at Emma, who was standing with a group of women near the women's shuffleboard lane. He wasn't doubting the Lord placing Emma and her girls in their lives as much as how he was handling their growing relationship. In fact, he was starting to think about Emma far too much.

As if she sensed his gaze on her, Emma smiled at him and started walking his way.

"Hi," she said. "Are you having fun tonight?"

"The best. Ben and Mark reminded me today that it wasn't healthy to never leave the farm. They were right. At home, I'm tempted to work around the clock."

Her eyes sparkled. "You raised some mighty wise young men."

"I think so, too."

"And one of them is surely in love," she murmured.

He whipped his head around to where he'd spied Ben and Tricia standing together a mere half an hour ago. Though they were still in the middle of a crowd of several young people, it looked as if they were hardly aware of anyone but each other.

"That boy of mine is truly smitten." When he noticed Ben lean down to whisper something in Tricia's ear and maybe—just maybe—brush his lips on her neck, he made a move to remind Ben of where they were. Ben wouldn't do Tricia any favors if he embarrassed her publicly.

But before he could move more than a couple of inches, Emma reached out and grabbed his sleeve. "Let them be. They are just fine, Jay."

"I don't think so." Lowering his voice, he said, "Ben is forgetting himself."

"I don't think he's forgetting a single thing," she said with a blush, then smiled as she quietly pointed to Lena and Mandy. "Look who else is keeping an eye on them."

Jay grimaced as he watched the little girls giggle, their eyes never leaving Ben and Tricia for a second. "Uh-oh."

"It's okay."

"I don't want your girls to be shocked. Ben and Tricia are

being entirely too free with their affection. I promise, I raised him to be more respectful and modest."

She waved a hand. "Ben and Tricia are of age. And they aren't doing anything out of the ordinary. Anyway, I think they look sweet."

"Sweet?" She'd surprised him. Since she was a parent, too, he had thought she'd feel the same way he did.

"*Jah*. Sweet. They are simply being affectionate. They're not doing anything shocking." She swayed a bit, letting her shoulder nudge his arm. "Look around you. No one except the girls and us are giving them a bit of notice."

As Jay scanned the area, he realized Emma was right. It wasn't that the other people at the park didn't see Ben and Tricia; it was that nobody was concerned by their behavior.

Maybe he was overreacting a bit?

"How did you get to be such an expert on kids courting?"

"I'm surely not an expert," she said with a self-conscious chuckle. "I was, um, simply remembering Sanford and me."

"Did you two act like that out in public?" He was a little shocked.

"Act so smitten?"

He nodded before thinking the better of it. "Actually, never mind. Forget I asked." His question was too personal and vaguely insulting. After all, hadn't he just acted like Ben and Tricia were making a spectacle of themselves?

She folded her arms across her chest. "Jay, why are you taking back your question?"

He noticed that she was looking at him in a direct way, too. Honestly, he hadn't felt so awkward in months. Years. Somehow he was managing to sound like a stick-in-the-mud and judgmental, too. "Never mind. I'm embarrassing myself and no doubt you, too."

"I'm not embarrassed. It's actually kind of fun to think about happy times with me and Sanford. Our families either dwell on his illness or never bring up his name." She glanced at Ben and Tricia again, then turned to face Jay. "I married Sanford when I was younger than Tricia. I was only eighteen but I had known him for years. Being with him was nice. Comfortable. I loved him." Emma pressed her palms against the fence, then continued, "We were happy together, and I suppose we had our romantic moments. But, well, we were never the sort of couple that Tricia and Ben seem to be."

"No?" She seemed to be circling around her past.

Emma shook her head. "Sanford and I were more like best friends." She shrugged. "I'm sorry. I guess women are usually romantic at heart. It kind of makes me happy to see Tricia and Ben so sweet on each other. Let them enjoy their moment."

Jay thought about his own courtship of Evelyn and realized that much of what Emma had just said could be applied to him. "I know what you mean," he said at last.

She blinked. "You do?"

"*Jah*. I grew up with Evelyn, too. She was always a bit delicate. A bit introverted. When we were teenagers, she would have stayed home on an evening like tonight. I would have been over playing basketball like Mark and the other boys." Thinking back, he forced himself to remember the evenings when he'd been frustrated with her bashfulness. Sometimes he'd wanted to complain, to tell her that he was tired of them never joining other couples at singings and such. He'd been so sure that if she tried a little harder to be out with others from time to time, she would have eventually overcome her shyness.

But after she'd gotten sick, and he'd realized that his time with her might be cut short, he'd been ashamed that he hadn't been more accepting of her quiet ways. He should have celebrated her strengths instead of concentrating on what he perceived to be her weaknesses.

"Did you ever wish she was more outgoing?"

"At times? *Jah*." The moment the words were out of his mouth, he was hoping and praying that the Lord would erase them from Emma's memory.

Especially since she was looking at him like he'd said the sky was falling. "Sorry. I did love her. She was a *gut* frau."

"Of course she was." She said it so quietly that he had to lean closer to hear her. "I was just realizing that my relationship with Sanford was *gut*, too."

"*Jah*. Of course it was."

"But it wasn't particularly romantic."

Since she was being so honest, Jay forced himself to put to words things that had only ever been vague thoughts—thoughts he'd done his best to push away. "I never thought I needed romance."

Cheeks flushed, she looked down at her feet. He noticed that she had donned bright pink rubber flipflops that matched her dress.

"Me, neither. But . . . but, maybe it would have been nice," she said at last.

Jay swallowed, too plagued by his regrets to say a word. He should have told Evelyn he loved her a whole lot more. He should have cared less about spending time with other people and treasured their time together more. He should have thanked her for giving him three fine boys and praised her for the wonderful way she'd raised them.

He should have been a better man.

Emma's silence meant as much to him as when she chatted about whatever was on her mind. It was if she understood completely just how hard it was to discuss things better left unsaid. Then she lifted her chin and looked at him, her blue eyes shining with honesty.

"I am only now beginning to realize that I don't have to always think that everything between me and Sanford was perfect."

"No one expects a marriage to be perfect."

Looking at him sadly, she shook her head. "I'm afraid some people do. My family and Sanford's family choose to remember my marriage that way. And while it was a *gut* marriage, it wasn't perfect. No relationship ever is, not completely, I don't think."

With that, she stepped back, just as two women who looked so similar to her that they could only be her sisters approached. After a curious look his way, they walked to either side of Emma and essentially escorted her away. The right thing to do would have been to avert his eyes and look someplace else, but he couldn't refrain from watching Emma walk away.

With the sun setting in the distance, the pink fabric of her dress highlighting her flawless complexion, and her tan toes peeking out of their sandals, he couldn't help but think that she was the prettiest thing he'd ever seen.

Remembering himself, he amended his thoughts: She was the prettiest thing he'd seen in years. Since Evelyn.

It was a shame that his thoughts didn't ring quite true.

THE MINUTE BEN'S FATHER turned and walked back to the shuffleboard courts, Ben sighed in relief, making Tricia grin. "That was close. I thought for a minute my *daed* was going to come over here and join us," he said.

She couldn't help but giggle. "Surely not."

"I'm not joking. He was looking like he thought we were making a scene."

Immediately she felt her cheeks warm. "Were we? I didn't think we were doing anything bad."

"We weren't. My father is simply being ridiculous. He doesn't believe in public displays of affection." Smiling, he said, "Unfortunately, Daed thinks even holding hands fits in that category."

Tricia was surprised. She'd been over to the Hiltys' home several times now and had noticed that their father always treated his boys with kindness, including the occasional pat on the back or a squeeze of their shoulder. But maybe Ben was speaking of the way he expected his boys to treat girls?

Leona Kaufmann, who was standing nearby, interrupted her thoughts. "Don't worry. You two weren't doing anything wrong." Smiling at her new husband, Zack, she said, "It's just that most parents don't like to think of their *kinner* doing the things they used to do."

Ben grinned. "I don't believe my parents ever held hands. I can't imagine such a thing."

"My *daed* is always giving my *mamm* a hug or teasing her," Zack said. Clasping Leona's hand, he grinned. "Once me and my sister Violet caught them kissing in the kitchen late one night. I thought my sister was going to fall on the floor, she was so stunned."

When Tricia chuckled, Ben raised his brows. "Really? I can't remember anything like that happening at my house."

Zack glanced over at Ben's *daed*. "I don't want to say the wrong thing, but maybe your father will be holding a lady's hand one day in the future."

Ben frowned. "What are you talking about?"

Gently, Tricia said, "It's becoming fairly obvious that your father and Emma Keim like each other."

He looked at his father for a few minutes and mused, "They sure were having an intense conversation."

Tricia thought of asking Ben what he thought about that, but knew he wouldn't want to say anything while they were standing next to other people.

But almost an hour later, when he was walking her back to the Orange Blossom Inn before taking the SCAT to his farm, she gathered her courage and asked, "Would you be upset with your father if he started seeing Emma?"

"Why would I be upset?"

"You know why. Because of your *mamm*. You might not want him ever having another relationship. If you don't, it's okay," she said quickly. "I am simply curious about what you are thinking."

"I'm starting to get the impression that you like to talk about things. A lot."

"I'm afraid so. I don't like to guess how people are feeling," she replied. Of course, she was also thinking about her volatile argument with Aunt Beverly a week ago. She'd been caught so off guard by her aunt's comments, she'd practically accused Beverly of not caring about her—which she knew couldn't be further from the truth. After all, Aunt Bev had taken her in when Tricia had arrived in Sarasota unannounced.

Since then, things had been a little strained between them, but they were getting better every day. Tricia had come to realize that she wasn't perfect and her aunt Beverly wasn't, either. Everyone sometimes blurted things they wished they would have said with more care.

Tricia was determined to use that strained conversation to her benefit now. She wanted to talk about things in a quiet, meaningful way. As often as she could.

After they walked another half a block, he answered her earlier question. "I don't mind if my *daed* likes Emma, Tricia." After another couple of paces, he continued. "My mother was the best. But she was sick for quite a while before she passed away. I don't know what my *daed* wants to do in the future, but if he chose to not remain alone, I wouldn't blame him."

Everything Tricia could think to say seemed a little too bold and blunt. Though Ben didn't talk about his mother much, she knew he still grieved for her. Therefore, she did the only thing she could think of to show her support. She reached out, took his hand, and gently squeezed.

He turned to her in surprise. Then carefully took her hand in return.

They walked the rest of the way to the inn hand in hand, neither of them caring that they made quite a sight.

All Tricia knew was that she didn't want to let go anytime soon.

Chapter 12

A whole lot of people were coming over after church and Emma was pretty sure she wasn't going to have enough food.

"You shouldn't have invited them over in the first place," she chastised herself as she chopped up another stalk of celery. "You should have left well enough alone."

But her practice of leaving well enough alone seemed to be a thing of the past. On Friday when Jay had stopped by to pick up William, they'd wound up sitting on her front stoop for a good hour, talking about nothing important, simply catching up on their week.

It had been so nice.

Remembering how comfortable she'd been, what with the porch's overhang shielding her face but allowing the sun to shine down on her bare feet and calves, Emma knew she hadn't felt so relaxed in ages. She and Jay had conversed about all sorts of topics, none of them taxing or particularly important. She'd smiled a lot and laughed some, too. As their easygoing conversation meandered along, each comment had led them off on another tangent. Before she'd known what she was doing, Emma had found herself inviting Jay and his family over after church on Sunday.

Then on Saturday, while she'd been pinning clothes on the line, Ben had stopped by and asked if he could bring Tricia. Of course Emma had said yes. Having Tricia there would make Ben happy, and no doubt help Emma, too. Then, that afternoon, Tricia had shown up to see if she could bring her aunt Beverly. Emma had simply smiled weakly and nodded. She liked Beverly very much, and she knew that she'd be helpful, too, but on the other hand, Beverly managed a whole inn. She was used to entertaining large groups of people all the time. Why, she might look at Emma's meager spread and think that it was hopelessly inadequate.

Which was why Emma now kept staring at all the food, feeling certain she hadn't made enough.

"Maybe I should make some potatoes?" she mumbled. "Or soup? But if I make soup, do I even have enough bowls?" Rushing to the cupboard, she pulled open the cabinet door and started counting.

Lena, who had been sitting at the table, looked at her curiously. "Mommy, who are you talking to?"

"Myself."

"How come you're talking to yourself?"

Realizing that she likely looked a sight, Emma shrugged. "I do that from time to time. It helps me think better."

Lena wrinkled her nose. "What are you thinking so hard about?"

"Serving lunch after church. I want to make sure we have

enough food for everyone. Wouldn't it be terrible if we ran out of food?"

Lena, being Lena, took her question seriously and nodded. "William would be sad."

"We can't have that now, can we?"

"What all did you make?"

"Tuna salad, chicken salad, taco casserole, and oatmeal cookies. And fresh bread. And I bought potato chips from the store and pickles and a relish plate."

With each addition she listed, Lena's eyes got bigger. "That's a lot, Mommy."

"It is." Sheepishly, she added, "Jay and his boys are bringing fresh berries, too."

"Oh, yum."

"*Jah.* And, um, Tricia said Miss Beverly was going to bring a chocolate cake and maybe even some banana bread."

"We're gonna get to have oatmeal cookies, banana bread, fresh berries, *and* chocolate cake for dessert?" Lena now was wearing an expression she usually reserved for her birthday and Christmas.

"We might have all of that, but you certainly can't eat all of those desserts. You'd get a stomachache." The moment Emma finished her explanation, she giggled. "I'm being silly, aren't I?"

Lena grinned. "Uh-huh. We're gonna have a lot of food."

"Maybe too much?" Though Lena didn't answer, Emma knew it was.

Then she looked down at her dress. It was dark purple; her girls were wearing matching shades of violet. All three were freshly washed and spotless.

And she'd put flowers in a glass milk jug, displayed on the table.

Ack! It was becoming obvious that she'd put a whole lot of time and effort and planning into this little impromptu meal. And it seemed she'd gone a bit overboard in her preparations. She hoped Jay wouldn't get the wrong impression. Though, who even knew what impression she was wanting to make!

Lena kicked the legs of her wooden chair. "Our *haus* is sure gonna be crowded."

"It is, for sure and for certain. It's a good thing that it's a pretty day. That way everyone can sit outside at our picnic table."

"I like sitting outside!"

"Me too, dear."

"Did Grandmommi get mad about us not going to her house today?"

"Of course not." But that was a lie. Her mother had been very upset with her. She loved having her granddaughters over on Sunday afternoons. Foolishly, Emma had at first tried to not give any particular reason for canceling their usual plans, but that hadn't gone over well. Her mother had asked so many questions that Emma had had no choice but to be completely honest. Yet the only thing her honesty had done was bring about an uncomfortable conversation.

"I fear you are making a mighty big mistake, Emma," her mother had said. "You are jumping into a new relationship and putting the needs of your girls second."

Oh, that had hurt. "I *always* put my daughters' needs first. And they're happy about me seeing Jay."

She'd blinked. "So, you are *seeing* him. It's serious, and you haven't even introduced me to him and his family?"

She'd never thought of her mother as being manipulative, but after that, it had certainly felt that way. Her temper—a temper she hadn't known she possessed—appeared and she'd let it fly. "Muder, enough." When her mother stared at her in shock, Emma said, "You are twisting things around on purpose. I don't appreciate it. I don't deserve it, either."

That was when the tears had begun to flow.

She'd felt awful for making her mother cry. However, she couldn't deny that she'd been excited to try something new. And, yes, she was now seeing Jay. After years of simply getting through each day, she was finally looking at another man. She was actually imagining that she could one day have another deep and meaningful relationship.

It might not happen anytime soon, or it might happen at lightning speed—only time would tell.

Until that time, she was going to take baby steps. And that first step for her was to host a gathering. It was only a taco casserole and tuna- and chicken-salad sandwiches, of course. But still, it was more than she'd done in a very long time.

"Lena, dear, let's get your sisters and go to church. We don't want to be late."

Luckily, all three girls were ready and, after giving Frankie a good-bye pat, they were on their way. As they passed the houses on one block, then another, several other men and women joined them. Emma knew everyone well enough to let go of Annie's and Mandy's hands. The girls appreciated the freedom and skipped ahead, chatting with some of their neighbors as they all made their way to the beautiful Pinecraft Amish Church.

Though most Amish never stepped foot in a church, often choosing to worship in each other's houses and barns instead, necessity had led to the building of the gray stone church with the metal roof in Pinecraft. Local Amish residents enjoyed not having to worry about hosting church and instead helped with the church's upkeep and landscaping.

Emma enjoyed the opportunity to worship among other people of her faith from around the country. Everyone was friendly, and it was a rare Sunday when she didn't return home with a new friend in her heart.

When they entered the building, she gathered her girls around her and sat down with the other women while the men sat on the other side of the aisle. As she spied Tricia and Leona Kaufmann just down the row, she smiled and settled in. It was time to cast aside her troubles and give thanks for the Lord's many blessings.

Two hours later, Emma was walking out of the service when she caught sight of her parents with Sanford's family. All of them stopped and waited for her on the front lawn. As always, the whole family greeted Annie, Mandy, and Lena with loving care. As Lena told them all about her week at school, Annie showed off her loose tooth, and Mandy told them about her skinned knee, her mother pulled Emma to one side.

Emma braced herself for another round. "Hello, Mamm."

"Emma, I don't want to argue again, but I would be remiss if I didn't caution you to be careful. I spoke with your father, and he, too, fears you're rushing into this relationship with Jay Hilty and his family."

"I don't want to argue, either," Emma replied. Measuring her words carefully, she added, "I'm glad you shared with me how you feel. But I don't happen to agree with you."

"Still . . ." Her mother's voice drifted off, and when she bit down on her bottom lip, Emma felt her irritation leave. Her mother was worried about their relationship changing.

"Mamm, it's going to be okay. You raised me to be a careful woman. I still am that way."

"But serving them all dinner sounds like a big step." She

glanced at her granddaughters worriedly. "Are you sure you know what you are doing?"

Sure seemed to be a bit too heavy-handed, but she did know that she wasn't making a misstep. "I know I am serving lunch to some friends today. Is that what you are referring to?"

Her mother frowned. "Of course."

"It is just lunch, Mamm. That is all."

"Still . . ."

She hated that her mother wasn't pleased with her decision but she wasn't going to back out of her plans. She was glad she had invited Jay and his boys and Tricia and Beverly over. She was looking forward to entertaining her new friends. "Would you and Daed like to join us?" she asked reluctantly.

"What would I tell Sanford's family?"

"Simply that I've made some new friends." Just then, Emma saw Jay visiting with William and another family. She'd meant to rush home so she'd arrive at least a few minutes before they arrived. "I need to get home to set everything up for lunch. But there's plenty. Why don't you and Daed join us?"

"*Nee.* I don't think that would be a *gut* idea. I'll come over to see you later this week."

"All right." She knew what her mother's visit would entail, too. A firm talking-to and a reminder of her place in the world as Sanford's widow. And though she knew her mother's advice would be given out of love, Emma was just as certain that her advice would be difficult to follow. She was growing closer to Jay and his boys every day and definitely did not want to give them up.

But despite this new resolve, little by little, all the good, warm feelings she'd gained from the service began to slowly drift away. In their place were a multitude of misgivings.

As she picked up her pace, encouraging the girls to run along in front of her, Emma felt even more flustered. Maybe hosting this meal actually had been a mistake. Maybe she should have listened to her head instead of her heart.

Oh, if only it were that easy.

AGREEING TO GO TO the Keims' house after church was a huge mistake.

As Jay walked down Kaufmann Avenue with Mark and William on the way to lunch at Emma's, he felt as if every person they passed was watching them with interest—and an occasional sly, knowing look. And who could blame them?

Word had spread around Pinecraft like wildfire that he and his sons were going to have lunch with the Keims.

He was a grown man with one almost-grown son, one teen in the middle of his rumspringa, and one boy who was still missing his mother. He was too old to be dressed in his best shirt and visiting single women.

He also knew better than to make himself a target for gossips. Hadn't everyone's interest in his private life been one of the reasons he'd left Ohio, anyway? He had been tired of always being viewed as Evelyn's poor husband. Or the sad widower with his hands full of boys.

"Wait a sec, Daed," William called out as he ran over to talk to one of his school friends.

Jay was happy to have an excuse to stop. Anything to delay what he shouldn't be doing in the first place.

Mark shifted restlessly. "Can I go on ahead?"

"Sure. I'll be right along in a minute."

"Everything okay there, Jay?" Michael Knoxx called out from the sidewalk.

"Oh, *jah*," Jay said as he walked over to say hello. "I'm just waiting for William." Though the man was fifteen years younger than him, Jay couldn't help but feel a little in awe. Until recently, Michael had traveled all over the world preaching to large groups about his experience of being trapped in a ravine several years ago. He'd lost the lower portion of his leg in the process, though one never would know it since he usually walked faster than most people.

"It was a nice service today."

"I enjoyed it." Looking for something to say, Jay said, "I heard you are writing a book."

"I am. I thought it was going to be easy, but I'm stuck at the moment."

That surprised Jay. "What's wrong?"

Michael sighed. "Have you ever had to do something that you know should be fairly easy but you keep thinking of reasons to doubt your progress?"

Since that was happening to him at that very moment, Jay nodded.

Looking down the sidewalk, Michael said, "See, I know what I want to say and what I want to write about, but I'm feeling afraid."

"What would you be afraid about?" He couldn't imagine Michael being afraid of anything.

"I'm worried my words are going to sound too simple. Or that my reasons for wanting to share my story might be misconstrued." Shaking his head in a self-deprecating way, he said, "What is striking me as odd is that I never had these doubts or worries when I toured with my family. I simply got up on stage, looked into everyone's faces, and spoke from my heart."

"You should simply write the words from your heart then."

"I wish it was that easy." Grimacing, he said, "For some reason, a white sheet of paper isn't giving me the same kind of feedback."

Jay laughed. "I'm no writer, but I can only suggest that you keep trying."

"You think it's that easy?"

"*Jah,*" Jay said, realizing that he was speaking to himself as much as to Michael. "After all, the only other option is to go backward, and you don't want that."

"You're right. I really don't want that."

Jay couldn't bear to slide back to that vacant place where his emotions were on hold and he didn't dare to feel too much. Living day to day, hoping to simply get through it while spending half the night unable to sleep was no way to live. Even worse, his boys had known he was living like that and they'd been worried about him.

Michael clasped Jay on the shoulder. "*Danke.* I knew asking you for help was a *gut* idea." He smiled at William who was returning from speaking with his friend, then went on his way.

"Daed, you ready?"

"I am, indeed," Jay murmured. He was suddenly ready for anything to happen. More than ready.

Chapter 13

*E*mma started setting up a buffet in the kitchen practically the moment she walked in her front door. Though she usually asked the girls to help her, she knew they were excited about having company over and restless after having to sit quietly during the service at church. Therefore, she'd simply asked them to play outside with Frankie.

As Frankie, whose favorite game was playing tag with the girls, barked and howled while Annie laughed and squealed, Emma finally relaxed. Her youngest could make even the cloudiest days seem brighter. She had certainly lifted Emma's mood after that upsetting conversation with her mother. Feeling back on track once again, Emma got to work with a new sense of peace.

Out from the refrigerator came the salads and two Mason jars filled with pickles that she'd jarred a few months back. Next came a tall pitcher of lemonade. She was just reaching into her small pantry for the bags of potato chips when Mandy wandered into the kitchen, leaned against one of the counters, and sighed.

"Mandy, why aren't you outside playing with Frankie?"

" 'Cause I've got something to ask you."

Impatience warred with curiosity. Then, seeing as how Mandy had that look on her face that said she was settling in for a good long while, Emma stopped and faced her daughter across the counter. "What is it, dear?"

"Mommy, I don't see why the boys have to come over," Mandy said, pouting.

Emma was surprised—and curious as to what had brought this on. But she couldn't resist teasing her middle girl a little bit before she got her answers. "That wasn't a question . . ."

"I know." Mandy plopped both elbows on the counter and rested her head in her hands, as if she were an old lady.

"What is wrong with the boys?"

"Boys are gross."

Well, this was certainly a new opinion for her six-year-old.

"Boys are not gross, and you like William, Mark, and Ben," Emma said. "Plus they have all been mighty nice to you. You shouldn't speak about them that way."

"I'm only telling you the truth."

"No, you're being mean," Emma retorted, deciding to nip her six-year-old's sudden, contrary mood in the bud. "I don't know what brought this on, but you have picked a bad time to start being unneighborly." Before Mandy could begin another outburst, Emma pointed to the stack of paper goods on the kitchen table. "Now help me put all the paper plates, napkins, and cups out."

"Mamm, you said we didn't have to help."

"I also said I wanted you to go out and play with your sisters and Frankie and Mark, who just arrived. You chose not to do that. Therefore, you can do this."

"I'm gonna go right now." Then, before Emma could chastise Mandy for ignoring her directions, Mandy darted out the door, just as Tricia, Ben, and Beverly came in the same way.

"Whoops!" said Beverly with a grin. "Someone is in a hurry."

That "someone" also knew how to behave far better than she was. If she'd been alone, Emma would have marched outside and told Mandy what she thought about her behavior. But if she'd been alone, Mandy would have likely not been causing so much trouble. Which, of course, was part of the problem, Emma realized. This situation was just as new and nerve-wracking for Mandy as it was for her mother. She should have thought about that and prepared the girls better.

Suddenly Emma felt exhausted by the weight of all of her responsibilities. Sometimes she was just so tired of trying to do everything. It was impossible. That knowledge, of course, brought back all of her worries and doubts. She was pretty good at pretending she was fine, though. And that was definitely what she needed to do now.

She smiled brightly. "Hello! *Wilcom!*"

"Hiya, Emma," Ben said as he led the way to the kitchen. "We saw the girls in your yard so we came on in. My *daed* and William are out there now, too."

"I'm glad you all could come over." Then, noticing that all three of them had full hands, she said, "What did you bring?"

"Berries," Ben said. "Blackberries and strawberries, too. My brothers and I picked them just this morning."

The fruit was in a medium-sized white stoneware bowl. As soon as he pulled the white dishcloth off the top of it, the delectable scent of fresh fruit floated across the kitchen.

She closed her eyes and sniffed deeply in appreciation. "They look *wunderbaar. Danke.*"

"It was nothing. We already washed them, too."

"Perfect! Would you mind setting the bowl over there with the other food?"

While Ben went to do that, Beverly stepped to her side. "That is quite a spread, Emma. Were you cooking all night?"

"*Nee.* Just a little bit."

Tricia chuckled. "That's not what Lena said. At church she whispered that you were cooking most of yesterday and this morning, too."

"Lena does like to talk. Let me see what you ladies brought."

"I baked banana bread. I think it turned out well, but Beverly's cake is what I can't wait to try," Tricia said.

Because truly, Beverly's cake was a thing of beauty. Three layers, covered with a thick, homemade chocolate frosting . . . it looked delicious. "Oh, Beverly. You honor us."

Beverly shrugged off the comment, acting as if she baked three-layer cakes from scratch all the time. Which, of course, she probably did. "It was nothing. You know how I like to bake."

"Tell me how the inn is going," Emma said as she waved Tricia and Ben back outside.

"It's going," Beverly said as she turned to watch Tricia and Ben go back out through the sliding glass door. "We're busy, which is a blessing."

"Sadie's shared that she often visits your inn for teatime."

"She does come over for tea almost every day." Smiling softly, she added, "She's so friendly and welcoming to my guests, I'm grateful that she joins us."

"I think she also enjoys your baking."

"I always bake too much, so I'm glad she does."

"I'm jealous. I'm going to stop by one day, too," she teased.

"I hope you will. My guests love to visit with locals."

Emma noticed that she said the last while gazing out into the backyard but Beverly was frowning, too. "Is everything all right?"

Beverly nodded. "Oh, sure. Fine. I'm just a little worried about Tricia and Ben."

That took Emma by surprise. "Why is that? I think they seem mighty happy together."

"Oh, they're happy. But I'm a little worried that they might be forgetting to be cautious."

"What do they need to be cautious about?"

"Everything."

Emma smiled before she realized that Beverly was being completely serious.

As if she sensed Emma's confusion, Beverly said, "Because Tricia is my niece and not my daughter, I worry about meddling. I want to help her, but I don't want to overstep my place, either." She sighed. "That said, I have some experience having my heart broken. Tricia needs to tread carefully and not let her emotions get the best of her."

"How would that happen?"

"Well, I'm worried she has already fallen in love with Ben."

"Would that be a bad thing?" Emma couldn't keep the surprise out of her voice. If she'd learned anything after Sanford's death, it was that love was a wonderful thing and shouldn't be taken for granted.

"I think so."

Though Ben wasn't her child, Emma felt protective of him. "He's a fine young man. She could do far worse."

"I agree that he does seem nice. But it takes time to really know a person. Don't you agree?"

If that was the case, then Emma *really* didn't know what to think about the feelings she'd been experiencing around Jay. "I'm not sure," she said at last.

"It's different for us. We're older. They're so young, Emma."

"Luckily, their relationship is out of our hands."

"That's what I'm worried about."

Emma felt sorry for Beverly's worries but she agreed that Ben and Tricia's relationship *was* out of their hands. If Beverly didn't realize that the couple was old enough to know how they felt—and that the Lord was already watching over them—Beverly wasn't going to want Emma adding her opinions, too.

Therefore, it was time to switch topics. "You know what, I think everything is ready. Let's go tell everyone."

"Good idea."

As they walked outside, Emma's attention was immediately drawn to Annie, who was sitting on the ground crying. Jay was kneeling next to her, obviously trying to comfort her. "What happened?" She brushed a strand of Annie's baby-soft hair away from her forehead. "Annie, are you hurt?"

Annie nodded, and Jay answered. "I think she's all right. She simply had a little scare. She tripped when she was playing." Jay's expression was tender as he looked down at her youngest. To Emma's surprise, she noticed that Annie was staring back at Jay with trust in her eyes.

"You better, Annie?" Emma asked gently. After Annie nodded again, Emma helped her to her feet. "All right, everyone, lunch is ready!" she called out. "Go on inside, fill your plates, and come back out here to eat."

Right away, the small crowd followed her directions. Lena raced to the house by William's side, Mark following on their heels. Ben and Tricia walked more sedately, looking oblivious to everyone around them. Beverly followed, holding Mandy's hand.

Emma breathed a sigh of relief. It looked as though Mandy had gotten over whatever she'd been upset about earlier and Beverly had decided to put aside her worries for the time being.

Just as she was about to follow and make sure everyone had what they needed, Jay clasped her elbow. "Wait a minute, Emma. They'll be fine. You, on the other hand, look like you could use a moment's rest."

Emma knew he was right. She did need a moment's peace. Besides, the only person there who would need help was now perched on Jay's lap. She pulled over one of her metal folding chairs and sat down next to him and Annie. "Thanks," she said, feeling a little sheepish. "I guess I am looking a little frazzled."

"You don't look frazzled at all. I simply hate the idea of you running yourself ragged for all of us."

"I'm not ragged." When his eyebrows rose, she giggled. "Okay, maybe I am a little ragged, but it's not your fault."

"What happened? Life?"

She nodded. "I like how you said that. I think God was simply reminding me this afternoon that even best-laid plans can come tumbling down."

"In spite of our best intentions."

She nodded. "I should have known that, too." Shaking off her mood, she said, "By the way, those berries look delicious. *Danke* for bringing them."

He grinned as William and Mark popped back outside, their hands filled with heaping plates. "It's the least we can do. My boys don't get lunches like this too often. Obviously, they're happy about it. Thank you for inviting us."

"I'm glad you could come."

Tilting his head down to peer at Annie, he spoke gently. "What do you think, Miss Annie? Are you ready to get some lunch?"

"Uh-huh."

Jay stood up and set her on the ground. "We'd better get our plates before everything's gone."

Annie nodded, then to Emma's surprise, slipped her hand into Jay's. He gave her a little smile before leading the way inside.

Watching them, Emma silently gave praise. Here she'd been so nervous and worried about the number of people, the amount of food, and how everything would look. But God had shown her time and again that it was the special people in her life who she needed to concentrate on the most. And today was no different.

Everything else would be just fine.

Chapter 14

$\mathcal{S}$oon after Emma had placed another pitcher of lemonade on the counter, helped Annie get her plate of food, and bent her head to silently say grace, everything that could possibly have gone wrong, did.

And it all started with Frankie.

As everyone sat down to eat, their usually lazy beagle became increasingly energetic. He barked. He whined for food. He propped his front paws up on the picnic table bench and the children's knees. He patrolled under the table for scraps. Continually. Like a shark.

He didn't listen to any of Emma's warnings, either.

She couldn't put him inside her bedroom because she didn't trust him not to scratch the door or suddenly start shredding her quilt. He had never done such things but she was worried that with all the company he was in an anything-goes mood.

Everyone, even the *kinner*, was becoming rather annoyed, and with good reason.

Then, just moments after Emma had chastised him yet again, she saw Frankie nudge William's knee with his nose and gaze soulfully up at him with his big brown eyes. For that award-worthy performance, William gave him a pickle.

Mandy, who was sitting beside William, did not like this happening one bit. "William, *nee!*" she snapped. "Frankie can't have pickles. You're gonna make him sick."

"Oh, come on. It was just one." He held up the other half of his pickle spear. "See," he said with a know-it-all grin, "only half of one."

"You shouldn't have done it!" Mandy's voice turned shrill and trembly. It was obvious to Emma that she was on the verge of tears.

Lena rolled her eyes. "Oh, stop, Mandy. It ain't like you've never given Frankie food before."

"Not pickles. Never pickles."

Lena shared a look with William. Even from where Emma was sitting, she recognized it as a superior smirk. The kind of smirk that said little sisters are nuisances. And while that might be true, Emma knew this was neither the time nor the place for it.

"Lena, be nice!" Emma called out, hoping to keep the little tiff from getting out of control. But she was too late.

Lena rolled her eyes.

Mandy pointed at her from across the table. "You canna do that, Lena. Mamm is gonna get mad."

Lena lifted up her chin. "Mamm's only gonna get mad if you mess up our lunch. Which you are doing, Mandy."

"Am not."

"Are to!"

"You're being mean."

"She's not being mean," William interjected.

Just as Emma was about to get involved, Mark leaned over to his brother. "Stay out of it, Will," Mark warned. "Mandy's problems ain't yours."

"But I didn't do nothing anyway," William snapped. "All I was doing was being nice to their stupid *hund*."

"Frankie ain't stupid," Lena retorted. "He's hungry."

"Then he's stupid *and* hungry." He paused, then added, "And fat."

"William, enough," Jay said, his tone brooking no argument. Looking a bit wary, Jay glanced at Emma.

She could tell he was worried that she might think he was being too harsh. But she happened to agree with his handling of the situation completely. If they didn't nip things in the bud the children would continue to needle each other until someone started crying.

Wanting to do her part, she said, "Lena, let's not worry about Frankie. He's fine."

"But he's not stupid! And he ain't fat, neither."

"Mind your manners, Lena," Emma said, unconsciously mimicking Jay's tone.

But her warning came too late. Things spiraled out of control, seemingly at breakneck speed. Mandy burst into tears. Lena seethed. William glared. Mark gloated.

And Frankie? Well, Frankie continued to annoy everyone, especially Beverly when he pulled a chip from her plate. *"Hund!"* she said.

Which made Mandy cry harder. Tricia tried to calm her

down, but when she put her arms around Mandy, Mandy's glass of pink lemonade fell onto the front of Tricia's dress. "Oh!" She jumped up from the table. "Oh, that's cold!"

Her jump made Frankie bark. And jump up for her plate. Which he caught.

"Stop, Frankie," Ben said as he, too, got up from the table and moved to Tricia's side.

"Oh, my dress," Tricia said. "What a mess." Frowning, she said, "I just washed it yesterday, too! I hope pink lemonade comes out of light yellow dresses."

"I'm sure it will, dear," Emma soothed. "We can even go soak it. You may borrow one of mine."

"*Danke.*" Still frowning at the fabric, she added, "I hope the stain comes out. I really liked this dress."

"You had better get used to things like that happening," Beverly said. "If you really do intend to have a houseful of *kinner* like you told me you did, things like this will surely be a daily occurrence."

Turning bright red, Tricia said, "Aunt Bev, I can't believe you said that!"

"What did I say? Surely you and Ben have talked about having children." Her eyes widened. "Or are the two of you not near as serious as you made it sound?"

Tricia froze.

Ben looked flummoxed. "Did you say *kinner*, Beverly?"

"Are you and my *bruder* gonna have a baby, Tricia?" William asked.

As Jay groaned into his napkin, Tricia turned an even brighter shade of pink. Then to everyone's shock, she burst into tears, too.

"It's okay," Ben murmured. When she merely cried harder,

he enfolded her in his arms. Over Tricia's head, which was now tucked into his neck, Ben glared at his father. "Daed. Do. Something."

By this time, Jay was on his feet, too. "William, no one is going to have a *boppli* anytime soon. Now, everyone needs to sit down."

His arms still securely wrapped around Tricia, Ben glared at him . . . and at Beverly. "Sitting down ain't going to fix this, Daed."

Emma couldn't help but agree with Ben as things continued to disintegrate. Tricia cried, Mandy cried. Beverly fumed. Boys argued. Food fell on the ground. Frankie foraged and ate too many pickles.

"Everyone, please calm down," Emma called out. Of course, it was a rather weak attempt to restore order. So weak, in fact, that not a single person listened. Except for Jay, but then even his efforts were foiled when he stepped backward . . . into dog poop!

"Frankie!" he yelled.

Frankie had struck again!

Emma felt like burying her head in her arms and crying, too, but someone had to remain calm. She walked to each of her girls, pointed to the house, and said, "Girls, please go to your rooms. Right now."

Her girls knew what her tone meant. Instead of arguing, Lena stood up and walked inside, with Mandy and Annie following behind.

"I hate to do this to you, but I think it might be best if I got mine out of your hair as well," Jay said.

Looking around helplessly, seeing Tricia and Beverly glaring at each other, Mark and Ben looking as if they would rather be anywhere else than here, and William almost as sad as her girls, Emma knew it would probably be for the best. Sometimes one had to cut one's losses and move forward. This definitely seemed like one of those times.

"Jah," she said wearily. "I, um, think that might be best, too."

He picked one of the plates up off the ground and set it on the table. "I'll help you clean up first. I mean, my boys and I will."

She knew his offer was sincere. She also knew if their situations were reversed, she would offer to do the very same thing. But at the moment she wanted nothing more than to be alone. "I appreciate your offer. However, if you don't mind, I'd rather clean up on my own."

"I can't let you do that." Looking around, he frowned. "I mean, it looks like a picnic exploded in the middle of your yard."

It kind of had, but Emma kept quiet about that. "I will be fine."

"I'll help her," Tricia offered.

When Emma noticed Ben's frown, she shook her head. "That's sweet of you, but no. Why don't you go change your dress? Go on now."

"I'll stay. Don't worry," Beverly said. "Emma and I will clean things up in no time. I promise, this is one instance when more hands will not make the chore easier."

With a sigh, Jay nodded. "I think you are right about that. I'll see you later. Thank you for the lunch."

Just then she remembered the banana bread and the cake. "Oh, hold on. No one has had dessert. How about I prepare a plate for you all? You can take it home."

All three of the boys shook their heads. "Maybe another time," Jay said.

Feeling the giant lump in her throat grow with each second,

she watched Jay and his sons walk back out the gate, Tricia by Ben's side. And then it was just her and Beverly. Emma walked into the kitchen, got a black plastic garbage bag, and started tossing dirty plates and cups into it.

"I am so sorry," Beverly said as she did the same. "I shouldn't have said a word to Tricia."

"Your words weren't the problem."

"I think they were. I shouldn't have mentioned anything about babies or children. She is a pretty sensitive girl."

"All girls her age cry from time to time. They can't help it," Emma said.

"I suppose. But I have to tell you, I simply don't know what happened," she continued as she gathered silverware and piled them into the bowl Emma had used to hold chips. "One minute, everything was fine, the next . . ."

"Chaos." Unable to help herself, Emma chuckled. It had been a crazy few minutes, but they'd survived.

After bending down to check on Frankie, who was lying on his side, looking rather like he was stuffed to the gills but otherwise fine, she walked into the kitchen.

"Don't worry about it. I'm sure you've seen things like this happen at your inn."

"Things have gone wrong," she agreed with a smile. "Though never with so many tears."

Emma stood at the sink and started washing dishes while Beverly put salads in plastic containers, handed serving bowls to her, and competently wiped down the counters and tables. After the first couple of minutes Emma felt herself relaxing. She rarely ever had help in the kitchen and she was finding Beverly Overholt's quiet industriousness to be a calming influence.

"Emma?" Beverly asked when they were almost finished. "If

you don't mind my saying so, I happened to notice that you don't seem all that shocked or worried about how fast things are progressing with Ben and Tricia. Why?"

"I guess because I was married at eighteen but I fell in love with Sanford years before that."

"That sounds so young."

"Because it was. It was young. But that doesn't mean it was wrong." She shrugged. "I just happen to believe that each of us has a match and when it happens it happens."

"So you think I should leave Tricia alone?"

"No. I mean, I know you love her and she loves you, right?"

"Of course."

"Well, if I am right and God has brought Ben and Tricia to each other and they are happy and in love . . . who are you to say that they are wrong?"

"I've been so used to guarding my heart because of some things that happened in my past . . . maybe I'm letting all that influence me."

"I suppose it's a possibility," Emma allowed. "I don't know."

"I think I need to pray on this."

Emma smiled. "I hope your prayers give you the answers that you need." Walking toward Beverly's beautiful cake, she said, "At least you'll have some cake while you're thinking."

"Oh, no. You keep it."

"It's too much."

"I'm sure you can find some folks to share it with." Smiling softly, she said, "Who knows? Maybe even Jay will get a chance to have a piece."

"I don't know. I think he was pretty upset when he left."

"He did offer to stay and help. I think he simply wanted to help you settle everything down."

"He did that." She really hoped their friendship hadn't been compromised. She was starting to realize that she really liked him. She liked him a lot. In fact, she wouldn't be opposed to sometimes seeing him alone. To spending a couple of hours when it was just the two of them. Instead of refereeing arguments, serving food, and washing dishes, they could talk.

They could simply enjoy each other's company.

Why, that would be wonderful, indeed.

Chapter 15

*W*ell, that was horrible," Tricia said after she and Ben said good-bye to his father and started walking toward the inn so she could change. "I think it was truly the worst lunch in the history of all after-church lunches."

"It wasn't that bad." When he caught sight of her incredulous look, he laughed. "Okay, it actually *was* that bad. And to think it all started with William giving Frankie a pickle."

"I'm starting to think that Frankie had the best time of anyone."

He chuckled again. "He was the only one who didn't seem out of sorts." After a pause, he said, "I didn't grow up around girls, but I would have thought that the three of them would have gotten along a lot better."

"I must say I'm kind of surprised myself. Every other time I've been around Mrs. Keim and her daughters I thought they were the most well-behaved siblings in Sarasota."

"I guess everyone can have an off day, hmm?"

Tricia looked up at him and felt herself warm. She loved how he took things in stride. He seemed to be a perfect foil to her constant emotional state. No matter how hard she tried to conceal her emotions, she always seemed to wear her heart on her sleeve. "When you put it that way, I have to agree. *Jah*, everyone can have an off day."

She also liked how he seemed to embrace life's imperfections easily. It made her realize that he wasn't expecting her to always be at her best. That thought kept her warm during their walk to the Orange Blossom Inn, where he waited for her on the front stoop while she ran inside and changed her dress.

When she reappeared dressed in a light rose-colored dress and matching flipflops and feeling much better, he smiled. "You look pretty."

"*Danke*. At least it's clean," she said as they started their walk.

"It's more than that."

His sweet words made her smile as they walked down Bahia Vista toward the center of town.

"Is there someplace special where you'd like to go?" Ben asked fifteen minutes later when they reached the sign for Pinecraft Park. "We could go to the park, walk around the shops, even go to Olaf's and get ice cream."

"I'll do whatever you would like." It was the truth, too. She was simply happy to be by his side.

"*Nee*, Tricia. I asked you what you wanted to do," he said gently.

"I just want to sit alone with you." She thought that sounded like the best thing in the world. Every day she counted the hours until they got to see each other and then, they were always in the company of his siblings or Beverly or their friends. Though it might make her seem selfish, she wasn't ready to share him with the rest of the world just yet.

"You mean that you want the two of us to have a real conversation without my little brothers eavesdropping?"

"Maybe. Or my aunt commenting on my behavior." Thinking about how much Beverly's rather personal comments had bothered her, Tricia felt sad all over again. She knew Beverly thought Tricia was being silly, and maybe she was. But her bold comment about Ben and Tricia having children when Ben hadn't even said anything about marriage had truly embarrassed her. It was the cherry topping to a series of cautionary conversations that had grown increasingly difficult to be a part of.

Tricia had come to Sarasota in the hopes of being around a family member who understood her. Or who at least wanted to try to see her point of view on things. But it seemed that Beverly had just as many notions about how she should behave as her parents ever did.

Ben pointed to an area of benches just beyond the park near the Phillipi River. "There's some shade down there. How about we sit there?"

The area was quiet and picturesque. Mossy trees hung over the river, and the wooden benches were spread far enough apart that it was possible to have a private conversation even if every bench was occupied. "I think that would be perfect."

Ben reached for her hand as they walked down the slight hill that was covered with soft grass. The closer they got to the river, the stronger the scent of water and the many flowers and shrubs that grew along the banks became.

"Do you come here a lot?" he asked once they got settled next to each other.

"I've never been here."

"I'm surprised. You like peaceful places."

Tricia smiled. She did like peaceful places, but what she really liked were peaceful places by Ben's side. "I'm glad we're here now," she said simply.

Though she'd tried to hide it, he caught the note of melancholy in her voice. "Are you still fretting about what your aunt said?"

"*Nee.*" She swallowed, hating to fib. "I mean, maybe." She shrugged. "Okay, *jah.*"

"What made you upset?"

She turned her head so she could see his face. He was tan now, his blond hair a little lighter. His blue eyes, of course, were exactly the same: light blue, framed by a dark blue ring and filled with as much compassion and sincerity as the first time they'd met.

"Everything. I didn't like her bringing up a topic that should be a private conversation between the two of us. I was mortified," she admitted. "Her insinuation that I was exaggerating how close we've become . . ." Just as soon as she spoke those words she was embarrassed. She didn't want him to know just how worried she was that he, too, thought that she'd embellished his feelings for her.

"You didn't exaggerate anything, Tricia," he said as he reached for her hand. "For what it's worth, I don't think she was trying to be mean, she simply loves you."

"Has your father warned you off?"

He chuckled as he squeezed her hand. "*Nee.*"

"What's so funny?"

"Nothing, except that, well, my father knows better than to start trying to warn me off of you. He knows I've fallen in love."

It took everything she had to close her mouth. "You have?"

"Uh-huh." He raised her hand with his and rubbed it along his cheek. "Don't worry, Tricia. I don't expect you to feel the same way."

"You don't understand. I've fallen in love with you, too," she blurted. "I didn't want to tell you because I was afraid it might scare you away!"

"I'm not scared." He smiled as he pressed her knuckles to his lips. "I'm mighty relieved, Tricia. I would hate to think I was the only one who felt this way." After he kissed her knuckles again, he released her hand.

Tricia couldn't believe it. Ben made falling in love seem so effortless and easy, as if he had no doubts about their future or his feelings for her. She wanted to feel the same way but her experiences made her not quite as trusting. "Do you ever wonder what will happen next?"

"Between us?" he asked, raising an eyebrow.

"*Jah.*"

"*Nee*, I don't wonder at all," he murmured as he looked at the river flowing in front of them, the current lapping along the shore. "I have a plan, you see."

There was no way he was going to keep that a secret! "What is it?" she asked, hating that her voice sounded as breathless as a child's.

"Well, after I confess my love for you . . . And after you realize that you love me, too . . ."

Her pulse began to race. "Yes?"

"And then, when the time is right . . ."

"Yes?" She knew she was starting to sound like one of Emma's little girls. But honestly, she was feeling so anxious. And excited. And almost sick to her stomach.

He turned to face her again. "I'll ask you to marry me."

She gulped. "And then?" she said softly.

Lines of humor fanned out from the corners of his eyes. "You tell me, Tricia. What will you say when I summon the courage to ask you to marry me?"

Ask you to marry me? She could hardly believe she'd just heard him say that. She felt like she'd jumped in the river and was floating along with the current, unable to stop. "I'd say yes."

All traces of amusement vanished. "Will you marry me, Tricia?"

His voice was solid and sure, without a drop of indecision or worry, making her realize that they were certainly not speaking in abstract terms anymore. He was completely serious.

So she answered in kind. "I will."

"You sure?" He stared at her intently. "Marriage is for a lifetime, you know."

"Ben Hilty, I have never been more sure about anything in my entire life."

He grinned broadly, and while she was still trying to come to grips with what had just happened—and what she'd just said—Ben folded her in his arms and hugged her. "You've made me mighty happy, Tricia."

For a few, brief seconds, Tricia contemplated asking him to slow down, thought about reminding him that they had known each other only a short time.

But that moment passed as quickly as it had come. Because one thing was for sure and for certain: Only a fool would have second thoughts about marriage to the very handsome, very wonderful Ben Hilty.

And though Tricia was many things, a fool was certainly not one of them.

"It was so awful, Eric," Beverly said into the phone as she watched the sun set over the tops of the citrus trees in the backyard. "It was the craziest, most disastrous meal I've attended in years. Years!"

Eric laughed. "I bet it wasn't all that bad. Matter of fact, I think it sounds like a lot of fun. Especially the part about Frankie virtually collapsing under the table at the end of it. Who knew pickles could cause so much trouble?"

Her lips twitched. "That was pretty funny, actually. He is one naughty dog."

"It sounds like Emma needs to be firmer with him. That dog needs to learn some manners."

"If you saw him in person, you wouldn't be able to be any stricter, either. He is really the sweetest thing. He lets all the children play with him, and his ears are so soft. I don't think he has a mean bone in his body. He simply likes his food."

"Well, I imagine we can both think of a person or two who might fit that description."

She giggled like a schoolgirl. "A sweet person who likes his food?"

"Come on. I dare you not to think of someone who doesn't fit that bill."

"I run a B-and-B. Of course I can think of many people who that describes." She shifted in her chair and watched two birds land on the back fence and then fly off in a panic as Serena, Mrs. Sadler's cat, hopped up onto one of her tables.

"So, what really happened to upset you? I know it wasn't cranky children or naughty beagles."

Beverly was tempted to ignore his invitation. But then she knew he would listen to her and help her decide what to do next. "I . . . well, I said something to Tricia in front of everyone."

"About?"

"About her and Ben, of course." Taking a deep breath, she forced herself to continue her confession. "Actually, I think I offended both Tricia and Ben. I pretty much sounded like a grumpy old woman and warned them about rushing into their relationship."

"How did that go over?"

Though she was embarrassed and upset, she forced herself to continue. "About how you would expect. Tricia started crying and Ben came to her rescue." She lowered her voice. "Later, I talked to Emma about my feelings and it was pretty obvious that she disagreed with me, too. So, I pretty much hurt my niece's feelings, offended her boyfriend, and there wasn't a person there who agreed with me."

He whistled softly. "I sure am sorry, Bev."

She blinked. "You're not going to give me a talking-to like you did when I interfered with Michael Knoxx and Penny?"

"Not this time."

Beverly heard the smile in his voice, which made her smile, too, and she hadn't thought that would be possible. "You know what? I'm really beginning to be glad we know each other."

"That makes two of us."

"What do you think I should I say to Tricia when she returns?"

"What do you want to say?"

"I want to tell her that I didn't mean to hurt her feelings. I just sometimes say things I shouldn't because I love her."

"I think she'll forgive you if you say that, Bev." He sighed. "Now, I can't believe I'm even doing this to myself, but tell me what you made for that shindig."

"A three-layer chocolate cake."

He groaned. "I have got to sell this house of mine."

"Yes, you do, Eric," she agreed. For many, many reasons, she added privately.

Chapter 16

$\mathscr{I}$t was close to eleven at night. Late, even for Ben, to still be out.

Sipping another cup of decaf, Jay tried not to watch the kitchen clock tick but he seemed unable to do anything else. Ben and Tricia had been together for hours now, ever since they'd left Emma's house after their disastrous lunch—and Beverly's rather insensitive comments.

Tricia's reaction had surprised them all. It had been obvious that Beverly had been insensitive but not malicious. However, when the tears came, Jay had felt awful. Young ladies in love had tender hearts and it was a good thing to remember that and tread softly.

When Jay had seen Ben go still and his expression turn hard, he'd known Ben had been just as unhappy about Beverly's words. Jay knew his eldest well; Ben was used to taking on the needs and worries of his younger brothers. Was he now trying to make Tricia feel better, too?

"Evelyn, I could sure use some help, here. What would you say if you were here?" he asked the empty room. He tensed, half hoping that her soft, sweet voice would come floating through the room, offering words of wisdom from up in heaven. But of course he heard nothing. Disappointment coursed through him, making him feel even more helpless. It was times like this, when there was no one to bounce ideas off of, that he missed his wife the most. Only the boys' mother would understand what Ben needed from Jay right now.

Then he recalled how Evelyn had dealt with almost any conflict in the family. She'd been patient. Content to wait. Content to let others shine.

"I guess that's my answer then," he murmured. "I'll wait and be patient and try not to meddle. *Danke*, Ev."

"Who are ya talking to?" Mark asked as he wandered in. He had on an old pair of cotton plaid pajama bottoms, slippers, and a white T-shirt. The outfit made him look both like the towheaded eight-year-old boy he used to be and the man he was on the verge of becoming.

"Your *mamm*," he said after weighing his answer.

"Really?" Mark raised his eyebrows. "Did she answer you?"

"*Nee.*" He smiled weakly. "I'm afraid you caught me at something I like to do from time to time. I ask Evelyn questions and hope she'll tell me what to do. But she never says a word."

"That sounds like Mamm," Mark said as he pulled out a chair and sat next to Jay. "I don't know how she did it, but Mamm could get Ben and me to do most anything without saying a word. And admit to anything we did wrong, too." He shifted, then leaned his chair back on two legs, balancing on them. "It was uncanny."

Jay opened his mouth to tell Mark to stop rocking on those back chair legs but then he decided to ignore it. His middle boy had taken to rocking in his chairs from the moment his legs were long enough to reach the ground.

Instead, Jay watched Mark's face as he said, "But not William?"

"William is the baby. Mamm let him get away with everything."

That was true. But Jay liked to think that maybe his *frau* had known she wasn't going to be around for much of William's life. She'd used their time together to give him love and attention.

"So, what are you still doing up, Daed? Besides talking to Mamm, I mean. Are you waiting up for Ben?" Mark asked.

"*Jah.*" There was no reason to pretend he wasn't.

Mark looked at the clock above the oven. "Ben doesn't have a curfew anymore."

"You're right. He doesn't."

"So, why are you waiting? Are you worried about him?"

"I know he's old enough to take care of himself." Jay shrugged. "But I guess some habits are hard to change."

"*Jah.*"

As the quiet settled around them again, Jay studied his middle son. From the time he was born, Mark had been his easygoing child. He was generally the most agreeable and even-tempered. But because of that, he was also the one Jay was always a bit in the dark about.

"Mark, how are you adjusting to being here? Do you wish you were back in Charm?"

"Sometimes. I miss my friends."

Glad that Mark was being forthright, he nodded. "*Jah.* It's hard making new friends here, I bet. Seeing that you are out of school." Before they'd moved, Jay had worried about Mark feeling lost and alone. He'd even told Mark he could attend high school here for a year or two if he wanted. It wasn't the norm, of course—most Amish stopped school after eighth grade—but most Amish boys didn't lose their mothers and move across the country, either. Mark had also been an excellent student. He'd loved to study history. Jay had thought letting Mark concentrate on his studies might also help him recover from his grief. But Mark hadn't even considered it. Maybe he was having regrets now? "Do you want to think about going to the public high school? You might enjoy it."

"I'm needed here on the farm, Daed. You, me, and Ben have more work than we can keep up with, especially because of all the rules and regulations about keeping things organic."

"I'd rather hire some help than see you unhappy."

"I'm not unhappy. I mean, not yet. My buddies from Charm will be out in November and I talk to them on the phone once a week. Plus, I'm meeting people. I played basketball with some guys at Pinecraft Park last week."

"All right."

Mark rocked back again, making the chair's legs squeak their disfavor.

"You're going to break that chair before long," Jay finally said.

"That's what you told me three years ago."

"If you break it, I'm gonna make you pay to get it fixed."

Mark smiled. "You told me that three years ago, too."

"As long as you remember," he warned.

"I'll pay to get it fixed if I break the chair. Which I won't." He rocked back again. "Hey, Daed?"

"*Jah?*"

"Do you think Ben and Tricia are serious?"

"It sure looks that way."

"Are you okay with that?"

"I think I need to be. Ben's old enough to make his own decisions. He won't thank me for interfering."

Mark seemed to stew on that for a moment. Then he blurted, "So you think she's the girl for him?"

Jay thought she might be, but he knew Ben wouldn't appreciate his father speculating about his love life. "I don't know if Tricia is or isn't. Only Ben can answer that one."

"She's funny. Remember last week when she decided to make us supper?"

"I do. Macaroni and cheese and hamburger patties." He smiled. It had been a simple meal, but tasty, too. William had asked for seconds.

"She made the mac and cheese from scratch. It was *gut*."

"It was." Unable to resist, he added, "Of course, our Ben made sure we knew that."

"Oh, yeah, he did. Like eight times."

"Mark, it wasn't that many. Probably only seven."

They were chuckling as the kitchen door opened and Ben stepped inside. Jay could tell Ben was startled to see them.

"Hey," he said. "What are you two doing down here? I thought you'd be asleep."

"I was just sipping a last cup of coffee when Mark came downstairs. We started talking."

"Oh." Ben's eyes strayed to the doorway and the stairs beyond. Jay knew his eldest would like nothing better than to dart out of the kitchen and escape their company. But tomorrow's focus would be the farm and all of the tasks that needed to be taken care of, and Jay knew he wasn't going to be able to concentrate on any of that until he knew his eldest was all right.

"So . . . were you with Tricia this whole time?"

"Jah." His cheeks flushed.

That took Jay by surprise. Ben was not a blusher. He was forthright and confident.

"Is she okay? I noticed she was a little upset with her aunt."

"She's fine."

"Oh. *Gut.*" A dozen other questions were on the tip of his tongue, but for the life of him, he couldn't imagine that any of them would be well received, especially not in front of Mark.

Luckily, Mark was not nearly so hesitant. "What did you two do? Where did you go?"

Ben sighed, pulled out a chair one-handed, and joined them. "I guess you two aren't going to let me go up to my room without being grilled."

"I was hardly grilling you, Ben," Jay said. However, Ben was right. He did want some answers.

"It's okay if you don't want to share." Mark's grin turned sly.

Ben glared. "We went over by the river. To talk," he said with a meaningful glare at his brother. "We did nothing to be embarrassed about."

"Of course not," Jay murmured.

After taking a deep breath, Ben added, "I asked Tricia to marry me tonight."

"No way," Mark said.

"Way." Ben lifted his chin. "And just so you know, Tricia said yes. We're engaged. Tricia Overholt is going to be my wife."

Mark's chair legs slammed to the floor and then, at last, one of the back legs cracked and gave way. With a bark of surprise, Mark jumped to his feet as the chair clattered to the floor.

Ben shook his head. "Looks like after three years of warnings, you finally broke that chair."

"Sorry, Daed," Mark said quickly. "I'll, um, get it fixed."

At the moment, Jay wouldn't have cared if the chair had broken into a dozen pieces. All he could think about was Ben's proposal . . . and the way he was so sure and certain about it. He was happy for his son but couldn't help but be worried, too. The last thing he wanted was for Ben to be jumping feetfirst into a situation he wasn't ready for.

Needing another second to gather his thoughts, he focused on the chair. "I'm not upset, Mark. I know you'll get it fixed. As a matter of fact, I think Frank Kaufmann might be able to help you. He's Zack Kauffman's *daed*. I think you know Zack?"

"*Jah*, I know him. I'll see him tomorrow," Mark mumbled, staring at his brother. "Ben, did ya really propose?"

His brother waited a second, then nodded. "*Jah*. I can't believe it."

Jay had always known this day would come, but he'd imagined it would be one day far in the future. He'd also always imagined that he would have the right words to say. And, well, that he would be more prepared.

Therefore, he clung to Ben's last words like the lifeline that they were. "You can't believe it?" he asked hesitantly. "Does that mean you didn't intend to ask Tricia to marry you?"

"Not at all. Tricia and I were sitting together, talking about her aunt Beverly. Then, next thing I know I'm telling her that I love her. Then she says that she loves me, too. And then . . ."

"And then . . . what?" Mark asked, leaning forward.

"And then I did it."

Mark's mouth was undoubtedly letting in flies, it was hanging so far open.

Jay could sympathize with him. It was something of a shock. But as he stared at his eldest, he saw something new in his expression. A contented happiness. And peace, too. He was happy about this. Really happy. "This is certainly big news," he said at last, because Ben was staring at him, likely waiting for his father to say something of worth.

"Daed, that's it? That's all you're going to say?"

"*Nee.* I'm simply trying to come up with the right words." Jay was also wondering how much to react . . . or if Ben and Tricia had gotten so wrapped up in their romance that they had let the moment get to them.

But then he remembered how he'd just been asking for Evelyn for guidance and realized exactly how she would have reacted. She would have put Ben's feelings first. Always, she put the boys' needs first.

It was time he did the same.

"Congratulations, Ben. I'm so happy for you," he said at last. "This is wonderful. *Wunderbaar.*" Standing up, he gave Ben a hug. "I love you and I hope you will be happy together. From what I know of Tricia, I think she's a fine girl."

"*Danke,*" Ben said.

"We'll talk more in the morning, but for now I think it's time I went to bed. Mark, move the chair out of the way."

Mark silently did as he was asked. Then, just as Jay was halfway up the stairs, he heard the words he'd been waiting for from his middle son.

"I'm happy for ya," Mark said. "Tricia's really nice. And really pretty."

"*Jah.* She is. *Danke.*"

Jay smiled to himself and as he climbed into bed he said a couple of prayers. Then, finally, he whispered into the dark, "You would have been mighty happy tonight, Evelyn. Our eldest is happy. God is very good."

TRICIA WAS RELIEVED TO discover that the inn was quiet when she slipped in the back door. The last thing she wanted to do was discuss what had happened with Beverly. Or worse, discuss it within the hearing of one of the guests. Although she wasn't eager to discuss what had happened earlier with Beverly, she couldn't resist continually reliving every moment that she'd spent with Ben.

He loved her. He wanted to marry her.

He'd asked her to marry him!

And just as important, she'd wanted those things, too! In the span of a few hours she'd gone from unsure of her future to being engaged to a wonderful man.

The difference was truly miraculous.

She knew she was going to be spending quite a few hours that evening in prayer. She had so much to be thankful for. God had led her to Sarasota, to working at the inn instead of turning tail and running back home. He had brought Ben and his family to the inn, too.

He had given her so many blessings, in fact, that it was difficult to remember just how forlorn she'd felt when she'd first climbed on the Pioneer Trails bus. She'd truly thought that God had forgotten about her. Now she was ashamed that she'd had so little faith in His plan. But perhaps that was what she was supposed to learn—that sometimes she needed to remember that with faith, all things were possible.

After taking off her shoes and setting them by the back door, she filled a glass with water and headed to her room. Then stopped when she saw a light shining under her aunt's door.

Though she was tempted to tiptoe by, Tricia knew that her aunt deserved better than that. She'd taken her in when Tricia thought she'd had nobody. That overruled any hurt feelings she might have about Beverly not completely supporting her relationship with Ben.

With that in mind, she tapped lightly on the door. "Aunt Bev, I'm home."

Almost immediately, the door opened. "Tricia, I'm so glad you stopped to tell me you were back," she said as she reached out and gave her a warm hug. "I feared you were upset with me."

"I was upset, but I'm better now."

"Really?" Beverly searched her face. "I want you to know that I'm sorry for speaking my mind like I did. I shouldn't have been so bold, especially not in front of Jay and Emma and their families."

"It's over now."

Beverly sighed, obviously relieved. "Did you and Ben have a good night?"

"We did." She debated the pros and cons of telling her aunt what had happened with Ben. It was true that she didn't want any negative words ruining her moment. However, on the other hand, Tricia knew Aunt Beverly would have to know before she called to tell her parents the news. It would be best to get her announcement over with instead of worrying about how and when it was going to take place. "Something happened, Aunt Beverly."

"Oh?" Her face looked impassive, like she was afraid to reveal too many of her thoughts. She patted the side of her bed. "Come sit beside me."

Tricia hopped up on the side of the bed and curled her feet underneath her. Then she bit her lip.

"You can tell me anything, Tricia. You know that, yes?"

"I know." Taking a deep breath, she said, "Ben asked me to marry him tonight and I said yes."

Aunt Beverly froze. "Oh. Well, my goodness."

Even though she knew her aunt was stunned, Tricia barreled on. "I know you're surprised, and I understand that. But Aunt Bev, I'm really happy."

Beverly smiled slightly. "*Jah*. I see that."

"I love him." Taking a deep breath, Tricia continued. "And don't say I don't know anything about love because I do. I know I love Ben Hilty. And I know this feels right. It feels as right as everything back in Walnut Creek felt wrong."

When she noticed that tears were filling her aunt's eyes, Tricia closed her own in frustration. Sliding off the side of the bed, she berated herself a dozen ways. She should have planned this announcement better. She should have thought more carefully about how to tell her aunt.

"I'm going to go to bed now. Good night," she whispered.

"Tricia?"

It took everything she had to turn around and face her aunt. "*Jah?*"

"I'm happy for you."

"That's why you're crying?"

"I'm crying because you're happy. And because I am so very happy for you." Scooting off the bed, she crossed the room and enfolded Tricia into a warm hug. "This is a *wonderful-gut* moment. I'm happy and excited, you sweet girl."

"Promise?"

"I promise. My goodness! We will certainly have a lot to talk about tomorrow."

"So much to talk about." Unbidden, tears slid down Tricia's cheeks. "This is the happiest night of my life," she said.

"*Jah*, dear. Some moments are so beautiful, only tears can tell our joy."

Tricia held those words close to her heart the rest of the night.

Chapter 17

*W*hat a commotion three girls and one boy could make while running down the street! As her girls and William ran toward her, all smiling as bright as you please, Emma quickly stepped out of the flower bed she was weeding and dusted off the front of her dress.

"Mamm!" Lena called out. "Mamm, guess what?"

"What? I canna begin to guess," she teased, looking just beyond the four *kinner* at Tricia and Ben, who were walking far more sedately behind them. Ben had offered to get the children from school from time to time as a simple way to thank her for helping William with his homework. Carefully, she scanned the children's expressions, looking for signs that one of the kids was in trouble or that something unexpected had happened at school.

"It's *wonderful-gut*," Mandy said as she practically skidded to a stop in front of Emma. "The best."

After giving her, Annie, and William hugs, she straightened and looked at Ben and Tricia again. "Now that all of you are here, please don't keep me in suspense any longer. What happened?"

"Ben and Tricia are going to get married!" William said.

"Oh!" Looking at the young couple, she felt tears prick her eyes. "Mandy was correct, this is *wonderful-gut* news. The best! Congratulations to you both."

Before Tricia or Ben could get a word in edgewise, Lena added, "And Mommy, guess what? They're going to get married at the Orange Blossom Inn!"

"Truly?"

"In four weeks' time!" Mandy exclaimed as all three girls joined hands and began jumping around again.

Emma sat down on the front step and reached a hand out to William. "And congratulations to you, too, William! Soon, you will have a new sister."

His eyes widened. "I never thought of it like that." He clutched her hand and made her very happy when he sat down right by her side.

"I'm sure Tricia has thought of that. Ain't so?" she asked the young lady.

Smiling softly, Tricia nodded. "I have a sister but no brothers, William. I'm glad you and Mark will be my *bruders*. It's a lovely blessing."

"Indeed, it is," Emma said. "Happy news is always a blessing, to be sure." When both Ben and Tricia sat down on her small front porch, she smiled. "Tell me how your parents took it."

"My *daed* was surprised but pleased, too," Ben said. "He married my *mamm* when they were young, so he remembered what being in love at our age felt like."

"I married at eighteen, so I remember that feeling, too," she said softly. Suddenly, all the years of building a home and a marriage flashed in her mind. Those had been busy years, stressful years. She and Sanford had been so young and inexperienced in the ways of the world. Luckily for them, though, they hadn't had time to wonder if they were doing things right. They'd had Lena almost ten months after the wedding and Mandy and Annie followed soon after.

Then, of course, came Sanford's heart attack. And after that? Well, her life had changed forever.

The rush of emotion she felt was an unwanted surprise. She didn't want her past heartache to interfere with the happiness Ben and Tricia were experiencing.

Suddenly she realized that she'd been staring off into the distance and that the couple in front of her was simply waiting for her to continue.

"I'm sorry. I guess my mind flew away with me. Ben, I'm so glad Jay is happy for you." Exhaling, she said, "Tricia, what did your family say?"

Tricia bit her bottom lip. "They were pretty shocked, of course. My parents don't know Ben and last they heard, I moved here to discover myself, not fall in love."

Emma noticed that Tricia looked a little hesitant but not devastated. "Will they let you get married?"

After a pause, she nodded. "At first they wanted me to go right back home, but after talking to them for, oh, hours, they began to understand how I felt." Looking sweetly bashful, she peeked at Ben. "I don't think a person can keep themselves from falling in love. It just happens whenever it's the right time."

"It sure does seem that way," Emma mused. "I'm glad your parents didn't forbid you to marry or demand that you return home."

"Me, too, though I wouldn't have agreed to move back no matter how much they yelled." Clasping her hands together, she said, "I'm so happy. I feel like everything in my life is coming together. I can't wait to get married!"

Beside her, Ben looked like he was trying not to start laughing. He held it together, letting her shine.

Emma smiled at the pair. She briefly wondered what Beverly's reaction had been but decided not to ask since Tricia hadn't mentioned her. "Soon, I'll have to have you two over for supper. We'll celebrate your *wonderful-gut* news."

When everyone started laughing, even the children, she giggled, too. "I know the last meal didn't go so well. But one can only hope that the next will go better. I'm sure it will. Well, with the Lord's help."

Ben leaned back on his hands. "Now, what I really want to know is what *you* are going to do, Emma."

She wasn't following. "What am I going to do about what?"

"You know, when my *daed* asks you to go courting." Lowering his voice, he said, "Will you say yes?"

"He wants to court me?" Her voice sounded as giddy as Tricia's. No doubt her cheeks were just as flushed with excitement. Remembering herself, she hesitantly asked, "I mean, what makes you think Jay and I would ever start seeing each other?"

Tricia wrapped her arms around her knees. "Miss Emma, I'm sorry, but it's kind of obvious that the two of you like each other."

Emma glanced to her left and right, worried that her girls were listening in. But they were currently bringing William through the back gate. Once she knew the coast was clear, she shook her head. "I don't know what to say."

"You could answer Ben's question. What would you say if Jay came calling like a proper suitor?"

"I don't know," she whispered. And her answer was true. Yes, she'd noticed that Jay Hilty was handsome. And she had spent an evening or two imagining what it would be like having someone special in her life again. To have a man who cared for her the way that Sanford had.

But there was a vast difference between wondering about something happening one day and what Ben and Tricia were talking about. Frankly, just the idea of Jay knocking on the door to see her was exciting. And it gave her a giant knot deep in the middle of her stomach.

Tricia looked at her closely. "Have you ever thought about marrying again?"

"I have," she said cautiously. "Well, from time to time. But I've always thought about it in a vague way, like when I wonder what it would feel like walking on the streets of Paris or Rome. I never truly thought I would find another man I would want to date."

"Never?" Tricia asked, her eyes wide.

"I loved my husband very much."

After darting a hesitant look at Ben, Emma said, "Now, I don't know what to think. My family and Sanford's family are very close. I suppose all of them thought I'd simply raise the girls on my own."

"I used to think my father should stay alone," Ben said. "But now I would feel bad if he did that. I would feel sorry for you, too, if you never considered courting again. Being alone forever is a mighty long time."

Emma was pretty sure Ben had no idea how true his statement was. "*Jah*. It is."

Tricia stood up. "Emma, I know you have been through a lot more than me, but I have recently learned that the Lord has put a whole lot of people on the earth and given us a whole lot of places to live and walk and explore. It would be a shame to ignore the chance for happiness because you were afraid you might like having a new man in your life."

Well, Tricia's words were certainly direct. *"Danke,"* she said slowly. Half of her was ready to disregard what the girl said. However, the other part was more than willing to accept Tricia's advice. After all, hadn't she been thinking just the same thing over the last few days? Clearing her throat, she changed the subject. "I should probably feed these *kinner* now. School gives one quite an appetite."

"I'll be back in two hours to get William," Ben said.

Just as Emma was ready to nod, Tricia's words reverberated in her head some more. She could either stew on them a little bit longer or do something.

Right then and there, she knew how Sanford would have reacted to such a statement. He would have grasped hold of it and held on tight. Furthermore, he would have convinced his parents to see his point of view. He would have not let anyone talk him out of doing something that was important to him.

And Jay was becoming important to her.

She knew what she had to do. "Wait. Ben, would your *daed* be upset if the girls and I brought William home?"

"Not at all."

"You sure?"

"If we don't need to stay around Pinecraft for William, I'll take Tricia back to the farm and tell my *daed* you're going to stop by. If it seems like he would be mad, I'll simply come right back to retrieve William."

"That's a lot of trouble."

"It's no trouble. Besides, I'm almost positive my father is going to be really happy about your visit."

"It's going to be fun. I'll make everyone supper," Tricia added with a happy smile.

"*Nee*, you don't need to do that," Emma said quickly. "I'm not planning to stay there long."

"Just long enough to say hello to Jay?"

Feeling like she was practically leaping off a cliff, she nodded. "*Jah*. I think, well, I think maybe I should give this courting idea a try. Just to see what might happen." She darted a look at Ben and was relieved to see that he looked pleased.

Tricia's green eyes sparkled. "Miss Emma, have *you* decided to be the one going courting?"

"Maybe. After all, the Lord doesn't say anything about women having to wait for the men to always make the first move. I think I would like to see what it feels like."

She only hoped Jay wouldn't be too shocked.

Chapter 18

Danke for coming to the farm," Jay said to a man about his age wearing a ball cap. "We appreciate your business."

"Are you kidding? We're glad y'all are open again. This is the best place in the county for fresh organic fruits and vegetables." Looking around, he pointed to the new display cases Jay, Ben, and Mark had built in the evenings. "I had heard you had opened a stand on the road, but this place is terrific."

"Thank you," Jay said, glad that the old building on the edge of the property had turned into such a perfect place to sell all their produce. With its quaint features, it looked like a cross between a gingerbread house and a rustic barn. The boys had painted it brick red and ordered a sign from a local woodworker declaring it the Hilty Organic Market in black and gold. The building had turned out to be a far better stand than Jay could have imagined. And its unusual, charming quirkiness had caught the eye of many locals.

When the boys had wanted to give the roadside spot a try, seeing that it wouldn't hurt anything to get people interested in the quality of their produce, Jay hadn't been too hopeful about it being successful. Luckily he'd been wrong. Word of mouth had been strong and every few days their number of customers doubled. The Lord had been working with them for sure.

Holding up his basket practically filled to the brim, the customer continued. "Everything you're carrying is top-notch. We're telling everyone we know about you."

"I am grateful for that. We'll be adding handmade soaps and other items eventually. Maybe even fresh baked goods, too."

"Sounds perfect. Thanks again," the man said after handing Jay his money.

After the man walked out to his car, hands laden with two large sacks full of fruits and vegetables, Jay gave a sigh of relief. At last they could rest for a moment.

"How many customers was that for the day, Daed?" Mark called out from the back of the stand where he was wiping down shelves.

"Twenty-seven."

Mark's grin was a replica of how Jay himself was feeling inside. "That's the best number yet and the day ain't even over."

"I was thinking the same thing," Jay admitted. "I hate to count my chickens before they're hatched, but things are looking up, for sure and for certain."

"They're getting better every day, Daed," Mark said as he walked to his side. "That man sounded like he loves your fruit and vegetables."

"*Nee*, that isn't right." Jay reached out and playfully tipped his middle boy's hat down low on his forehead. "The customer loves *our* fruit and vegetables, son. You've put as much effort into this stand as I have, and any success we have is because of your hard work and Ben's, too. I'm right proud of both of you. I could have never done all of this on my own."

Mark beamed, reminding Jay once again about how important it was to compliment his boys on jobs well done.

"Before we know it we'll be running the store full-time," he said.

"Maybe so." Jay wasn't willing to sound any more optimistic than that, but he was beginning to feel cautiously eager about their plans.

Almost since the moment they'd moved into the house, he, Ben, and Mark had gotten up every morning before dawn and spent practically every waking hour on the business. Each day either he or Ben would return to the house at half past six and wake up William. After the four of them had a big breakfast together, one of them would take William to school, then head back to the farm to put in a full day's work.

It had been a hard schedule. And Jay would be lying if he didn't admit that he'd spent at least a few minutes a day fighting the guilt that ate at him for spending so much of his energy and time on the business. He hoped the boys, especially William, weren't feeling as if he didn't care as much about their needs.

But neither Ben nor Mark had taken nearly as much time for himself as Jay had tried to give them. Instead, they threw themselves wholeheartedly into the business. Little by little Jay had come to realize that this organic farm wasn't just his dream; it was his sons' dream, too.

Together, they'd decided to start small with the sales part of the business. Eventually, Jay would concentrate more on expanding the farm, but for now they had decided to take advantage of the fruit and crops that had already been planted.

"What do you think we should do? Wait another hour or celebrate by taking off an hour early?"

Mark pointed past Jay to the couple walking toward them. "Stay and hear what Ben and Tricia have to say."

"They're here already?" Concerned, he walked over to them. "Ben, why isn't William with you?"

"Because Emma said she wanted to bring him home."

"Why?" Automatically, he feared the worst. "Did something happen? Should you have left him?"

"William is fine." Looking a bit mischievous, Ben stuffed his hands in his pockets. "What's more, he ain't the reason Emma wants to come over tonight."

"What is the reason?" He held up a basket of berries. "Does she need some fruit? We can get that ready for her."

"She isn't coming over for fruit," Tricia said.

Jay thought Tricia looked like she was hiding a special secret, too. "What does she want?"

Ben and Tricia exchanged small smiles, then Ben spoke. "She, ah, wants to come courting."

He froze. "What?"

Behind him, Mark stifled a chuckle. Barely.

Jay decided to ignore his son's amusement. "Tell me what you mean, son," he bit out as he tried to ignore the flush of embarrassment that was surely staining his cheeks.

"We were talking to her about our engagement," Tricia began. "Then we started talking about courting . . ."

"And then I asked her if she was ever going to date again," Ben continued. "And, well, I might have also asked about you and her."

"You did not."

Ben nodded. "It wasn't any big deal, Daed."

"You and I will speak about keeping my business private later, son."

"We can talk about that all you want, but I wasn't wrong. She knows you are becoming a friend and I think she admires you, too."

Jay's next gripe got stuck in his throat as his son's words registered. "She said all that?"

"More or less." Ben shrugged. "We didn't talk about you all that much. But she is going to come over." Giving him a look, Ben added, "And before you start getting upset with me for sticking my nose in your business, I need to point out that this visit was her idea, not mine."

"Really?" he asked before he remembered to stop sounding like a lovesick fool.

Tricia nodded. "Really."

"You ought to be nice to her, Daed," Mark said.

"I'm always nice to her."

"You ought to take her out walking or something, then. Girls like that."

He was completely taken off guard, both by his middle boy's dating advice . . . and what his words meant. "Mark," he ventured hesitantly, "do you want me to see Emma?"

"Maybe." He paused, then added, "I hate seeing you alone."

"I haven't been alone. I have all of you."

"It ain't the same, Daed." Mark looked down at his boots, as if he was wary about revealing his thoughts.

Jay could understand that. He didn't want to reveal just how much he was starting to care for Emma. "We'll see what happens," he murmured, attempting to keep his voice and expression neutral. "After all, it hasn't been that long since your *mamm* passed away."

Raising his chin again, Mark said, "I know, Daed. But Mamm was sick for a long time before then." He held up a hand. "I know I'm not supposed to ever speak of that. Or talk about how I feel. I'll stop."

"You can always tell me how you feel, Mark. Always." When his son looked at him like he couldn't quite believe that, he added, "I know your heart is in the right place. I know you loved your *mamm*, and just as importantly, she knew it, too. Because of that, you can be as honest as you would like about your feelings."

He looked back down at the floor. "I only meant that when she was so sick, it was like we'd already lost her," he mumbled.

Mark's words hit him hard. Not because they weren't true or he was surprised. It was because Mark was brave enough to voice how long and difficult Evelyn's illness had been for everyone. Jay had always felt disloyal whenever he dared to be so honest. "I know," he said at last. "I know what you meant. But that doesn't mean I need to start getting serious about another woman."

Ben groaned impatiently. "You don't have to be like Tricia and me and fall in love right away, Daed. But anything is better than sitting home alone all the time. Ain't so?"

He privately agreed, but he didn't know how to handle both his feelings and his sons' feelings. Or how much his eldest sounded like a love and romance expert.

But because William was not there—and he'd always been sure that William was suffering the most from the loss of Evelyn—he admitted, "I don't know how to do all of this correctly. I don't want either of you to feel like I'm replacing your mother."

"You could never replace Mamm," Mark said. "But I don't think she would be happy to know you were home by yourself and sad."

He'd never thought about it like that. He'd only concentrated on his promises to her . . . not what she might have wanted him to do. Evelyn was the most generous woman he'd ever met, and though her body had always been weak, she'd had innate strength about her. A backbone. "I think you're right."

Ben smiled. "If we're right, then that means you ought to go home and wash up, Daed. We'll finish up here."

He looked down at his clothes. He supposed he was a bit muddy. "You think I need to clean up a bit?"

Tricia nodded. "It couldn't hurt, Jay."

As he went inside the house to take that shower, he felt lighter. As if the weight of guilt and worry he'd been carrying around had finally been lifted. To his surprise, he also felt a little nervous. He was going courting again. And as he thought of Emma, with her perfect skin, dark blue eyes, and heart of gold, he knew he wanted to be worthy of her.

Actually, he wanted to eventually mean as much to her as she already meant to him.

That was something to truly aspire to.

JAY HAD JUST MADE a pitcher of fresh-squeezed lemonade when the kitchen door opened and William came in with Lena, Mandy, and Annie right behind. Emma brought up the rear, looking a bit like she was herding sheep.

After greeting them all, he couldn't resist teasing Emma. "What, no matching dresses today?"

"Mamm changed," Mandy said, her mouth in a tiny pout. "She said she needed a fresh dress. I don't know why."

It took everything Jay had not to smile when Emma flushed. "I gardened today," she said. "It's always a very warm job."

"I had to change, too. I was out selling produce."

William looked around and frowned. "Where are Mark and Ben?"

"They are finishing up business this afternoon at the stand. They'll be here within the hour."

"Oh."

Jay noticed the three girls were staring at him like they were just waiting to be visited with. Pulling up a kitchen chair, he sat down on it so he wouldn't be towering over them. Gentling his voice, he asked, "What did you three do today?"

Annie walked right up and showed him her finger. "I got a Band-Aid."

He held her little palm in his and examined her finger closely. "My goodness! What happened?"

"I don't remember."

Jay couldn't help it, he burst out laughing. "You don't?"

"Annie likes bandages, I'm afraid," Emma said. "To her, it's a cure for most anything."

Jay was about to nod when Annie surprised him and crawled onto his lap. Immediately, a feeling of warm protectiveness settled deep inside him. William had recently informed Jay that he was too old to be cuddled. Jay supposed it was true. But as Annie rested her head against his chest, Jay felt a warm surge of affection flow through him. Having Annie be so trusting of him made him want to shield her from the rest of the world and make her happy all the time. He wrapped an arm around her so she wouldn't fall.

Annie turned her head and gazed up at him, her blue eyes seeming to take in every line and wrinkle on his face.

"You okay?" he asked.

She nodded, then said, "Your beard is short."

Her statement was so blunt—and so out of the blue—he couldn't help but chuckle.

"Annie!" Emma cried. "You mustn't be rude."

"It's not rude if it's true," Jay replied as both Mandy and Lena stepped closer. "I trimmed most of it six months ago. I, uh, needed that symbolism, I think," he said quietly as he met Emma's eye. Men grew beards after they married. Most never trimmed them. But in the days after Evelyn's death, he'd felt it was a symbol of something he'd lost. In a moment of weakness he'd trimmed it close. Now, in the Florida heat, he'd elected to keep it short. It was too hot otherwise.

"I understand," Emma murmured.

"Do you like peanut butter?" Mandy asked.

He blinked. "Yes?"

"Oh." She frowned as Annie crawled off his lap.

Confused, Jay looked at Emma. "Did I say the wrong thing?"

"Not at all." Emma shook her head. "Mandy is allergic to peanuts and peanut butter so she doesn't like to be around it."

"I'll make sure I don't keep any around."

"That's not necessary," Emma said.

"How about I'll make sure none of us eat it when you are around?" he said to Mandy.

Emma smiled. *"Danke."*

"Daed, can we go out and wait for Mark and Ben?" William asked, obviously bored with the concerns of little girls.

"As long as you stay near the front porch," he said just as the kids ran out.

And then he and Emma were alone.

Suddenly, he was tongue-tied. Should he say anything about

how he'd heard from Ben and Tricia that she was going courting? He ached to have it out in the open so they could both laugh at the idea of such a thing . . . and so she wouldn't discover somehow that he'd known her intentions but never let on.

But for the life of him, he couldn't think of a way to tell her without embarrassing her. Getting to his feet, he said, "I squeezed some lemons and made lemonade. Would you care for some?"

"Please," she said. "I guess you had to learn to make all kinds of things after Evelyn passed on to heaven."

"I did. But she was ill for a long time before that, too." He pulled out the ice tray from his freezer and put several cubes in each glass. "Growing boys need to eat."

She tilted her head to one side, as she watched him pour. "Did your family not help you?"

"They did. Though, to be honest, they wanted to do more than I let them. I didn't want them to always be in the house. I needed control, you see. Taking care of my boys let me pretend that I had some control of the situation, though of course Evelyn's fate had always been in God's hands." Handing her a glass, he said, "I love my family but I needed space, too. I guess that's another reason why the boys and I moved to Florida."

"I understand." Emma frowned. "But I've never been quite brave enough to refuse my family's offers of help. Or Sanford's. They are around all the time."

"There's nothing wrong with that. It's a blessing."

"It is," she said slowly. "And it was. But now I feel like I'm not really very independent. What's more, I don't think they want me to be."

"I'm sure God will help you find the right way to extricate yourself. Or not. Everyone moves at their own pace, I think."

Her blue eyes widened and Jay stared back, thinking what a pretty shade they were. A true blue, not veering toward gray or brown or green. Her eyes were slightly almond shaped, too.

She set her glass down on the kitchen countertop. "Jay, I'm afraid I have a confession to make."

He set his glass down, too. "What is it?"

"Well, I had a talk with Ben and Tricia this afternoon. And for some reason—I'm not rightly sure how—we started talking about their engagement and courting and then, well, me courting."

Her last words were so hesitantly spoken, so very embarrassed sounding, he stepped closer and gently ran one calloused finger along her knuckles. "I wasna going to tell you, but Ben and Tricia told me about that conversation."

"They told you?" she squeaked.

"They did. They were excited about the idea, you see."

She closed her eyes. "I'm so embarrassed. If I keep my eyes closed, can we pretend I'm not here?"

He chuckled. "Not a chance."

"Couldn't you try real hard?"

"Nope. Because I'm glad you're here, you see." In for a penny, in for a pound. "I was glad to hear what Tricia and Ben told me."

Her eyes popped open again. "You were?"

"*Jah.* I'm proud of you for being braver than me."

"I wasna brave."

"You were." Taking a deep breath, he said, "Emma, if you came over here just so your girls could say hello to my boys, that is fine with me. We will always enjoy your company and friendship. But . . ." His voice drifted off. He was warring between being as honest and brave as she had been and guarding his heart.

"But?" she prompted.

"If you really did come over because you'd like us to be closer in an . . . um, romantic way? If you'd like to see whether there could be a relationship between us—us as in you and me—I have to tell you that makes me really happy."

"It does?" Wonder lit her voice.

As Jay nodded, he realized that he was telling the absolute truth. "There's something about you that makes me want to know you better, Emma. And it has nothing to do with the fact that we have had similar experiences with losing a spouse. It has to do with how kind you are. With the way you love that *hund* of yours, even though he has to be the worst-behaved beagle in history. It has to do with the way that you brought over supper and didn't expect even my thanks in return."

Lowering his voice, he reached out and took one of her hands. "And it also has something to do with the fact that you have the prettiest blue eyes I've ever seen in my life. And that I think all of you is just as pretty."

In that moment, he felt as vulnerable as he'd ever been. Actually, Jay felt more fragile and uncertain than Ben probably had ever felt around Tricia, more hesitant than he'd ever felt around Evelyn. Funny how life's experiences made one wiser but also made one realize just how fragile the heart was. Now that he knew about loss, and knew how fleeting happiness could be, he was far more hesitant to put himself at risk.

She blinked again and smiled. "So you are sayin' coming over was the right decision?"

"The very best. But from now on, I think I would like to do the calling and courting. I may be rusty but I'd like to give it a try."

She giggled, a light, girlish sound that lit up his kitchen. "That's a deal."

Outside, the children were chattering up a storm—it was obvious that Ben, Mark, and Tricia had returned—but inside the kitchen, under the pale glow of a kerosene lamp, there was only a thick silence.

Jay was so struck by what had just taken place between them, he had to force himself to remain in the here and now. Otherwise he would be too tempted to reflect how one day had changed things completely for him.

As they stared at each other, the air was warm with the intangible heat of their new awareness. Emma's lips were slightly parted, her cheeks flushed. In the dim light, she looked as young as Tricia and just as hopeful and naïve. The sight before him made him want to pick her up and twirl her around and make a dozen promises about how he would always make her happy.

Though his mouth had suddenly become dry, he said, "Emma, may I take you out to supper on Friday night? Just the two of us?"

"You may."

"I'll come get you at six o'clock?"

As if she was too overcome to talk, she nodded.

He was pleased. Really pleased. He reached out, needing to touch her, needing to skim a finger over her lightly flushed cheeks . . . when the back door opened and a pack of kids came roaring inside.

Instantly, the subtle tension dissipated into happy smiles and teenaged needs. Quiet had ended, replaced by talking and laughter, chattering and interruptions. Noisy boots on the hardwood floor, the clattering of bags on chairs and tables.

Life with children. Something that was just as precious to their lives as hope and romance and quiet moments filled with shy flirting.

"Emma, I'm mighty glad you came over," Mark fairly called out over the din. "Any chance you brought us some cookies?"

"As a matter of fact, I did," she teased. "I brought all of you lots of them."

As Jay watched Emma hand Mark a cookie from a plastic container before passing them out to all the kids, he stood to one side and smiled.

He had a date with the prettiest girl in Pinecraft on Friday night.

He felt like the luckiest guy in town.

Chapter 19

$\mathcal{B}$everly was in the kitchen making loaves of zucchini bread on Thursday morning when the phone rang. Thinking it was sure to be Eric, she debated answering it. Recently, she'd discovered that his phone calls had become the highlight of her day. She had also, to her dismay, even begun to wonder if their friendship could eventually evolve into something more romantic. Which was just silly.

Really not good!

After all, Eric was an Englisher, and a successful financial planner. He was worldly, and had obviously dated a lot. He would never be remotely attracted to her, and she would be a fool to entertain such thoughts.

In fact, it would be best to start distancing herself from him. On the other hand, anyone could be on the line. And, well, she was the innkeeper, which meant she had no business ignoring a ringing telephone.

"Hello?"

"Hiya, Beverly," her older brother Edward said. "What is going on out there in Sarasota?"

Oh! This was what she got for hoping and praying that it wasn't Eric on the line. It was worse! Now she was going to have to walk the line between defending her abilities to look after Tricia and taking the blame for letting the girl fall in love and get engaged.

Then there was the fact that she was somehow going to have to try to be supportive of both her niece and her brother, which was likely going to be impossible.

"Beverly, you there?"

"Everything is, um, moving along," she said at last. "I'm busy keeping the inn going. Which is, well, a busy job."

"Sounds like you've been far busier than that." There was a definite edge to his voice now.

"Hmm?" Growing up with Edward, she'd learned it was helpful to play innocent.

"Beverly, who is this Ben? Is he really everything Tricia says he is?"

"Well, um . . ."

"And what about his family?" he added. "Tricia said his father is a widower. When did his wife pass away? What happened to her?"

"Edward, that ain't something that's any of our—"

"She said they just moved to Sarasota, too. What brought on the move? And where do they hail from?"

She was starting to realize that not only had she not done a very good job of looking out for Tricia, she had definitely not asked enough questions about Ben. "Edward, if you have so many concerns, you should simply come down here and get the answers yourself. I'm the girl's aunt, not her parent. And I'm, you know, busy with the inn." There, that would show him!

"That's why I called you. Me and Kathleen are getting on the bus tomorrow. We'll be there on Saturday."

"You're coming out here to visit?" As she heard her voice, she grimaced. She'd practically squeaked.

"*Jah*. That's what I just said," he said impatiently. "What's wrong? Do you not have room in that busy inn of yours? If not, tell me where I should stay."

"Of course I will have a room for you both." She was pretty sure she would. But even if she didn't, she would find them someplace, even if it meant she had to give up her own room or share with Tricia. "I'm glad you're coming down." And, she realized, she *was* glad. Edward and Kathleen had never had the opportunity to come visit her. She'd understood, knowing he was busy with his farm. "I've missed you, Ed," she said, voicing her thoughts.

"I feel the same way." Lowering his voice, he added, "Kathleen has been fairly vexed with me. She's been wantin' to come down for a few weeks now."

"I'll look forward to seeing her."

"You'll see her soon enough. Now, give me some answers."

"Well, let's see. Ben is a nice young man. He seems very smitten with Tricia. He's also the eldest of three sons. He looks after them and helps his father with their organic farm." She thought of his other questions. "As for his father, I'm not sure when his wife passed on to heaven and I haven't asked. I do know he came down here to start fresh."

"Tricia already told me most of that."

Now, more than ever, Beverly wished she could go back and apologize to Tricia for sounding so doubtful. Not that she had changed her mind about her concerns, but it was obvious poor Tricia had already been grilled over the phone.

"If Tricia told you everything, why are you asking me?" she snapped.

"I want your thoughts about this man. Tricia acts like he's wonderful. Is he?"

Oh, for heaven's sakes! "That's not for me to say. I am not engaged to him, *Edward*."

"Come on, *Beverly*. Do you really not care that my youngest is ready to get hitched to a man she barely knows? I would have thought you, of all people, would have cautioned her about giving in to her heart."

For days, she'd thought the very same thing. But now, hearing her brother speak about her misalliance in the past? Well, it didn't feel too good.

In fact, she was kind of tired of being Marvin's poor ex-fiancée. "Tricia is her own woman and she is smarter than you are giving her credit for," she replied, no longer even trying to keep the vinegar out of her voice. "As far as I can tell, Ben Hilty is a good man and he seems to care for her very much. She certainly looks happier than I've ever seen her. That says a lot, I think. And if you're wondering if he's going to break up with her before the wedding, I don't think so."

Edward sighed. "Sorry. I didn't mean to hurt your feelings."

"This isn't about me, Ed. It's about Tricia and Ben."

After a brief pause, he mumbled. "*Jah*, that's what Kathleen said."

He sounded so sheepish, she grinned. "I knew you married a smart woman. Now I really *can't* wait to see Kathleen."

"We're looking forward to being there. I suppose it's still hot there?"

"Hot as July," she said with a smile. "Bring plenty of cool clothes. And don't forget water for the bus ride. That twenty-hour ride seems to last forever."

"I wrote that down. Okay, we'll be getting off that Pioneer Trails bus on Saturday."

"I'll be in the parking lot waiting with the rest of Pinecraft. Does Tricia know you're coming?"

"*Nee.* I wanted to talk to you first." For the first time, his voice sounded hesitant. "Will you tell her?"

"Of course I will. Safe travels, Edward."

After she hung up, Beverly poured bread batter into the three lined pans on the counter, put them in the oven, and set her egg timer. Then she went to go find Tricia and deliver the news.

WHAT SHOULD SHE WEAR? What should she say? What should she do? Staring at the clothes in her small closet on Friday, Emma's choices became too many and the decisions dire.

It was time she got some help.

Though Emma had plenty of weeds to pull and even a sewing project to finish, she put a leash on Frankie and walked around the block toward Dorrie's house. Around noon every day, her best friend took a thirty-minute walk. Though it was hot as could be, Emma figured she and Frankie could handle it if he could keep his paws mainly on the cool grass.

They'd passed five houses and just turned up Miller Avenue when they saw her. Dorrie had on her usual: sunglasses, sporty tennis shoes, and a bright smile. Today, she was wearing a bright coral-colored dress. Frankie, recognizing Dorrie and her penchant for giving him lots of doggie treats, wagged his tail and picked up his pace. When Dorrie saw them approaching, she waved.

"Fancy seeing you two out and about!" she said with a happy smile.

"We thought it was a good time for a walk."

"At noon?" Dorrie stopped and looked at her carefully for a moment. "Well, it is *my* favorite walking time. How's my favorite beagle?" she asked when Frankie nudged her with his nose.

He sat down in a spot of grass beside her so she could give his head a rub—and so she could pull out a dog biscuit from a hidden pocket in her dress. Chomping away, he had the gall to look at Emma as if to say it was really too bad that she hadn't ever learned about dog biscuits.

"Gut hund," Dorrie murmured as Frankie crunched. When he wagged his tail, she gave him a pat and pointed to a small, shady spot under a tree in someone's front yard. *"Jah*, it is a warm one. Hop up there and take a break where it's nice and cool."

Stunned, Emma watched Frankie do exactly as Dorrie suggested. She wasn't sure if she was impressed or jealous of Frankie's obedience. "How do you do it, Dorrie? Frankie doesn't behave that well for anyone else in the world."

"Nee?"

"You know he doesn't."

"Well, it's all in the dog treats. I always carry one when I go for a walk, just in case I run into Frankie."

"Hmm." Maybe *that* was why Frankie was always on the loose.

Still looking pleased with herself, Dorrie continued. "I bake them myself, and from my own recipe, too. Dogs love them. They're tasty."

"Have you tried them?"

She grinned, showing off her dimples. "Of course I have. I give them to my pair." Dorrie and her husband had two rescued greyhounds. Emma had long ago decided that those dogs were the luckiest in the state of Florida. "I just noticed that you are all alone. Where are Amber and Lace?"

"Ach, Amber was looking a little peaked this morning. I think one of her front legs is bothering her a bit."

"I hope there's nothing wrong?"

"Nothing that a little rest and a treat or two won't help. Now, what are you doing out? I don't care what you say, you walking out and about at noon is most unusual."

"I need your help."

Immediately her friend's easygoing smile vanished. "Of course. Anything. What happened?"

"Jay Hilty is coming over tonight to take me to supper."

Immediately her look of worry slipped into another beautiful smile. "Emma! Good for you!" She pulled her into a quick, fierce hug. "Isn't that good news? The best! *Wunderbaar.*"

"It is. I mean, I think it is."

Dorrie chuckled. "Oh, it is."

"I would feel more positive if I wasn't so nervous. I don't know which dress to wear. Or what I should say or do. Or what I *shouldn't* say or do."

Her girlfriend looked her up and down, shaking her head in dismay. "Dear, you're a mess."

Emma wasn't even going to try to say she wasn't. "This is true. I am. I am a complete mess."

Dorrie turned around, leading the way to Emma's house. "Come on, Frankie," she said. "Let's get you out of the hot sun and settle your owner down." As if Frankie understood every word she said, he woofed and trotted forward, leading the way home.

Once they walked inside, Dorrie went straight to Emma's bedroom, scanned her seven dresses, and pulled the tangerine-colored one off the hanger. "This one."

"Really?" She hardly ever wore that dress. Though she liked the bright color on her daughters, she'd always thought it was a bit too flashy for a woman like herself. She was a widow and a mother of three. Surely such women didn't wear such shades of orange. "Um, I was thinking maybe the blue. Because of my eyes."

"I'm sure he's already discovered you have pretty blue eyes, Emma. This dress is happy. And you are always tan, so it looks pretty on you, too."

"You don't think he will think it a bit gaudy?"

"He will think you look fetching. Trust me, Emma. Tangerine."

"Okay. *Danke.*" She carefully laid the dress on the bed. "Now, what do you think I should talk about with him?"

Her lips twitched. "Probably whatever you want to talk about, dear."

Emma noticed that Dorrie was trying not to tease her. "I'm serious. I don't know what men like to talk about on dates. What if I say the wrong thing?"

"If you say the wrong thing then he's not the man for you." Sitting down on the edge of the bed, she added, "I don't think you have a thing to worry about. Don't forget, you already are friends. He already knows you are sweet and kind."

Sweet and kind didn't necessarily sum up the person she wanted him to think she was. "I hope it's that easy."

"It will be if you allow it to be. Don't make good things difficult, dear. We all have enough troubles, you don't need to go borrowing them."

"You might be right about that."

"I know I am." Shifting, she rested one of her hands on Emma's lemon-and-blue log-cabin quilt. "Now, how is your family taking it?"

"They don't know. I only asked my parents to watch the girls for a few hours this evening."

"They're going to be here when Jay comes over?"

"Oh, *nee*! I asked if I could bring the girls over to their *haus*."

Dorrie tilted her head. "And they agreed without asking the reason why?"

"I'm sure they'll ask." Thinking of how difficult navigating that conversation was going to be, she murmured, "I'm sure they're going to ask a lot of questions."

"They are. And I know you won't like me sayin' this, but they're going to try to convince you that you're doing the wrong thing."

"They may be right."

"They aren't, Emma. Even if you and Jay Hilty realize that the Lord only wants you two to be friends and nothing more, it is important that you take this first step. You need to open your heart to the possibility that you could find love again. And what's more, Sanford would want you to."

"Do ya really think so?" Emma wanted to imagine that Sanford would be happy for her, but she just wasn't sure. She sighed. "I've tried to imagine what he would say if I told him that I was doing this."

"I know what he would say, and I think you know, too."

"And what is that?"

"That it is about time you allowed a man to take you to dinner." She wagged a finger. "It's been three years, Emma. Three years is a long time to be alone."

It had been. "Our families are going to worry about me."

"I am sure they will." She pursed her lips, then added, "Forgive me, but I think they are also worrying about themselves."

Dorrie had lost her. "That makes no sense."

"Of course it does. Change is hard, Emma. If you move on, that means they'll have to move on, too. They've already had to adjust to Sanford leaving this earth so quickly. They're going to fight tooth and nail if you make them adjust to something else."

She was starting to think that Dorrie made a good point. Emma's parents had told her that they would be happy to take care of her and the girls for the rest of their lives. At first, she'd been so grief-stricken that she'd clung to their promise and hadn't dared to think that anything could possibly be different. But now, with the girls all in school and her having more time on her hands, she'd started to feel that she needed something more than they could give her.

Of course, until Frankie had found Jay and his boys, no other man had made her even contemplate falling in love again.

"Change is hard."

"*Jah.* But change is a part of life. We grow older in spite of our best intentions. And with that age, it's best to become wiser, too."

Emma nodded. "*Danke*, Dorrie. I knew going to find you was the right thing to do."

"See, you're already getting wiser!"

"And you are getting prideful," she teased. "Thank you for your help."

"It was nothing." Standing up, she pointed to the tangerine dress lying on the quilt. "Wear the dress and take the girls to your parents early so that whatever they tell you can roll off your shoulders before Jay comes over."

"I'll do that," she promised, though she didn't think her parents' criticisms were going to roll off her shoulders at all. No, they were going to remain firmly settled there like a twenty-pound flour sack.

Heavy and burdensome.

Chapter 20

*A*s Jay drummed his fingers on the hard plastic seat of the SCAT shuttle, he couldn't help but reflect on the path the Lord had shown him. Here he was, sitting beside his eldest son near their new home, on the coast of Florida. Furthermore, they were both on their way to go courting. Courting by his son's side!

Jay had never pictured that happening. Ever.

As the shuttle made its way through the streets of Sarasota and people got off and on, he glanced out the window and tried to tell himself that he had no reason to be nervous. He was a grown man. He'd survived all kinds of things, from Evelyn passing away to all three boys having chicken pox together to Mark breaking his arm when he was thirteen.

He could take a woman out on a date.

"You okay, Daed?" Ben asked.

"I'm fine. Why?"

"No reason." Smiling he added, "Well, no reason besides the fact that your right hand is gripping the rail like we're on a roller coaster and you're about to fall off. And your left hand has been tapping the edge of your seat. Loudly."

Immediately, Jay clasped his hands in his lap. Ben had been right, he'd been holding on for dear life, in the metaphorical sense. "I guess I'm a little nervous," he admitted.

"You'll be fine, I promise. Emma likes you. I saw the way she was looking at you the other night."

There was no way he was going to ever admit how happy Ben's words about Emma liking him had made him. "It's just a walk and supper. We've shared several meals together now."

"That you have. You're going to be fine."

"And if we realize we don't suit, that's not gonna be a problem." Best to keep expectations low and all.

"It won't be a problem. You will suit each other fine. You already suit each other fine."

"Maybe you are right."

"I know I'm right. All of us have noticed that there's something special happening between you and Emma Keim."

"All of us? You mean you and Mark?"

"And William. And Tricia. And I think, even Lena." Grinning, Ben stretched his hands out in front of him. "We're all counting the minutes until both of you know it, too."

"Great."

Discovering that Emma and he did suit each other well was actually what he was most afraid of. If that happened, he'd have to think about another date. And then, maybe even a future. And what then? It was one thing for their *kinner* to be all right with him taking Emma out every now and then, but surely their children would react differently if they thought things were about to change drastically.

Would Emma's little girls ever be okay with the idea of sharing their mother?

Suddenly, his collar was way too tight. He pulled on the fabric around his neck. It didn't stretch a millimeter, of course, but the action did somehow make him breathe a little easier.

Ben noticed. "Daed, quit worrying so much."

"Do you think William was being truthful when he said he didn't mind me doing this?"

"I do."

"Really? Because his acceptance kind of took me off guard, if you want to know the truth."

"Really, Daed. I'm sure. William is not upset."

"Wait a minute. How come you sound so sure about this?" For the first time Ben looked a bit hesitant. "Ben, what do you know that I don't?"

"Nothing. It's just that I know William misses having a mother." He swallowed. "We all do, of course. But me and Mark had Mamm for a lot longer than he did. Plus, William is kind of sensitive. He needs a woman's ear from time to time."

Jay thought about that and realized his son was exactly right. For the last few years now, Jay hadn't been giving Will as much attention and care as the young boy needed. First he'd been looking after Evelyn, then mourning her passing. Then had come all the planning and preparation for their big move to Sarasota, and lately Jay had needed to spend every waking hour getting the farm up and running. Besides all that, there were the simple chores of everyday life that took up so much time: laundry and grocery shopping, cooking and cleaning. That left little quality time for him to spend with his boys. But while Mark had taken it in stride because that was his nature, and Ben was more than ready to be an adult, little William had been floundering.

"Maybe I should be spending more time with Will instead of with Emma."

"Daed, not to be mean or anything, but Will don't need more of you. He needs a mother."

"Maybe if I go courting, I should be looking for a woman who doesn't already have a bunch of *kinner*." Not that he had ever even looked at another woman twice before he'd met Emma.

"Daed, William likes Emma. He likes going to her *haus* every afternoon." Flashing a smile, he added, "He likes all of those little girls, too. We all do."

The comment reminded him of just how cute those girls were. And so different from William, Mark, and Ben! "Little girls are sure silly."

Ben smiled. "Yep. And they squeal."

"And cry easily, I'm learning."

"But that Annie is so cute, Daed. The other day she wanted to hold my hand. And when we said good-bye, she asked for a hug."

"They're sweet girls, for sure. No matter what happens with Emma and me, I am glad that we've gotten to know them."

Ben looked at him in appreciation. "*Gut* for you, Daed. You are ready at last." Chuckling he added, "And it's a *gut* thing, too."

"Why is that?"

Ben stood up as the SCAT bus stopped with a small jerk and quiet squeak of brakes. "Because we're here," he said before he led the way out.

As Jay hurried to catch up with his boy, he had a feeling he was behind him in more ways than one.

WHEN HE WAS ALMOST at Emma's doorstep five minutes later, Jay paused and closed his eyes. *Lord, help me have the strength to follow my heart,* he prayed silently. *Help me not let doubts and worries overtake a glad and hopeful heart.*

Figuring that was good enough—and since the Lord was probably about to send out a swarm of bees to hurry him along—Jay knocked on Emma's door. When she opened it, he was struck by two things: one, her bright orange dress made her lightly tanned skin look even prettier than ever and her eyes look even bluer than they usually did.

And two, she'd been crying.

"Emma, what's wrong?" he asked, walking right in and shutting the door behind him.

She bit her bottom lip. Obviously, she was trying to keep it from trembling. "It's nothing."

"It's obviously something. What is it?"

"When I dropped off the girls at my parents' *haus,* they worried that I was encouraging the girls to forget their father."

"That couldn't be further from the truth. Seeing someone new doesn't erase the past."

"I agree." She bit her lip. "When I tried to explain that I needed to do something for myself, they ignored me."

He couldn't imagine how anyone could ever find fault with the way Emma conducted herself or raised her daughters. He couldn't name a woman who led a more Christian life. "I'm sorry, Emma."

"*Jah.* Me, too." She swiped at a tear. "I'm sorry. I didn't want you to see me like this."

Jay knew some men would have had all the right words for her. But all he could think of doing at the moment was holding her in his arms. "Come here," he murmured as he gathered her close. When she slowly wrapped her arms around his waist, and then, with a quiet sigh rested her head on his shoulder, he knew he hadn't felt anything so special in a very long time.

When her tears finally subsided, she pulled away. "Oh, I bet I look even worse!"

He thought she looked very sweet. "Nope. You still look pretty."

"Really? Because my skin gets all splotchy when I cry."

To be honest, her skin was splotchy. But that didn't bother him any. He liked the fact that she'd leaned on him for comfort. In fact, there was little about her that he didn't find enchanting at the moment.

"Do you want to talk about things or go?"

She looked at him in wonder. "I didn't ruin everything? You still want to go?"

"Of course. And I'm not letting you back out, either. We both have waited quite some time to go out to supper. We're not going to let a couple of grumpy parents derail our plans."

Her lips twitched. "They weren't exactly grumpy. More like mighty determined to get me to see things their way."

"I can be mighty determined, too, Emma," he said, realizing that all of the doubts he'd shared with Ben had vanished the moment she'd shared her worries. "Go wash up and let's go."

After looking at him a good long moment, she nodded and walked to the washroom.

He sat down on the couch next to Frankie, who was reclining with two feet stretched out in front of him. "Beagle, you are a couch-hog. Move over." Frankie yawned, gave him a small look of disgruntlement, then curled into a beagle ball.

"I'm ready." She led the way outside, a tentative smile on her lips. She was happy again. And he'd helped her get there.

"*Gut.* Let's go then."

Ben had been right. They did suit. They suited each other well. Very well, indeed.

"Do you feel different, now that you are an engaged woman?" Ben asked.

Tricia was cuddled against her fiancé's side in front of the fire pit on the inn's back patio. They'd been sitting that way for the last hour and Tricia hoped she'd never have to leave. It was so rare for them to have any time completely alone.

Tricia thought about Ben's question before replying. "I suppose I feel a little different," she said at last. "I know I feel happier than I can ever remember being. I think I feel a little bit more grown-up, too." She was now thinking about her future by Ben's side. She'd gone from being centered on herself to focusing on Ben's needs. Instead of making plans with only her wants in mind, they were dreaming about their future as a married couple.

"Our meeting today with the preacher went well," Ben said.

"I agree. Though Eli has seen us together at church a couple of times, I thought he might try to convince us to break the engagement. Or, at the very least, postpone things."

Ben grunted. "I would have been really upset if he had asked us to break up."

"Me, too." Stretching her bare foot toward the fire, she added, "Instead, he simply wants us to pray about our future."

"And to be open to the possibility of talking more with him about our relationship."

"That wasn't a difficult thing to promise," Tricia decided. "I want to talk to you about marriage and your goals."

He squeezed her shoulder. "Only *my* goals?"

"Well, my goals, too. And all my questions."

"Sounds like you've got lots of them."

Tricia heard the amusement in his tone and she supposed she didn't blame him. She did sound a little anxious. "I do have questions, but what I am most concerned about is making sure we're secure in our faith and our future together. Especially since we're going to say our vows near the end of October."

Especially that. Because nothing was going to prevent her from following through with those plans. She didn't care if they had no decorations, no fancy luncheon, nothing but time to pray and make promises to each other. She wanted to be Ben's wife in a month's time.

"We will be," he promised. "By the time we say our vows, neither of us will have a bit of doubt that we've made the right decision."

Hearing him say the same things she was thinking made her relax and cuddle a bit closer.

"So, are you nervous about your family arriving on the bus on Saturday?"

"*Jah*, but not as nervous as I thought I'd be." When he merely looked at her and smiled, she added, "Ben, I realized that I have started worrying less about what will make them happy and more about what will make me happy." Looking into his blue eyes, she said, "You make me really happy."

"*Gut*," he said simply.

Another moment passed as they gazed at the dancing flames before he added, "I'm happy, too. I have a new sense of purpose and something to look forward to. I knew proposing to you and planning a wedding would make me happy, but I kind of didn't expect to feel so free." He shook his head. "I would have never imagined that tying myself to another person would make me feel lighter. It's like all my burdens about the future have been lifted."

Tricia knew exactly what he meant. Now that she'd found the person she wanted to spend the rest of her life with, she felt like a tremendous weight had been taken off her shoulders. In its place was a sense of security stronger than anything she'd ever known.

"After Beverly told me they were coming, I went down to the kitchen and called my *mamm*."

He chuckled. "And?"

"And after she quit asking me if I'd lost my mind and started listening, she told me about a cartoon she'd once seen," Tricia said. "It had a picture of a perfectly straight arrow and beneath it said, 'our plan.' Then, right below it was another arrow that was twisted and full of bumps and valleys. That caption said, 'God's plan.'"

He grinned. "I like that. It's fitting. As much as we might want things to go the way we think they ought to, the reality is that the future is out of our hands."

"I thought it was fitting, too. And at first, I only compared the differences between the two lines, but then Mamm pointed out where they ended . . . at the same place." She paused. "I think she was trying to remind me that life is full of hills and valleys and twists and turns. But in the end, the Lord wants us to achieve our dreams. He wants us to be happy."

Ben nodded. After a moment, he said, "I can't tell you how hard it was to watch my mother get weaker. I hated to see her suffer. I prayed with everything I had that she would get stronger and recover. Get healed by a miracle. But it was God's wish that she go up to heaven early."

This was the most he'd ever shared about how hard his mother's illness had been for him. She was so proud of him for opening up to her. She hoped she would always be worthy of that trust. "Maybe we were never meant to meet in Ohio but to meet here," she said softly. "Maybe we had to go through our own trials in order to appreciate the happiness that we've found in each other."

He smiled. "I'm glad the Lord gave me you, Tricia. And at the perfect time in my life."

"I feel the same way," she said as she laid her head on his shoulder and enjoyed the feel of his strong body against hers. If she closed her eyes, she was sure she could hear his heartbeat, steady and sure. She never wanted the night to end.

A few minutes later, he shifted and pulled away from her. "Tricia, as much as I want to stay here with you, I think I need to go. The shuttles don't run all night, you know."

"I know." She got to her feet, hating to say good-bye but finding comfort that in just a month their late-night farewells would be a thing of the past.

Reaching out, he brushed a finger along her cheek. "I'm going to be at the farm all day tomorrow, which means I won't see you until you bring your parents over to my house in the evening."

"I know."

"Are you sure you won't change your mind and have me be by your side when the bus arrives? Mark and William can work the market without me."

"As much as having you there would comfort me, I think I need to face them by myself. Plus, if they say anything mean, I don't want you to hear it."

His expression hardened in the flickering light. "If they say anything mean to you, I want to be there to make sure they stop."

Tricia knew he would, too. Ben was used to looking out for

his brothers and he'd already shown her that he was the type of man who looked out for his fiancée. He wouldn't be happy if her parents made her cry.

"Let's keep things the way we have it. I'll bring them to your house at five o'clock tomorrow. We'll grill chicken and sit in your kitchen and talk."

"I'll see you then. But first, let me do this," he murmured, just as his lips brushed against hers.

She closed her eyes, wrapped her hands around his neck, and gave herself over to his touch and his kisses. Now, this, she thought, was one of her most favorite parts of being engaged.

One of her most favorite parts of all.

TRICIA AND BEN WERE kissing again.

That had been a mighty close call! Beverly quickly stepped back and turned around. Thank goodness she'd had the foresight to peek through the back door's window before pulling it open and reminding Ben of the time. Just imagining how awkward it would have been for all of them . . . It would have been *worse* than awkward.

Beverly decided to wait a minute or two. Or five. Ben needed to catch that shuttle but she didn't want Tricia to think she was spying on them. Hopefully, they were simply kissing each other good night. With great, um, enthusiasm. It certainly was becoming obvious that Tricia and Ben were very much in love. It was also obvious that she had completely misread their situation. She'd been looking at Tricia through her own fears and worries.

But now she was realizing that what was happening was meant to be. Surely no couple as happy as they were could be making a mistake.

Suddenly she felt not just alone but lonely. And maybe a little envious. Oh, she wasn't jealous of Tricia's romance, but envious that she didn't have anyone in her life that she was as close to. Except, maybe, Eric.

Just then the back door squeaked. Realizing that they were about to come inside, Beverly sat down abruptly on the chair by the phone.

"Aunt Bev, what are you doing, sitting down here in the dark?" Tricia asked.

She turned the light switch on the battery-powered lamp. "I, um, was thinking about calling Eric."

"This late?"

"*Jah.* I had forgotten how late it was. That's why I'm sitting here. I decided not to call."

"Um, okay," Tricia said as she slipped her hand in Ben's. "Well, I'm going to walk Ben to the front door."

"All right. Good night, Ben."

" 'Night, Beverly."

Feeling even more foolish, Beverly opened the drawer under the phone and pulled out a pen and paper. Since it was too late to call, she decided to give in to temptation and write Eric a letter. It wouldn't quite ease the ache she was feeling, but it wouldn't wake him up, either. That was something, she supposed.

WHEN THEY'D GOTTEN OUT to the sidewalk, Jay had pulled out a sheet of paper listing a couple of restaurants that were within easy walking distance but were outside the heart of Pinecraft. They had ended up having Italian food. Emma had wanted to take the SCAT and dine someplace where it was unlikely that they'd see anyone she knew.

And they hadn't.

Therefore, instead of feeling like she and Jay were being observed, they were able to simply enjoy each other's company. Instead of wondering what the gossipmongers would say or rush to tell her parents, she'd focused on herself and her feelings and slowly let down her guard.

And they'd talked. Oh, how they'd talked! About childhoods and school while eating Caesar salads, about hobbies and what they'd done during their rumspringas, while eating far too much of the chef's delicious baked ziti. They'd talked about favorite foods and foods they hated as they split a decadent plate of cheesecake with a fresh strawberry sauce.

And as each course came and went, Emma found herself opening up even more. She laughed a little more easily, shared more personal stories. And she listened to Jay a little more closely. She soaked in every sweet look and kind gesture.

Now, after taking the SCAT bus back to Pinecraft, Jay was walking her home down Kaufmann Avenue. She felt flirty and giddy. Found herself smiling whenever he glanced her way . . . and discovered she couldn't seem to stop gazing at him. None of this felt especially mature or anything like the behavior a mother of three should be exhibiting! Actually, she felt just like one of the teenagers she saw off in the distance—light and carefree.

"You've gotten quiet all of a sudden," he said. "Did I talk your ear off?"

"Not at all. I guess I was simply thinking about what a nice time I had with you tonight."

"I enjoyed myself, too." He looked like he was tempted to add something more, but he said nothing else. "You're easy to talk to. I, um, shared more with you tonight than I have with anyone in the last year."

"I feel the same way. I was actually hoping you didn't think I was talking *your* ear off," she admitted, "or that I'd revealed too much about myself." Maybe she'd told him too many stories about being a single mother.

"I liked hearing all of it from you."

"It's been a long time since anyone wanted to know so much about me."

He smiled. "That's the price of parenthood, I guess. It's never about us anymore. It's about the *kinner*."

"It's always about the *kinner*," she agreed. "And that is as it should be. Though sometimes . . ."

"Sometimes it is nice to remember that there is more to us than just being someone's father or mother."

"Exactly." She was glad he understood.

But as she looked around, she realized they were just steps from her house. After all that worrying and fretting she'd done, her date was finished and she felt slightly empty. "I canna believe it's over," she murmured.

"What is?"

"Our date."

He held out a hand to help her up the steps. She liked the way it felt in hers, liked the way he seemed to enjoy her touch as much as she enjoyed his. "I'm sorry it's over, too. But maybe we'll do it again sometime soon?"

"Are you asking me out again?" She really hoped he thought she was merely teasing.

"*Jah*, though it seems I'm doing a poor job of it. Will you go out with me again?"

"Yes."

"What about your parents? Are you willing to go up against them again?"

Until that moment, she hadn't been sure if she was strong enough. But now she knew she wasn't going to let anything stop her from having another night like this. "I'm willing. They are going to have to find a way to accept my decision." Just as she was going to have to find a way to convince them of it.

He smiled as they walked up the steps, her hand still securely clasped in his. When they reached her front door, he held out his hand for her keys. She handed them to him and stood quietly while he unlocked the door. Then she felt a moment of panic. Did she invite him in? Did he expect to kiss her good night? Would he be shocked if she actually *did* kiss him good night?

His expression was warm as he watched her. "It's okay, Emma. All I'm going to do is say good night to you right here."

"You knew what I was thinking?" She wasn't sure if she was mortified or extremely relieved.

He nodded. "As clearly as if you were saying it out loud." Folding his arms over his chest, he grinned. "I know what you were thinking because I'm pretty sure I was thinking the same thing."

"Which was?"

"That I don't want to leave you yet. I would love for you to invite me in, but I'm afraid every one of your neighbors is watching quietly from their windows. I don't want to do that to you."

Feeling a little sheepish, she said, "I fear you are right. My neighbors are wonderful, but they're not exactly afraid to be nosey, either."

"I don't want tonight to end because I like being with you. But the only remedy I can think of for easing our unhappiness is to make plans to see each other again. Will you go out with me again soon?"

"*Jah,*" she answered. She didn't know how she was going to manage it but she would make it happen.

"I'll see you soon, then." Reaching out, he ran a finger along her cheekbone. "If we weren't likely being observed, I'd try to kiss you good night. Would you let me?"

There it was. That gentle flirting again. It made her smile . . . and made her want to flirt a little bit back. "Maybe."

"Maybe?"

"If I told you all my secrets you'd have no reason to want to see me again."

"You would be wrong about that, Emma. I would want to see you soon, even if I knew every one. *Gut naught.*"

"*Gut naught*, Jay. *Danke.*"

With one last lingering smile, he turned and walked away.

And when she went inside, she could practically hear the pounding of her heart.

Chapter 21

*B*y Saturday afternoon, Beverly was wishing she *had* called Eric on Friday evening, even if it would've meant waking him up. She was going to need his frank speaking and easygoing manner to get through her brother's visit.

The moment Edward and Kathleen had gotten off the bus, they'd fussed over Tricia like she'd been away for years. That was understandable. But their constant questioning of everything Tricia did was becoming hard to watch. At first, Tricia had held up fine under their barrage. But now, after sharing a lunch at Yoder's, Tricia looked as if she was about to burst into tears or lose her temper. Probably both.

As they walked back along the streets of Pinecraft toward the inn, Beverly knew it was just about time to step in. If she didn't, it was very likely that Tricia was going to lose her very last thread of composure.

She wondered if Kathleen realized that.

Beverly decided she probably didn't. Otherwise Kathleen wouldn't have wrapped an arm around Tricia's shoulders, keeping her firmly in her grip as she spoke. "Tricia, there isna reason for you to have the wedding here. You don't know anyone and all of your family is in Sugarcreek. Besides, this Ben's relatives are in Charm."

Tricia pulled away. "But *we* are here in Pinecraft, Mamm. Ben's family is here, too."

Kathleen stopped right in the middle of the sidewalk. "We are *not* here," she said sharply, oblivious to the attention she was drawing from everyone around them.

"I want to say my vows here," Tricia retorted. "It's important to me."

"I don't see why," Kathleen huffed as she began walking again.

Tricia trotted to her side. "You will, once you spend some time here. Pinecraft is special to me. Aunt Beverly's inn is special to me, too. It's where Ben and I first met."

"I understand that, but marrying here makes no sense."

Tricia stopped again. "It does to me, Mamm."

"Come along, Trish. I'll arrange a date for next November, when things have gotten quiet on the farms."

"Next November?" Tricia shook her head. "*Nee*, Mother. That's over a year from now."

"You need that much time."

"Why?"

"To be sure of your feelings," she said impatiently. After glancing at Edward, who Beverly noticed was pretending he wasn't within earshot, she said, "You know what I mean."

"*Nee*, I don't know. Mamm, Ben and I have already talked with the preacher and the bishop. They have given us their blessing."

"It also takes at least a year to plan a big wedding," Kathleen said as she picked up her pace. "We're going to have to pick colors for your attendants' dresses, decide on flowers, think about a cake . . ."

"I don't need all that. And Aunt Beverly is the best baker around. I'm sure she could make my cake." Glancing at Beverly over her shoulder, she said, "Right, Aunt Beverly?"

Beverly gulped as she scurried to catch up. "Of course, dear. I would love to make you a cake."

While Kathleen glared at her, Edward at last entered the discussion. "Tricia, no one is saying that you can't marry this boy. We simply have to wait a bit. There's nothing wrong with that." Glancing at Beverly, he said, "Right?"

Oh, no. He was *not* going to rope her into his side. "This has nothing to do with me, Edward." Seeing the inn in the distance, she said, "Perhaps we should finish this conversation at home?" Pointing in front of her, she added, "See? We're almost there."

"We might as well finish it right now," Edward said. "It's not like it's going to get any easier."

To Beverly's surprise, Tricia smiled broadly. "That's exactly what I've been saying! There is no reason for me to wait to marry. So I'm not waiting." Tricia's tone was firm. "I am getting married next month."

"But that won't work out for us," Kathleen blurted.

"That is too bad," Tricia said in an airy way. "I would have liked to have had you here." Then she darted around a pair of Amish teens who'd been eavesdropping and strode toward the inn.

Beverly groaned under her breath.

Edward got the same look on his face that he'd had at age eight, when he didn't get his way. Raising his voice, he said, "Tricia, you are my daughter—"

"I know that," she said over her shoulder.

"Let's talk about this later, Ed," Beverly interrupted, "when you aren't still recovering from a long bus trip." And, well, when half the residents of her street weren't witnessing their argument.

"Stay out of it, Beverly."

"I'm afraid I cannot."

Edward glared. "Now I'm starting to understand why Tricia is suddenly sounding so headstrong."

Oh! "Just as *I* am starting to understand why she got on that bus to come here in the first place!" she snapped. "Tricia, please stop," Beverly called out. There was no way she was going to deal with Edward and Kathleen without her right there. To her relief, Tricia did stop.

When they were by her side again, Tricia quietly said, "Mamm, Daed, I truly feel as if the Lord has been listening to my prayers. I've been asking and asking him to give me a partner who can love me for me. Ben does. He doesn't want me to change. He isn't asking me to obey him or to be different. He simply wants me in his life." After a pause, she looked at all three of them, one by one. "Why would you expect me to ignore this blessing?"

"Oh, Tricia," Beverly said, feeling incredibly humbled by Tricia's faith.

"I . . . I don't want you to," Kathleen said as she looped an arm through Tricia's. Looking tired but also far more at peace with the situation, she added, "Edward, I think it might be time to take a little rest. We have a lot of thinking and praying to do."

Edward stared at her blankly. Then, to Beverly's amazement, he nodded. "You know we only want you to be happy, Tricia."

"Then please listen to what I am saying. Ben is wonderful and I love him."

Her parents gazed at her, then at each other.

"You *are* happy, aren't you, Tricia?" Edward murmured.

"*Jah*," she answered just as quietly. "I am as happy as I've ever been."

"All right then."

"*Danke*, Daed."

When Tricia started chatting to her mother about how much she liked the scent of the magnolia blossoms on the tree they were passing, Edward stepped to Beverly's side. *"Danke,"* he whispered.

She slowed her steps to put some distance between them and Tricia and Kathleen. "For what?" She was genuinely surprised. "I thought you were mad at me."

"I was. But maybe it was more that I'm simply used to getting my way."

"Some things never change," she teased.

"That seems to be true. It's also true that you still have that ability to simply see what is important in most every situation. You have done that with Tricia."

"I appreciate your words, but I honestly don't know if I've done anything right. I haven't raised any *kinner*, you know."

"She is so much more confident and sure of herself. So happy." Lowering his voice, he added, "While I believe what Tricia said about the Lord answering her prayers, I must admit that I, too, have had many long conversations with the Lord about why my daughter went running to you instead of reaching out to her mother and me. Now I understand that He knew you would have the right words for her."

Edward's words practically took Beverly's breath away. She hadn't expected to ever be thanked. She hadn't expected anything. Hadn't even thought that far ahead. "What you just said, Ed . . ."

"Yes?"

"It . . . It means the world to me."

He turned his head and smiled. There was a sweet, new warmth in his eyes. "I am so glad we came to see you. So very glad," he said at last.

And truly, there was nothing else that needed to be said.

As Tricia walked between her mother and father up the long, winding, graveled driveway to Ben's house, she suddenly realized that the nerves she'd been sure would be jangling in her stomach were nowhere to be found. Instead, all she felt was happiness and excitement. She was looking forward to introducing Ben to her parents and talking about their wedding.

Much of the change had to do with the shift in her parents' attitudes. She was so glad they'd finally listened to what she had to say. Maybe Mamm and Daed could finally see how happy and content she was.

"You look as bright as a penny, Tricia," her mother said. "I don't know if I've ever seen you so happy. Are you that excited about seeing Ben?"

"I am," she admitted. "But I am even happier that you and Daed don't seem as cross with me. I hate it when I disappoint you."

"You have not disappointed me or your father," her mother said quickly.

"I know you were disappointed when I left Ohio."

"We were concerned," her mother corrected. "We also weren't happy that you left without letting us know first."

Thinking back to the first time she'd talked to them on the phone after arriving in Pinecraft, Tricia thought that was putting things mildly. "You were rather cross."

Her father looked down at her and frowned. "We were caught off guard."

"You still weren't happy when you got off that bus."

"There is no reason to go over everything again. Though I haven't made up my mind about this Ben of yours, I listened to what you had to say."

"I'm glad you are following your heart," her mother said. "Though, at times, I've often wished you'd be less impulsive, I also think it's a blessing that you know your mind."

Tricia hoped her mother was being honest. She knew there had been times in her life when her mother had been quite put out about her nature. More than once she'd advised Tricia to be more reserved.

They were on the front steps now. "I hope you will like Ben."

"I hope we will like him, too," her father murmured.

Though it was too late to worry about such things, a momentary panic rushed through Tricia. Was there anything about Ben that she should have warned them about? Anything she could do in order to make this first meeting go more smoothly?

Her mother gestured toward the door. "Knock on the door, child. No doubt they are wondering why we are simply standing here."

Her father raised a brow. "Unless you want to argue about that, too?"

Practically rolling her eyes, Tricia stepped forward and knocked three times. Immediately the door was opened . . . by William.

"Hiya, Tricia," he said with a smile. "Daed, Ben, and Mark are still washing up so I said I would answer the door." Looking on either side of her, he puffed up his chest. "Hi. I'm William Hilty. Ben is my big brother."

That seemed to be all that was needed to endear her parents

to him forever. Her mother rushed inside and shook his hand, then brushed her hand across his blond hair. Her father shook his hand, too, and patted him on the back.

"You want to see what we got today?" he asked, his blue eyes shining with hope.

"Of course," her mother said, immediately following the boy into the living room.

Sharing an amused glance with her father, Tricia followed them. She was learning that William was an excitable boy but also surprisingly sensitive. She was glad he'd seen something in her parents that drew him to them.

When they entered the living room, William pointed to a large cardboard box in the center. Inside was a thick fleece blanket and on top of that was a cat and two squirmy black-and-white kittens.

"Oh, look at that," Tricia gasped.

William grinned. "Yep. We've got kittens!"

Just as Tricia was about to caution William to lower his voice so he didn't frighten the babies, her mother knelt by the box and peered inside.

"My goodness! Aren't they sweet?" She reached in the box and gently petted one. "Where did they come from?"

"We were working in the store this morning and saw their mother carrying them by the scruff of their necks to a little nest she'd made," Mark said, stepping down the stairs. "She was so sweet, Daed said there was no way we couldn't adopt the three of them."

"Plus, I knew that Tricia would be mighty upset with me if we didn't rescue them," Ben said as he entered the room.

Waiting with bated breath, Tricia felt the tension in the room heighten as her parents turned to Ben.

"Mamm, Daed, please meet William's *bruders*. This is Mark and Ben." She could practically feel her skin flush when she heard how her voice changed as she said Ben's name. It was full of bright happiness.

Mark stepped forward and shook their hands, as did Ben. After greeting Mark politely, her father focused completely on Ben. So much so, why there might as well have been no one else in the room. "So you are the man who has claimed my daughter's heart?"

Without missing a beat, Ben replied, "I hope so. She has certainly claimed mine."

"I'm Kathleen," her mother said with bright pink cheeks.

"Pleased to meet you, Kathleen." Looking at both of her parents, he said, "I'm sorry I wasna downstairs when you arrived. Time got away from us, I'm afraid."

"I understand about work. But not so much about adopting three cats at once," her father joked.

Tricia exhaled. If her father was joking, everything was going to be all right.

"My father said the same thing," Ben replied. "But they are cute, and we'll always need mousers."

"And a sweet cat for our future home," Tricia said.

Ben's expression softened. "Indeed, we will need that, if it will make you happy," he murmured and kissed her forehead. Right in front of everyone!

"You wouldn't mind?"

"Tricia, if you think we need a kitten, then we will have one."

Tricia felt a lump rise in her throat as she realized her parents were watching her intently.

Then, to her surprise, her father chuckled. "It seems we better meet your father and start planning a wedding. The sooner the better, too. I have a feeling you two are determined to marry with or without our blessing."

"I want your blessing, sir," Ben said. "I love Tricia. I want to be everything she's hoped for. That means I want you to feel the same way, too." He straightened his shoulders. "I'm willing to do whatever it takes to earn your respect and trust."

Tricia was blown away. She had known Ben was upstanding and she knew he cared deeply for her, but for some reason, she'd never imagined he would make such statements.

Looking from one of them to the other, her father nodded. "Then you shall have it."

"Forgive me for making you wait," Jay announced as he joined them. "I was the last to have the shower."

"That's okay," her mother said after all the introductions were complete. "We've been doing just fine getting to know your sons."

Moments later, her parents followed Jay into the kitchen. Tricia had offered to accompany them, but all three of the parents told her and Ben to relax with the boys and the kittens.

She needed no further instruction. Sitting down next to the box, she peered in and saw that the mom cat was sprawled on its side and one of the kittens was fast asleep. But the other kitten, one with tawny-colored eyes, was staring right at her. She carefully picked it up and set it in her lap.

Ben sat down next to her. "You doing all right today? I've been worried about you. Actually, I've been praying for you all day."

"Your prayers were answered, because it's true. I really am good. Better than I thought I would be, actually." After glancing around the room and seeing that Ben's brothers were busy eating some cheese and crackers that someone had set out on the coffee table, she said, "We had kind of a rocky start, but after I spoke from my heart, everyone settled down. Isn't that something?"

"It's a blessing, that's what it is."

She grinned. "Indeed. God truly works in mysterious ways."

"Have you thought of a date?"

"Yes. Is October twenty-second too soon?"

"As long as the preachers and bishop agree, I'm fine with any date."

"And you are still okay with having the wedding and reception at the Orange Blossom Inn?"

"Perfect. I don't want a huge wedding anyway."

"Me neither." They shared a smile, and for a moment, Tricia was sure Ben was going to kiss her cheek, but the tension was broken by the kitten wiggling in her arms. When she set it on the braided rug, it darted right over to William. In the box, the other kitten began squirming and Mark took it out.

Next thing they knew, the four of them were laughing at the kittens' antics, just as if it was the most natural thing in the world for them to be together. But when Tricia heard her father laugh at something Jay said in the other room, she relaxed completely. This moment was worth everything.

Everything in the world.

Just then they heard a knock at the door.

Jay came out from the kitchen. "I'll get it."

"Who's here, Daed?" Ben asked.

"Emma and the girls." Looking a little self-conscious, Jay added, "I didn't think you would mind, Ben."

"I don't mind about Emma and her girls being here at all. I think it's *wonderful-gut.* Don't you agree, Tricia?"

Tricia smiled. "I'm glad they are here."

William scrambled to his feet and trotted to the door. "I didn't know Lena was coming over."

"I hope you don't mind," Jay said, looking over at Tricia's parents who had followed him in from the kitchen. "Emma and her girls have become special friends of ours. I thought they might enjoy meeting you, too."

"And seeing the kittens," William said with a beaming smile.

"Yes, of course. And seeing the kittens." Resting a palm on his youngest boy's shoulder, he said, "Let's go let them in, Will."

When they disappeared from view, Ben winked at Mark, who was grinning broadly.

"What is going on here?" Tricia's mother whispered in her ear.

"Jay has recently started seeing a nice lady in Pinecraft. Her name is Emma. He likes her a lot."

"But—"

"They're both widows. They have a lot in common, and all the kids are kind of excited about what is happening."

Tricia didn't have time to say another word because Annie rushed in to say hello, followed by Lena, Mandy, and William, and at last, Jay and Emma. Jay and Emma looked a little bit awkward about being on display, but also happy to be by each other's side. Tricia's *mamm* walked over and introduced herself. When Emma smiled and greeted Tricia's *daed*, then formally introduced her girls, Ben nudged Tricia.

"It's going okay," he whispered. "Look, your parents don't even care about us now, they are so focused on my *daed* and Emma."

Tricia thought that might be true. Her mother seemed enchanted by the idea of two people who had lost so much finding love again. They also seemed to enjoy how Jay's boys were already looking after Emma's girls. Somehow, everyone was becoming one, big, happy group in spite of a somewhat rocky beginning.

LATER THAT NIGHT, WHEN they were on the last shuttle back to the inn, Tricia's mother said, "Tricia, I'm starting to think there must be something special about Pinecraft."

"There might be. All I know for sure is that I'm starting to think that maybe I'm special, too." She smiled. "I know I've always been special to you and Daed and God. But now I'm starting to realize that I have value, too."

"You've always had value, dear."

"I know. But when those girls back in Walnut Creek were making me so miserable, I starting believing everything they said. I started thinking that I wasn't ever going to be good enough. I started thinking that no man was ever going to fall in love with me. That I was always going to feel a little out of place. That I wasn't capable of keeping friendships."

"They were wrong, Trish. If you had trusted me more and talked to me, I could have told you that."

"Mamm, I love you, but that wasn't what I needed." Her voice cracked as she continued. "For some reason, I needed to do something on my own. I needed to grow up and become a little more independent. And it's done wonders for me. Now I am working at the inn and I've become friends with Emma and her girls and have even been able to help them from time to time."

"And you fell in love with Ben."

"*Jah*. Once I loved myself again, I fell in love with Ben." As her mother smiled softly, Tricia added, "And he fell in love with me."

Chapter 22

I don't quite understand why you are making so many place mats, Emma," her mother said a week later. As she slid her scissors through another layer of checkered fabric, she frowned. "Twelve seems excessive."

Glad she was facing her treadle sewing machine, Emma rolled her eyes. Her mother knew exactly why Emma wanted to have such a large set of place mats. She simply didn't want to think of Emma, Jay, and all their *kinner* sharing a meal together.

"*Muder*, we've discussed this already."

"No, we haven't. Not really. Daed and I told you that we thought you were jumping into a relationship far too quickly. You refused to listen."

Thinking again about how much her mother's lack of faith in her had hurt, and how she hadn't even tried to temper her words before Emma's date with Jay, Emma knew that as far as her parents were concerned this would always be moving too fast. She hadn't even bothered to tell them about the two other dates she'd been on with Jay in the last week. There had been no need, since Ben and Tricia had volunteered to babysit at the farm.

"I listened, Mamm. I simply didn't agree."

"So you've decided to make place mats to prove me wrong."

"*Nee*, Mamm. I decided to make a set of place mats because I want to make place mats. If I want to serve a meal on them to Jay and his boys, I'll do that, too."

"Why are you making twelve?"

Emma was just irritated enough to give her mother a little jab. "I had hoped that maybe you and Daed would one day want to join us. Maybe even Tricia. Maybe even all sorts of people."

"Perhaps you would like me to leave?"

"I would love for you to stay if you are ready to apologize. If not, then *jah*, it might be best if you went on your way."

When Emma heard her mother's chair scoot back, she bit her lip to try to stay tough. But inside, her heart was aching. She truly didn't want to have to choose between her parents and Jay. Especially not when their grandchildren were involved.

But instead of walking out the door, her mother walked to her side. "Emma, you know I don't like arguing with you. However, I simply cannot help but think you are making a mistake."

Emma turned to face her. "Why?"

"You are forgetting yourself. You already have been married. You were married to a *gut* man who loved you. You had a nice life with him."

"I know all of that. Don't you think I knew how blessed I was to have Sanford?"

"Then why would you even think of trying to replace your

husband? God doesn't give you two mates in life, dear. You are setting yourself up for heartbreak."

"Mamm, I need you to try and see my point of view. I will always honor Sanford's memory, but he is gone! Jay is a *gut* man, too. I need you to wish me well. Or, if you can't do that, at least promise me that you'll at least try."

As her mother stared at her, little by little, all the love that she'd always shown Emma glimmered in her eyes. "I will try," she said at last. "Because I love you, I will start to try."

"*Danke*, Mamm. I love you, too."

After giving Emma a quick hug, her mother muttered something about the time, picked up her purse, and walked out the door. Emma went to the window and watched her mother walk slowly down Kaufmann Avenue, her head bent. She looked sad.

Crossing her arms over her chest, Emma expected to feel justified and pleased that her mother had finally listened. Instead, she felt more confused than ever. Though she knew Jay was a wonderful man, a small part of her wondered if her mother had been right. Was it too much to ask for two successful relationships? Was she foolish to expect Jay to ever love her like he'd loved his first wife? Could she herself ever fall in love again?

Turning away from the window, she looked at the remains of the project she'd started. Though her mother hadn't liked the task, she'd dutifully cut out the rest of the fabric. It was now arranged neatly on one corner of the table. Two completed place mats were on the arm of her couch. Scraps of fabric and thread littered the table and the floor near her sewing machine.

It all kind of looked like how her life felt: in disarray.

Maybe it was time to slow things down. Just to make sure she wasn't making a terrible mistake, that she hadn't simply latched on to Jay and his sons because she'd been so lonely.

Her eyes stung as she quietly folded the extra fabric, gathered the scraps and completed place mats, and stuffed them all in the sack from the fabric store. Then, before she could change her mind, she walked to her bedroom and shoved the sack under her bed.

Out of sight.

Only later did she realize that although she had indeed put it all out of sight, she had also opted to keep it close at hand.

As HE APPROACHED EMMA'S house, Jay felt a hum of anticipation that he now understood went hand in hand with his visits to her. He was anxious to see the Keim girls. He missed Annie's hugs, Mandy's tentative smiles, and Lena's shy welcomes. He missed Emma's pretty face and sweet nature. Most of all, he'd missed the way he now only felt whole when they were nearby—each had truly taken a piece of him.

It was amazing how quickly the change had taken place . . . though maybe not.

Another two weeks had gone by but, as far as Jay was concerned, it might as well have been two hours. He was slowly discovering that planning a wedding took far more work for the father of the groom than he'd originally thought.

It was also far more nerve-wracking than he'd imagined it would be.

When he and Evelyn had gotten married, he'd been filled with the surety that what they were doing was the right thing. He'd been eager to have Evelyn by his side for the rest of his life. To be honest, he'd been looking forward to a lot of things about being married.

Now, as the groom's father, though he rejoiced in his son's

happiness, he couldn't help but worry about Ben and Tricia. A dozen questions continually floated through his mind: Were they too young? Had they known each other long enough? Were they compatible enough to withstand the hundreds of little adjustments that came with married life? Had they considered those pesky things called patience and compromise?

Jay simply wasn't sure.

Though he was relieved that they'd visited with the bishop and the preachers several times. Jay figured if the leaders of their church hadn't insisted that they wait longer to speak their vows, then their discussions must have been going well.

He had also been delighted to discover that he had much in common with Edward and Kathleen Overholt. He'd found Tricia's parents to be faithful, kind to their daughter, and a lot of fun, too.

After that first awkward hour, which had involved several minutes of cautious conversation, they'd settled in and ended up having a good time. They had enjoyed the following two evenings as well when they'd begun playing Rook, which had allowed the two families to spend time together without fumbling for conversation. Little by little, Tricia had come out of her shell and Ben had gained his confidence. It soon became obvious that the young couple knew what they were doing.

The night before Edward and Kathleen were to leave, Beverly had invited everyone over to the inn for supper. She'd made a beautiful buffet and served it outside on her back patio. She and Tricia had even strung up white lights around the porch.

It was an evening of fun and laughter. The food had been delicious, but spending time with family and friends had been even better. He'd especially enjoyed watching his eldest fuss over Tricia and become friends with her parents. He'd also liked watching Beverly and her brother. She'd seemed to relish the family time even more than Ben and Tricia.

Now, the wedding preparations were in full swing *and* just this week Jay had opened the market full-time. Life was busy and full and rich with new experiences—including the knowledge that it had been a very good decision to follow the Lord's plan and relocate to Sarasota.

The only area he wasn't sure about was his relationship with Emma. He liked her—he liked her a lot—but he also knew that being "in like" wasn't enough to build a relationship.

Furthermore, she seemed to be having some of the same misgivings. She'd canceled the last date they'd planned, citing that she needed to be home with the girls. Perhaps that was true. But he also wondered if there was more to it. Which was why he'd told Ben that he would be the one to get William from Emma's house that afternoon. He wanted to spend some time with Emma and gauge how she was feeling about him.

They were all in the backyard when he arrived, and Frankie alerted the girls to his approach with a happy howl.

"Who's here, Frankie?" Mandy asked. Then, when she spied Jay, she opened the gate and rushed to him.

"Mandy, don't leave the backyard!" Emma cried.

"I'm not leaving. I'm lettin' Jay in," she called back, then looked up at him happily. "Hiya, Jay."

Jay knelt down to give Mandy a little hug. "Hello, Miss Mandy. How are you?"

She giggled. "I'm *gut*. We went on a walk today at school."

"That sounds like fun. Where did you go?"

"To Yoder's. A lady there showed us how they make pies."

Her pretty smile turned into a bright, blinding grin. "And guess what?"

"What?" he asked, unable to keep from mirroring her excited expression.

"We got to have pie, too!"

"That sounds mighty special," he said as he led her into the backyard. "What kind of pie did you have?"

"Peach."

"Yum."

"Uh-huh." She smiled again. "It was yummy." Then she let go of his hand and ran to where William and Lena were climbing on Emma's small jungle gym.

And that, Jay decided, was the difference between little girls and boys: His boys would have simply shared that they'd had pie at school and been done with it. But for little girls like Mandy? A walk to Yoder's, followed by a slice of peach pie?

It was very big news, indeed.

Spying Emma kneeling next to Annie on the ground he walked over to say hello. "What's going on here?" he asked as he noticed they were both peering into a plastic sand pail.

"We found a frog, Jay," Annie said. "I'm going to keep him forever."

After peeking at the little green frog sitting rather forlornly at the bottom of the pail, he teased, "Is that right? Are you hoping he will turn into a prince?"

"*Nee.* I just want him to be a frog. He likes being a frog, I think." She looked so intent and serious and sweet that it took everything he had not to press his lips to her brow. Each time he was around Lena, Mandy, and Annie, it seemed that they let him into their hearts just a little bit more. And as they became more comfortable with him, he felt more comfortable reaching out to each of them.

When he turned to Emma, her expression was soft . . . and a touch guarded. He was glad he'd decided to stop by.

"What brings you here this afternoon?" she asked.

He knew he needed to be as honest and direct as possible. "I wanted to get William, but I also wanted to see you, too. I think we need to talk, Emma."

"Now isn't a good time."

He knew she was hoping he'd nod and retreat, but he was pretty sure that giving her more time was not the answer. "How about in five minutes then?"

"Five?"

"Come on, Emma. Don't make me beg."

Her eyes widened in that cute way he had come to realize was a mixture of happiness and shyness. He found it endearing that a woman like her, who'd had a rich married life and three daughters, could still be as sweetly shy as she was.

"All right. We'll talk. Annie, dear, go play with your sisters for a few minutes, 'kay? I need to visit with Mr. Jay for a minute."

"Okay, Mommy," she said as she trotted off to Mandy's side.

Jay smiled at Annie's retreating back. "She listened to you right away. That's impressive."

Emma chuckled. "It doesn't happen all that often, though my Annie is the most agreeable of my girls." She looked as if she was about to add something more about her daughters, but she swallowed instead. "So . . ."

"So, I wanted to make sure I hadn't done anything to upset you the last time we went out."

"You mean when we went out for ice cream?"

He nodded. Because it had been a school night, he and Emma

had simply gone for a walk to Olaf's for ice cream while Tricia and Ben watched the girls. Mark had stayed back at the farm with William. Ever since he'd said good night to her, Jay had been replaying everything they'd done and said, but no offenses came to mind.

"You haven't seemed as open the last couple of times we've talked," he said. "I may be overthinking things, but I wanted to hear what you had to say."

After glancing at the children again, she nodded. "You're right. I've been having second thoughts about us."

Her explanation was surprisingly painful to hear. "What did I do?"

"Oh, goodness, Jay. It isn't you. It's me. I, well, I've been worried that maybe we've been rushing into things."

"I see." Of course, he really didn't. Though he had been honest about his feelings toward her, Jay had made a concerted effort not to push Emma. He'd been careful not to talk about the future. He certainly hadn't done anything more than hold her hand.

"I had another conversation with my mother," she added. "She reminded me that I might be asking for too much."

"What were you asking for?"

She shrugged but didn't meet his eyes. "You know. To have another relationship."

"Emma, surely you don't imagine that the Lord wants you to live the rest of your life as a widow?"

"I don't know."

"Do you think He wants you to be alone? I thought all of us being together made you happy."

She blinked. "It did. I mean, it does."

"Then why isn't that enough? Why can't we simply be happy for now . . . and let the future take care of itself?"

"Do you think that is possible?"

He nodded. "Isn't that what happens anyway? I was happy with Evelyn and you were happy with Sanford. But they both got sick. How would you feel if you had spent all your time with Sanford doubting yourself or wondering if you deserved your time with him?"

"I would regret it."

"I'm going to regret it if you give up on us," he admitted. "Please don't give up on us yet."

She stared at him for what seemed like an eternity. Then, at last, she nodded. "All right, Jay. You win. I won't give up on us."

Only then did he release the lungful of air he hadn't even realized he'd been holding.

Chapter 23

*T*he next afternoon, Emma was sitting outside in the back-yard with the kids when Jay came over again. The *kinner* reacted to his arrival much like they had the day before. Lena and William looked pleased to see him but tried hard to act far too old to get excited. Annie and Mandy, on the other hand, rushed to him with outstretched arms. Jay got down on one knee and gently hugged each of them. And then gave Frankie a pat, too. Only after the girls went back to the tent they were making out of an old sheet did he walk to Emma's side.

"Hi."

"Hi, Jay. It's nice to see you two days in a row."

He grinned. "Ben and Mark have been teasing me, saying I'm smitten."

"Are you?"

He winked. "Maybe."

And just like that, her heart started beating a little bit quicker.

He took a seat next to her at the picnic table. "Do you have plans for supper?"

"Nothing too special. The girls and I were going to have soup and sandwiches."

"Then, would you consider going out for pizza?"

"All of us?" a small voice said.

"Of course." When he turned and saw that Annie had just walked up to them and had heard, he tapped her nose with his finger. "I couldn't get a pepperoni pizza without Annie, could I?"

"I like pizza," she said. "My frog does, too."

"Everyone likes pizza. Well, except for frogs. I doubt they care for it."

Annie frowned. "You don't think?"

"I think he'd rather have a fly or something, dear." While Annie stewed on that, he raised his gaze, meeting Emma's eyes again. "So, what do you say? Will you and your girls join William and me?"

"Say yes, Mamm," Annie coaxed.

Smiling at her daughter, she nodded. "I would like that. *Danke.*"

After Annie went to go tell the others, she asked, "Do you want to go right now?"

Jay and Emma looked around the yard. William was playing with Lena, Mandy was tossing a tennis ball with a happy beagle, and little Annie was now sitting at the picnic table with her frog. It was a nothing-special kind of day.

It was exactly the kind of day she'd used to take for granted.

"Do you mind if we wait a little bit?" he asked. I would like to simply sit right here."

She pointed to the bucket with Annie's frog in it. "You don't mind sitting here, keeping company with a frog?"

"I would be content to sit with you all afternoon. And four

kinner, and a beagle, and a frog." He shifted, waving a hand in the air. "The *kinner* aren't arguing, the sky is clear, the day is warm. I can't think of any place I'd rather be."

"I agree with you, Jay. Days like this are special. Too special to take for granted."

Ten minutes later, Annie asked, "Jay, what should we name my frog?"

"How about instead of naming him, we let him go?"

She frowned. "But I don't want to."

"That's your decision, but he looks kind of lonely, don'tcha think? He would probably rather be with his frog friends."

Annie stared hard at the frog, then at the grass, then at last at Jay. Then, with a sigh, she held out her hand. "Will you help me put him back?"

"Yep." Over her head, he caught Emma's smile. "Don't move, Em. I'll be right back."

As she watched Jay walk with Annie's hand nestled in his, Emma thought that this was not simply a good day.

It was the best day she'd had in a very long while.

A FEW HOURS LATER, Emma was sure her girls had never been so spoiled. Jay's pockets seemed to be filled to the brim. There was no other explanation for the bounty of food he'd ordered for the six of them.

He'd ordered not one but three pizzas. Three! Then he'd ordered Em some Stixs—Village Pizza's famous breadsticks. And soda!

"The *kinner* are not going to be able to eat all of this," she exclaimed, staring at the plain cheese pizza, the Pinecrafter, and the Veggie Delight all sitting in front of them. "I hate to see you waste your money on so much food."

He laughed. "It's not a waste if they enjoy it. Plus, you forget I've got Ben and Mark. They'll think they've died and gone to heaven when they forage in the refrigerator later tonight."

"I suspect boys are always hungry."

"Always!" William chirped.

"See?" Jay asked. "Now, let us pray and then eat."

Automatically, they bent their heads in silent prayer. Emma gave thanks for the bounty of food, the hands that made it, and her new relationship with Jay and his sons. After everyone raised their heads, Emma and Jay handed out paper plates and plastic utensils. And napkins! Lots and lots of napkins.

Finally, Emma took a slice of veggie pizza for herself, neatly cutting a piece with her fork and knife and savoring her first bite. "It is wonderful."

"It is," he said, amused.

"What are you smiling about?" She grabbed a napkin and pressed it to her lips. "Do I have pizza sauce on me?"

"*Nee.* I was simply thinking how cute it is that you eat a pizza with a fork and knife."

"It's neater that way."

"I'm sure it is," he agreed, just as he folded his pizza in half and took a generous bite.

She laughed. "It would serve you right if pizza sauce spilled on your shirt."

"Since I do the laundry at my *haus*, I guess I'll have to deal with my mistake."

She laughed, enjoying the silly conversation about nothing important. Then froze.

Because right there, walking toward them from the post office, were Sanford's parents, Rachel and Samuel. And they were staring at her with pained expressions.

Immediately, her hands began sweating.

Jay noticed her discomfort. "What's wrong, Emma?"

She shook her head, not trusting herself to try to explain. Instead, she did what she knew was the right thing and stood up. "Hello, Rachel. Good evening, Samuel."

A little bit of the worry eased from Rachel's expression, though it was evident that she was uncomfortable. "Hello, Emma."

"Grandmommi! Dawdi! Hi!" Lena said as she hopped up and ran over to them. Mandy and Annie followed.

As William watched them curiously, Jay got to his feet as well. "I'm guessing these are Sanford's parents?" he asked Emma quietly.

"*Jah.*" She swallowed. "They are nice folk."

"I'm sure they are." He gave her a smile before introducing himself. "Hi, I'm Jay Hilty."

Sanford's parents had always been gracious. Right away Samuel shook hands with him and introduced Rachel. Then Jay found a way to usher the girls back to their places at the table, introduce Sanford's parents to William, and then, to Emma's bemusement, invite Rachel and Samuel to join them!

In the midst of all that, he'd somehow made it obvious that he was important to Emma . . . and that he would not appreciate them being distant or rude to her, especially not in front of her girls.

Though they politely declined his offer to join them for supper, Rachel and Samuel did linger. After eyeing the children all together, Rachel said awkwardly, "Emma's mother told us that she and the girls had been spending time with another family. I'm, uh, glad to know you . . ."

"I'm pleased to know you, too." Jay smiled. "Since we each have three *kinner*, we sometimes tease each other that we have too much in common not to be friends, though of course, our losses are not something we wish others would share."

Samuel exchanged a glance with Rachel who then smiled awkwardly. "I imagine not."

Emma noticed that Samuel was obviously waiting to help Rachel if the conversation became too much. Then, to her surprise, she realized that Jay was doing much the same thing for her. He, too, was being protective. Unable to help herself, she lifted her chin and shared a smile with him.

He squeezed her shoulder as he said, "I know this is hard, but I really would like us all to be friends. Emma has told me how much you both mean to her and the girls."

Rachel's lips parted slightly. "You still want to know us, Emma?"

Emma felt her throat tighten as she suddenly understood her mother-in-law's concerns. "Of course I do, Rachel! I love you and Samuel, and the girls do, too." When she saw that Rachel, too, was trying to hold back her tears, she added softly, "Lena, Mandy, and Annie will always be your grandchildren. They'll also always be Sanford's daughters. I want them to know you both. I want them to grow up hearing stories about their father. Only you two can help me do that." Aware that a tear was now slipping down her cheek, she reached for Rachel's hand. "I promise, you will always have a special place in our hearts. That hasn't changed."

"Our feelings haven't changed, either," Samuel said. "I think we can make this work."

"I think so, too," Rachel said as she clutched Emma's hand. Then, with a sigh, she smiled. "I promise, I am happy for you both."

Emma had never expected such words to come out of her mother-in-law's mouth. "Thank you for saying that."

"It's the truth," Samuel said. "I miss Sanford. I miss him every day. But no amount of prayer or tears is going to bring him back."

"As hard as it is to admit it, we need to move forward," Rachel murmured.

Samuel nodded. "Rachel and I have been talking." Looking at his wife fondly, he said, "She and I have been married for forty years. I can't imagine what life would have been like if one of us had lost the other. I do know that I would never have wanted my wife to spend the majority of her life alone if I had passed on to heaven thirty years ago."

"Plus, those *kinner* need two parents," Rachel said. "They are a handful."

"Would you like to join us?" Emma asked, repeating Jay's earlier offer.

Rachel looked at the empty seats, her eyes cloudy with what Emma recognized as a mixture of hope and hesitation. Emma had felt the same thing when she'd first brought over that meal to Jay's farm but wound up staying several hours.

"You really wouldn't mind?" Rachel asked.

"I would be sad if you didn't want to join us."

"Well, since you have so much pizza laid out, I think sharing it would be the least we could do," Samuel said. "Someone's eyes were a little too big, I think."

"Come sit by William and me, Dawdi," Lena said. "William has kittens. He can tell you all about them."

Samuel winked at Emma. "I was just thinking that I needed to hear about some kittens. Move over, Lena, and hand me one of those paper plates, too."

As Rachel took the chair next to Annie and reached for a slice of cheese pizza, Emma met Jay's gaze. His eyes were filled with patience and understanding, making her realize that she wasn't simply feeling hope; it was something far stronger.

She had just fallen in love for the second time in her life. That was surprising enough in and of itself.

What was even more miraculous was that she didn't feel a single drop of guilt about it.

Chapter 24

*T*oday was the day.

A large white tent stood erect in the back of the Orange Blossom Inn. Inside the voluminous structure lay at least twenty tables and four times that many chairs. The tables, chairs, and even the plywood floor were painted white.

And now, some of Beverly's friends were in the lodging business, too. Winnie and Sadie had graciously taken in some of Tricia's and Ben's relatives. Even the Kaufmann family had opened their spacious home. In fact, it now served as a home base for Edward and Beverly's other siblings and their parents. Other guests from Charm and Walnut Creek were staying at local hotels and inns. It seemed an October wedding in Sarasota, Florida, was an excellent excuse for a weekend getaway.

Or maybe it was the chance to see two young people who had overcome their share of hardships celebrate a most glorious day.

Standing in her kitchen at five in the morning, Beverly wondered how it was possible to feel so tired. And then she recalled just how frenetic the last week had been. She had been entertaining relatives, soothing Tricia's nerves, cooking every spare minute in between . . . and making the most glorious cake.

She'd been working on it for three days now. It was five layers, filled with an orange ganache, and iced with thick buttercream frosting. She'd also made delicate white-chocolate leaves and arranged them on the top around a small bouquet of real, pale orange roses. It was the prettiest cake she'd ever made and it was her gift to Tricia, her way of letting her niece know that she loved her and was genuinely happy for her, too.

But all the cooking and wedding preparations weren't the only cause of her jangling nerves. No, the cause of that had much to do with the man who had arrived yesterday afternoon and been given the best room in the inn.

Eric Wagler—her boss, her friend, her pen pal, her support system—had returned.

She'd known he was coming to the wedding, of course. He'd promised he would, even if his house still hadn't sold. And she'd been slowly learning that Eric kept his promises. No matter what.

Her hands shook as she poured herself another cup of coffee and attempted to tell herself that the trembling had everything to do with too much caffeine consumption. It didn't take but a moment to realize that excuse was a fantasy, for sure.

They'd all been sitting in the living room last night—Tricia and Ben, Jay Hilty, Edward and Kathleen. Frank and Ginny Kaufmann had been there, too, along with Leona and Zack Kaufmann. They'd been laughing at a story Kathleen had told about Tricia when she was a little girl. It seemed sweet, impetuous, energetic Tricia had been fond of mice and was constantly trying to save them.

Since mice and barns were not necessarily a good combination, their barn cats were kept very busy. But one of the barn cats had the unfortunate habit of always, always bringing her catch directly to Tricia. No matter where she was or how the other family members might have praised the cat. And every time, Tricia would squeal and run and cry and insist on a mouse funeral.

"Every. Single. Time," her older sister Kate had said as they'd all laughed.

"Tricia, what are we going to do with our kitten?" Ben asked.

"Hope it's lazy," Kate had said.

Which, of course, had made all of them erupt into even more gales of laughter. Beverly had started crying, she was laughing so hard.

And that was the scene Eric had walked into.

"Eric!" Tricia had said before running over and giving him a welcome hug. "You're just in time to save me."

He'd tossed his green canvas duffel on the ground, cast a concerned glance Beverly's way, then wrapped his arms around Tricia. "Save you? My favorite bride-to-be? What's going on?"

Pulling away, she smiled at Ben and then at her parents. "I'm getting teased about my, um, childish love for mice."

Eric had thrown back his head and laughed like it was the best thing he'd heard in a year. "This is why I couldn't wait to return," he declared. "I missed this place."

Beverly stepped closer to him. "Everyone, this is Eric. Eric Wagler. He's my . . . uh, he's my boss."

Almost immediately, Eric's relaxed smile and look of happiness had vanished, replaced by a shadowed look of concern and then disappointment.

Beverly had known right then and there that it had been a mistake to refer to him as only her boss. He was so much more to her than that. He'd become her friend and confidant, her voice of reason and best encourager.

But in her haste to classify him easily, she'd hurt his feelings.

Now, the next morning, Beverly was wondering how she was ever going to make things right. How did a woman fix a clumsy mistake like that? Holding her cup of coffee, she stared hard at the cake and tried to form the right apology to Eric.

"Hey." His deep voice carried across the room and, just like it did over the phone, gave her a little shiver.

She'd been so consumed with her regrets that she hadn't heard him enter the room. Of course. Because it seemed she was destined to be perpetually awkward around him.

She quickly set her mug down on the counter. "*Gut matin*, Eric," she said, trying not to notice how handsome he looked. His dark hair still seemed to be damp from his shower, and he had put on aftershave. It smelled fresh and tangy and so very appealing.

Too appealing.

"Would, um, would you like some *kaffi*?" Mentally, she berated herself again. Could she be any more apprehensive? Her use of Deutsch was telling, for sure. She used it with him whenever she was nervous or on edge. In today's case, she was both.

His brown eyes remained steady on her. "Yeah. Coffee is good."

She turned to get a cup from the cupboard but he reached it first. "I'm good, Bev," he said quietly. "You know you don't have to wait on me."

"I'm not waiting. I was simply, um . . . trying to make you feel welcome." Of course, the moment she said that, she wished she could take it back. Could she sound any more distant?

His eyes narrowed. "Because I'm your boss?"

His words sounded bitter though his tone was mild. She needed to fix this.

"Eric, I'm sorry," she said in a rush. "Of course, you're much more than simply my boss. We're friends. Of course we are."

"It didn't sound like that last night. I walked into a roomful of laughter and a hug from Tricia but you made me feel like I was about as welcome as a case of the flu."

"I didn't mean to make you feel that way." She hated that whenever he was around she became a person she was definitely not proud of. "I don't know why I told everyone you were my boss."

He set down his cup and turned to her. "I never want to be treated like your boss, Bev," he said quietly as he approached her. "I thought we'd gotten through all that."

"We have." She swallowed as he drew to a stop barely a foot away.

"Are you sure? Or is there something you're confused about?"

"I'm not confused. I mean, we talk to each other all the time."

"Then why are you keeping me at a distance? Why didn't you tell everyone I was your friend? Your very good friend?"

Because she didn't trust their relationship. Because she wasn't completely positive that he wouldn't still change his mind about her and hurt her badly. Because she was thirty-four years old and unable to get over a hurt that it seemed anyone else could have moved on from.

Because he smelled really good and at the moment seemed to be staring at her lips.

But instead of saying any of that, she lied. "I don't know."

He blinked. Then, to both her relief and disappointment, he took a step back. "Oh, okay. Thanks for explaining that to me. I feel a lot better now."

"Eric, I'm sorry." She lifted a hand. Then, as she realized that she'd been just about to press it to his chest, she dropped it back down by her side. And felt her cheeks heat.

He inhaled and a new glint appeared in his eyes. "You know what? It's okay." A hint of a smile appeared on his lips. "Don't worry about it. So, tell me about the day's schedule."

She was so relieved to be talking about something else, she practically chirped. "I can do that. Let's see . . . the wedding starts at nine this morning."

"And when will it be over?"

"Around noon or so."

"So we'll be sitting together for three hours?"

Her pulse started racing again. "*Jah*. It's the way of an old order Amish wedding. It's customary for three preachers to speak."

"All in Pennsylvania Dutch. It's going to be a long morning." He smiled again. "Don't be surprised if I start passing you notes."

She was as taken aback by his teasing as she was by how charmed she realized she'd be if he actually did something like that. "It is a long service, but don't worry, you won't be expected to be there for the whole thing."

"Of course I'm going to be by your side for the whole thing. What would Tricia think?"

She was starting to think that they were talking about more than just Tricia's wedding. "If you'd like, I could simply bring you in for the important parts. It's customary for folks who put on the wedding to come and go. A wedding is a *part* of our lives, you know. It isn't meant to take over everything." Of course, as she said the words she couldn't help but smile. Her little speech was in direct contrast to what had been happening; the wedding had taken over her life for weeks.

"Let's play it by ear, okay?"

Again came the little tingle of awareness she felt every time he gazed at her directly. Suddenly tongue-tied, she simply nodded her head.

Looking satisfied, he glanced at the clock. "It's now five thirty. What do you want to do first?"

"I'll make you some breakfast. Then, how about we start putting out the tablecloths and setting the tables? After that we can start gathering all the food."

"What do you mean, 'start gathering all the food'?"

"Oh, Eric. You have no idea. I've got plates and dishes stashed all over this town. It's going to be a wonder if I can find it all."

He chuckled. "I'll help you gather all you want, Bev. Just tell me where to go and I'll do it."

The tension between them had dissipated and she was so, so relieved. "Thank you."

"You're welcome." After taking another sip of coffee, he asked, "You got any cereal?"

"I do. I have a brand-new box of Cheerios just for you."

"I'll have a quick bowl of cereal, then start on those tables."

"Thank you for helping."

"No worries. I may be your boss, but today you are in charge, Bev."

His warm expression conveyed everything they'd been hinting around for the last few minutes. There was more to them than a simple working relationship. A whole lot more. It made her giddy and a little flustered. Therefore, she said the only thing she could say. "All righty, then. Eat your cereal, then roll up your sleeves. The next four hours are going to be the fastest of your life."

He winked. "Yes, ma'am."

Oh, that wink. "I'm just going to, ah, go get something from my room that I forgot. I'll be right back."

"Take your time, Beverly. I'll still be here when you get back."

And that, of course, was what she was afraid of.

Now that they were together again instead of miles away from each other, Beverly knew it was going to be even harder to ignore her feelings for him. Yes, he was her friend. And yes, he was also her boss. But he was also becoming something else to her—almost her secret crush.

Chapter 25

*J*ay should have realized that it didn't matter how many times he practiced his father-son speech or how many times he prayed for strength and guidance, nothing could completely prepare him for the day his son got married.

He'd woken up at four, said his prayers, and quietly gone about the morning chores: gathering eggs, feeding the cat and kittens, watering the small garden they'd recently planted next to the house. And as he'd done so, he'd wondered where the time had gone. It seemed like Ben had just been a shy boy starting school, then an irritable teenager fending off two younger brothers, and, most recently, a handsome young man with a look of despair in his eyes as he tried to push his grief to one side in order to comfort his brothers.

Through it all, Jay had been proud of him. He'd told him that, too. He'd also made sure Ben had known he was loved.

But this day? This day called for something special to say

about his son. He simply didn't know how to begin. After waking up William and Mark and serving them their breakfast, Jay had sent them back to their rooms to get ready so he could concentrate on what he wanted to say to Ben.

Time was running out and it was making him a nervous wreck.

Just then, Ben entered the kitchen. After pouring himself a cup of coffee, he offered to help with the chores.

"*Nee*, Ben. You have a seat. I, um, made you breakfast."

As Ben sat and ate, Jay couldn't help but notice that his eldest was looking as cool as a cucumber. Almost as if he didn't have a care in the world. How could that be? Had the Lord seen fit to simply lay all the burdens and worries on Jay's shoulders?

"More coffee?" he said when Ben's plate was almost empty.

"I'm good, Daed."

Jay looked at the remains of the breakfast he'd made for him. "More eggs? Piece of sausage?"

"No, thanks. I can't eat another bite."

"Oh."

Ben glanced at him curiously before letting his gaze stray to the pile of dishes on the counter. "I'll help you with the dishes. I don't know where William and Mark are."

"I think they're upstairs getting ready." Actually, Jay knew they were upstairs staying out of the way. Because he'd asked them to give him some time alone with Ben.

Ben looked irritated. "They shouldn't have left us with the dishes. It's Will's turn to do them, too. Want me to go talk to him for you?"

"*Nee.*"

"Daed," he retorted impatiently, "William is not gonna start doing what he's supposed to if you don't—"

"I asked him and Mark to give us some time alone together."

Wariness filled his eyes. "Why?"

"Because it's your wedding day, son. We need to talk."

Ben stared at him like an animal caught in a trap. "What do you want to talk about?"

Here it was. His time to impart something worthwhile. But instead of finally saying everything he needed to, Jay found himself unbuttoning his collar. And then he flushed. "I'm afraid I don't know how to begin. I feel a little awkward, I guess."

Ben looked alarmed. "Listen, uh, Daed. This talk of yours doesn't have anything to do with wedding nights, does it? 'Cause, um, well, I think we're going to be just fine."

Jay's mind went blank. "What?"

Ben stared at him. "Tricia and I will be *fine*, I promise. I don't need your advice on the matter. *Really.*"

It took a moment for Ben's point to sink in. "Oh! Oh, um, no. I wasna thinking about that." Could a grown man ever be more embarrassed? He wasn't sure. "Not that I don't want to talk about such things," he said in a rush. "I mean, if you have any questions . . . I'm sure I could answer them."

Ben was now staring at a point right above Jay's head. "I do not. Not a one."

Jay breathed a sigh of relief. "That's *gut*." But the moment he blurted that, he wondered if it was the right thing to say. "Um. Well, I meant—"

Ben scooted back his chair. "Daed, I think I had better go make sure I've got all of my things gathered together."

"*Nee*. Listen, Ben. I simply wanted to tell you that I'm proud of you."

Ben's head popped up. "What?"

"*Jah*. I don't think I've told you that enough. And though

you're merely moving into an apartment in town and not across the country, I wanted to make sure I told you that I have no doubt you are going to be a husband that Tricia will be proud of. I know this because you already are a man I am proud of."

"*Danke.*"

Jay heard the new rasp of emotion in Ben's voice and breathed a sigh of relief. He wasn't messing everything up. "I know you and Tricia are going to be fine. And I know you don't need me offering advice about, um, anything . . . but I wanted to share with you something that I've learned that you might feel is useful."

"Yes?"

"When you choose to share a life with another person, one finds out all sorts of things about themselves, and about his bride. Some of it is wonderful. And some of it might take some getting used to. But whatever you do, please don't take it for granted. Not the days when everything goes right, or the days when everything goes wrong. Don't spend any time hoping something passes or wishing it hadn't happened. Try to remember that your time together is a gift, son. A beautiful, amazing gift that was bestowed on you both. Do . . . Do you think you can do that?"

Ben's expression had turned soft. "*Jah*, Daed. I can. I can try."

"If you even try, that's all that matters. I will be praying for you, son. I will be praying for both of you. Because I love you."

"I love you, too, Daed." After a pause, he whispered, "I loved Mamm, too."

"She knew you did."

"You sure?"

"Very much so. Who do you think gave me that advice to give to you?" he asked with a watery smile. "She knew our life together was a blessing to us all."

Ben stood up and clasped his arms around Jay, hugging him

tight. "*Danke*, Daed. I'm glad we talked."

"Me, too," he murmured when he was alone in the room again. He was also mighty glad that talk was over.

It was happening! They were getting married!

As she sat next to Penny Knoxx and faced the men on the other side of the aisle, Tricia knew that she had never been so happy. Here she was, wearing the traditional blue dress with a white apron and black *kapp*, minutes away from exchanging vows. Across from her sat Ben. He was wearing his wedding finery, too. She thought he looked handsome in his white shirt, dark navy vest, and dark pants. Due to the heat and humidity, he'd rolled up his sleeves about an hour ago. At the moment, he was resting his elbows on his knees and staring directly at her.

As the preacher continued to talk about trust, respect, love, and duty, they shared a smile.

Tricia remembered a friend had told her long ago that Amish weddings were a lesson in patience. She had thought the comment had been simply irreverent at the time, but now she understood what her girlfriend had meant. It took all her years of self-discipline to sit patiently while three preachers spoke about marriage and relayed stories from the Bible. The three-hour service was lovely and meaningful.

And, Tricia thought, rather long.

She was jarred from her musings when the preacher cleared his throat, and Penny Knoxx gave her a little nudge. "It's time, Tricia," she whispered.

She wiped her palms and breathed in. Finally, it was time to say their vows.

When they were directed to stand up, Penny squeezed her hand. Tricia's heart started racing as the preacher recited several verses from First Corinthians. Tricia stepped closer to Ben and took comfort from his warm expression. Then, as carefully as possible, she repeated the promises the preacher spoke about. She promised to love and cherish and obey and care for Ben in good times and bad. And in sickness and in health. And when he did the same, it suddenly felt as if they were the only two people standing under the tent.

She forgot about all the people gathered with them. All that mattered was Ben and the way he was looking at her—as though she was the most special thing in his life. She knew that look well, because she was feeling the same way.

At last she was Tricia Hilty. At last she was no longer alone.

AN HOUR LATER, AS Tricia looked around at her sisters and parents and Aunt Beverly, at Ben's family and all the friends she'd made during her short time in Pinecraft, she knew she had never been happier.

In fact, the only thing that would make her any happier would be if she and Ben were finally alone. But that wouldn't be for hours. Most likely, not until the sun began setting on the horizon.

As she walked around and greeted everyone, thanking them for coming and accepting gifts, she kept finding herself looking for Ben across the way. They'd had a few moments to sit down by themselves, but after that, they'd been pulled in opposite directions. Every time she thought there might be a break, someone needed something else. Though she didn't mind it too much. Everyone was so welcoming and seemed to enjoy their story. Apparently, no one was immune to tales of couples falling in love practically at first sight.

After leaving a group of ladies, Tricia was ready to sit quietly for a few minutes, but then she saw Emma Keim sitting by herself.

"Do you mind if I join you?" Tricia asked.

"I would love to sit with you. I'm very pleased to see you looking so happy."

"*Danke.* It's a wonderful day."

"Indeed it is."

"Did it make you a little sad?"

"Remembering my wedding day?" She shook her head. "This may sound bad, but no. My Sanford and I had a wonderful wedding day, and I enjoyed it very much." Smiling softly, she said, "Goodness. Our wedding was the culmination of years and years of waiting. I was so eager to marry Sanford at last, I don't think anything could have dimmed my joy. I count myself fortunate that I can look back on things without regrets."

Tricia knew what she meant. "Though Ben and I had a whirlwind romance, I feel the same way. I couldn't be happier today."

"It was a lovely marriage service, Tricia, and this is a beautiful reception, too." Emma waved a hand. "I love this tent. I love how everything is white except for all the flowers. It smells like heaven in here!"

"I agree! I can't imagine having a prettier wedding or reception. Beverly outdid herself."

"I saw her and her boss, Eric, talking about an hour ago. They're funny together."

Tricia laughed. "That's a *gut* way to describe it. They are constantly, *constantly* bickering. It's funny. I am really glad he came."

"For an outsider, he sure seems to know a lot of people. I saw him speaking to Michael and Penny Knoxx."

"I think he likes to get to know people. I know he's anxious to move back here. He's waiting for his house in Pennsylvania to sell."

Emma frowned. "I wish him all the best with that."

"So, I saw you and Jay sitting together during the service."

She smiled softly. "The *kinner* like sitting together."

"Yes, I noticed that." She'd also noticed that Jay and Emma liked sitting together, too. "I'm glad your families have become close."

"Me, too. I—" Her eyes got wide, then she bolted to her feet. "Oh, no," Emma moaned under her breath.

On her feet as well, Tricia turned to where Emma was staring, and gasped. "Oh!"

Somehow Emma's beagle had barged in and was trotting through the maze of tables as if he were in a race. Tricia hadn't known he could move that fast.

And then she saw where he was headed.

"Frankie!" Emma called out. "Frankie, *nee!*" she yelled again as she darted through the crowd, practically knocking over a pair of toddlers in her haste to get to the beautiful five-tiered wedding cake that Beverly had spent almost every spare moment on.

On the other side of the tent, Tricia saw Aunt Beverly stiffen at the sound of Emma's cry. Then they both stood frozen in horror as one forty-five pound beagle scrambled up onto a white folding chair, paused to gain his balance, then hopped onto the table where the cake was waiting—and took a huge bite.

Tricia was so shocked, she could only watch in dismay.

"Frankie, *nee!*" Emma shrieked, reaching the cake table.

The shriek startled the dog, which caused him to topple to the ground . . . along with all five layers.

As the entire crowd stared in stunned silence, the beagle began furiously devouring white wedding cake with orange filling and buttercream frosting like it was the most delicious thing on the earth. Which it probably was.

Frankie had struck again.

Chapter 26

*E*mma had married at eighteen, then given birth to three children and buried her husband. She'd mourned, taken care of her girls without complaint, and had even recently stood up to her parents when the situation warranted it. She took care of her house, paid the bills, and now was raising three little girls on her own.

Because of all this, she secretly prided herself on the fact that she could handle almost any situation with calm and patience.

But none of those things had prepared her for the humiliation of having to detach her dog from the remains of what was once a stunning, five-layered wedding cake.

"Come, Frankie," she hissed under her breath.

Frankie—whether it was because he was on the verge of a diabetic coma or he somehow knew that he'd finally crossed the line and was in danger of being given away to anyone who would take him—walked obediently by her side through the crowd.

Every single guest stepped aside as she passed, though Emma had no idea if that was because she was now a pariah or because Frankie was covered in sticky white frosting. All she did know was that she was never going to be able to look Beverly Overholt in the eye again.

"Girls!" she called out as she walked. "Girls, we need to go. Now."

Ben walked toward her. "Hey, um, Emma—"

Though it was one of the hardest things she'd ever done in her life, Emma made herself stop and meet his gaze. "Please tell Tricia I'm sorry. I am so very sorry."

"It's okay."

"It's most definitely not okay." Then Emma reached down, grabbed hold of Frankie's collar, and guided him out of the tent before she burst into tears or Frankie decided to go in search of leftovers.

"Mamm!" Lena said. "I've got Mandy and Annie."

Turning around to see that all three of her girls actually were there, she nodded. "Let's go home."

Mandy ran forward to open Beverly's back gate. "And then we'll come back to the party after we put Frankie up?"

"*Nee*. We will not be coming back." As soon as Annie stepped through, she said, "Annie, don't forget to shut the gate."

"All right, Mommy," she replied in a sad little voice.

"Mommy, we're not really going to stay home, are we?" Mandy asked.

"We really are."

Lena rushed to her other side. "But, Mamm . . ."

"Not right now, Lena." Emma was fairly sure if she didn't

get home soon she was going to start bawling like a baby in the middle of the street.

"But Mamm, I wanna go back," Lena whined. "Two girls I met at school are there. We were having fun."

"I am glad, but we are staying home."

Mandy pulled on her apron. "How come we have to stay home?" she asked, her tone turning belligerent. "We didn't do anything wrong."

"Because I said so."

"But—"

"Not another word, Mandy."

Immediately, Mandy quieted. Looking for Annie, Mandy grabbed her hand and started leading the way down the street. After a pause, Lena followed her. Tired of bending over to hold Frankie's collar, Emma hefted him in her arms. Frankie squirmed uncomfortably then snuggled close, as if he was grateful for the ride.

She was so ashamed. She should have given the dog away years ago. She should have been harsher to him, maybe. Meaner. Something to have made him mind better. And that was what she was going to have to do. Tomorrow, she was going to take Frankie to the pound.

After two seconds passed, she sighed. Oh, who was she kidding? She could never give her sweet, silly dog away. He curled up next to the girls when they were reading or sad. He slept next to each of them every night. And after their father had died, he'd let them cry all over him for hours without complaint. She loved this silly, ill-mannered dog. Loved him completely. And he loved them, too. It was simply a real shame that he managed to ruin lots and lots of meals.

"Mommy, how do you think Frankie got out this time?"

"I guess he dug himself another hole."

"It's good he found us, though. Ain't so?" Annie added helpfully. "We don't want him lost."

She was wondering how to answer when she heard someone jogging toward them.

"Emma, girls, slow down, wouldja?" Jay asked.

Her heart in her throat, Emma turned and watched him approach, bracing herself for his anger. After all, she'd just single-handedly ruined his son's wedding day. When he stayed silent as he closed the gap between them, she decided to get her apology over with.

"Jay, I'm so sorry. I really am so embarrassed. I don't know how to apologize enough."

His gaze softened. "There's nothing to apologize for."

"Yes there is! I ruined Ben and Tricia's wedding."

"*Nee*, Frankie ruined the cake." When Frankie yelped in her arms, he shook his head. "Put him down, Em. I'll deal with him now."

"But he might run off—"

"I'll make sure he doesn't. Set him down, dear," he murmured. "Girls, why don't you go on ahead? We'll be right there."

Once the girls were on their way, Jay helped Emma set Frankie on the ground. Then, after giving the silly dog a pet, he snapped his fingers. "Come on, Frankie."

To Emma's amazement, Frankie lumbered forward. He was, no doubt, feeling awful.

She grimaced. "He's going to be so sick tonight."

"I'm afraid he will." His lips twitched. "He ate a lot of cake."

"He did. In mere seconds, too."

"It was impressive. He practically inhaled it. People will no doubt be talking about his display for years to come."

The tears that she'd been holding at bay pricked the corners of her eyes. "I feel so bad about this."

"Don't feel bad. It was only cake."

As they approached her house, she saw all three of her girls sitting on the front steps, each one looking more dejected than the last.

"What's wrong with them?"

"They are upset that we had to leave the wedding. They'll be all right."

"Sure they will." Reaching for her hand, Jay said, "Please stop worrying. I heard Eric tell Beverly he was going to run over to Yoder's and buy a bunch of pies. No one is going to go hungry."

That made her feel slightly better. "At least no one will miss dessert."

"I promise you, the only people we need to make happy are Tricia and Ben. And I promise, they are. I can almost pretty much assure you that the last thing they're thinking about is dessert."

Emma figured Jay had a point. She and Sanford had only been thinking about each other on their wedding day. After taking a deep breath, she looked at him curiously. "Why are you here? You better hurry back to the reception. Ben might need you."

"I will. I just wanted to make sure you were okay."

"I will be." She summoned up a watery smile.

"Why don't you come back, too?"

"Jay, I can't. There's no way I can face everyone right now."

They were at the house now. After guiding Frankie inside, Jay turned back to Emma. "Of course you've got to go back. Everyone's waiting for you. And I don't want to go back without you, Em."

"I'm so embarrassed. Frankie ruined everything." And then, to her horror, those tears finally started to fall. And then she started crying. Really crying.

"Mommy?" Annie rushed forward. "Mommy, what's wrong?"

Before Emma could reply, Jay took control. "Girls, go inside and get Frankie some water. I'll take care of your mother."

The moment they were in the house, Jay pulled Emma into his arms.

At first she was too surprised to do anything but freeze, but then her body gave in and she rested her head on his chest with a sigh. Jay felt solid and strong, warm and protective. And for a minute she imagined that she would be very happy standing in his embrace for the rest of her days. Little by little, she let her muscles relax. Giving a small sigh, she cuddled closer. She couldn't remember the last time she'd leaned on another person for support.

All she knew was that it had been a very, very long time.

Though she heard the girls talking to each other in the kitchen and knew she should step away, she wrapped her arms around his waist and held on. Just for a moment or two longer.

Still holding her close, Jay ran a path along her spine with his fingers. "I promise, everything is going to be okay. No one is mad at you."

"Ben and Tricia—"

"Are perfectly fine. But they won't be if you and the girls don't come back."

"That's sweet, but—"

He leaned back so their eyes could meet. "Do you understand, Emma? We aren't fine without you, Lena, Mandy, and Annie. We want you there. Frankie, on the other hand, can stay home."

She swiped at her eyes. "I don't know . . ."

"I think you actually *do* know," he said gently. "Don't you understand what I'm talking about? What this means?"

"Jay—"

"I'm trying to say that life is better with you in it."

"Even if I ruin things?"

"Especially if you do. Or if I do. Or any of us does." Smiling, he added, "Emma, between us we've got six *kinner*, eight grandparents, and two spouses in heaven. Things are going to get messy. Things are going to be noisy. Things are going to be imperfect and crazy and full of surprises. We're going to be late, the house is sometimes going to be messy, and things are going to get ruined. But because of all that, it's going to be wonderful."

She looked at him in wonder. "You really mean that, don't you?"

"Of course I do. In one year's time, I want to be back at this Orange Blossom Inn saying vows to you. My boys are going to be there, and your girls are going to be so happy, and Frankie is going to have his own bone and be leashed. And perhaps, if we say enough prayers, the good Lord will keep Frankie out of trouble for a solid six hours."

"Six hours?"

"That's all the time we would need, Emma. Just long enough to enjoy our day and get a chance to taste our wedding cake."

She giggled. "And if Frankie still gets loose?"

His expression softened. "You know the answer, Emma. If we can't have cake, we'll simply have pie."

When he smiled, she did, too. And she realized that he was exactly right. Life was unpredictable and things didn't always happen how one hoped they would.

But that didn't mean one had to roll into a ball and mourn forever.

"I can't give up Frankie. If it wasn't for him, I wouldn't have you."

Leaning forward, Jay kissed her lightly on the lips. "Put that way, he's my favorite beagle in the whole world. Now, let's go get those girls and return to the party. I don't know if you've heard, but there's a pretty big wedding going on over at the Orange Blossom Inn."

"I did hear," she replied as she clasped his hand with a smile. "I heard it's the most exciting wedding in town."

About the author

About the book

Insights,
Interviews
& More...

Read on

Meet Shelley Shepard Gray

PEOPLE OFTEN ASK how I started writing. Some believe I've been a writer all my life; others ask if I've always felt I had a story I needed to tell. I'm afraid my reasons couldn't be more different. See, I started writing one day because I didn't have anything to read.

I've always loved to read. I was the girl in the back of the classroom with her nose in a book, the mom who kept a couple of novels in her car to read during soccer practice, the person who made weekly visits to the bookstore and the library.

Back when I taught elementary school, I used to read during my lunch breaks. One day, when I realized I'd forgotten to bring something to read, I turned on my computer and took a leap of faith. Feeling a little like I was doing something wrong, I typed those first words: *Chapter One.*

I didn't start writing with the intention of publishing a book. Actually, I just wrote for myself.

For the most part, I still write for myself, which is why, I think, I'm able to write so much. I write books that I'd like to read. Books that I would have liked to have in my old teacher tote bag. I'm always relieved and surprised and so happy when other people want to read my books, too!

Another question I'm often asked is why I choose to write inspirational fiction.

Maybe at first glance, it does seem surprising. I'm not the type of person who usually talks about my faith in the line at the grocery store or when I'm out to lunch with friends. For me, my faith has always felt like more of a private thing. I feel that I'm still on my faith journey—still learning and studying God's word.

And that, I think, is why writing inspirational fiction is such a good fit for me. I enjoy writing about characters who happen to be in the middle of their faith journeys, too. They're not perfect, and they don't always make the right decisions. Sometimes they make mistakes, and sometimes they do something they're proud of. They're characters who are a lot like me.

Only God knows what else He has in store for me. He's given me the will and the ability to write stories to glorify Him. He's put many people in my life who are supportive and caring. I feel blessed and thankful . . . and excited to see what will happen next! ❧

Letter from the Author

Dear Reader,

Many of you know my husband and I have Butch and Suzy, two very spoiled dachshunds. What some of you might not know is that long before we had Butch and Suzy, we had a sweet beagle named Phoebe! We got her soon after my kids started school. Almost immediately, she became the center of our household. Beagles are naturally gentle dogs who like being with children. Our Phoebe was no exception. She became my children's tag partner and hiking buddy. Their favorite cuddle companion and all-around best friend.

Phoebe was a great dog. However, she wasn't perfect. She had a terrible fondness for pizza. And ham. And eggs. And anything else she wasn't supposed to have. In the blink of an eye, she would go from steadfast companion to stealth pizza thief. Whenever there was a particularly tasty-looking snack (and for Phoebe, this was all food), she hopped on chairs, climbed on tables, and nosed her way inside closed cabinets. Once, when she had a torn ACL, she got up on her hind legs and pulled down two large pizza boxes. She then wolfed down the entire contents, all in under ten minutes. It was remarkable.

About four years ago, soon after she turned sixteen, Phoebe passed away. Her death left a huge gap in our family. And, well, it was almost a full year before we ordered another pizza to be delivered. Funny how the things that used to drive us crazy became the things we missed the most!

I was delighted to feature a naughty beagle named Frankie in this book. Though I truly loved writing about two likable people and their six *kinner*, you might have gotten the impression that my heart belonged to that beagle. I guess enough time had finally passed to remember how perfect that imperfect dog had been for us.

So if you, like me, have ever had a pet who wasn't perfect but claimed your heart just the same, this book is for you. I hope you enjoyed *A Wedding at the Orange Blossom Inn*, my ode to *The Brady Bunch*, and my tribute to one very sweet, very hungry beagle.

Thank you for picking up the book!

With blessings and my best,
Shelley Shepard Gray

PS. I love to hear from readers, either on Facebook, through my website, or through the postal system! If you'd care to write and tell me what you thought of the book, please do!

Shelley Shepard Gray
10663 Loveland Madeira Rd. #167
Loveland, OH 45140

Questions for Discussion

1. The theme of renewal and rebirth is highlighted in each book in this series. In this novel, the focus is on two people who have already found love once before. What obstacles do you think they might have had to overcome that someone who isn't a widow might not?

2. Why do you think Jay needed to move to Florida in order to be happy? Was that fair to his boys? How do you think they would have coped if they had stayed in Ohio?

3. There were a lot of characters and a lot of relationships to explore when writing this novel—romances between Emma and Jay and Tricia and Ben, as well as new bonds forming between all of the kids and their parents. Which relationship appealed most to you?

4. Beverly Overholt is a central character in the series. How have you seen her grow and change throughout the first three books?

5. I loved the Amish proverb I found to guide me while writing: "It takes both sunshine and rain to make a rainbow." I thought it worked well for Emma and Jay. How might it be applied to your life?

6. I used a verse from Psalm 119 while writing the novel. "Your word is a lamp to guide my feet and light for my path." How has God's word guided you? Has there ever been a time when you didn't listen?

7. I can only imagine what problems Jay and Emma might encounter when they become parents to six children! What do you think will be some of their surprising

blessings? What do you think they might find to be an obstacle?

8. Finally, Frankie the beagle had my heart from the moment he first appeared in the novel. Do you have a pet? How has that pet enriched your life? ❧

Cranberry Orange Bread

1 cup fresh cranberries, chopped
½ cup sugar
1 teaspoon orange zest
1¾ cups flour
2½ teaspoons baking powder
¾ teaspoon salt
1 egg, beaten
¼ cup orange juice
½ cup milk
⅓ cup vegetable oil

Preheat oven to 400°F. Mix cranberries, sugar, and orange zest. Set aside. Sift together flour, baking powder, and salt in a large bowl. In a separate bowl, combine egg, orange juice, milk, and vegetable oil. Add to dry ingredients, stirring until just moistened. Fold in cranberry mixture. Put in greased bread pan and bake 30 to 35 minutes or until done. Serve warm.

(from Mrs. Perry [Susan] Miller, Sarasota, Florida)

Taken from Simply Delicious Amish Cooking *by Sherry Gore. Copyright © 2012 by Sherry Gore. Used with permission of Zondervan. www.zondervan.com* ∿

Shelley's Top Five Must-See Spots in Pinecraft

HONESTLY, I fell in love with everything about the tiny village of Pinecraft, nestled in the heart of Sarasota and nearby Siesta Key! Here are five places to start your journey:

1. *Yoder's Restaurant.* I've been to a lot of Amish restaurants. I've eaten a lot of coconut cream pie at each one. But nothing has compared to this well-known restaurant. The line to get in is always long, usually at least a thirty-minute wait. But the long lines allow everyone to chat and make friends.

2. *The Produce Market at Yoder's.* The market next to Yoder's is full of beautiful Florida-fresh produce. We couldn't resist picking up two pints of strawberries and five oranges. Just to snack on—in between servings of pie, of course!

3. *Pinecraft Park.* It's the social center of the community! The night we were there, kids were playing basketball, men and women were playing shuffleboard (women have their own lane), and there were at least another forty or fifty people standing around and visiting.

4. *The bus parking lot.* Behind the post office is a large parking lot where everyone meets to either board one of the Pioneer Trails buses or to watch who is arriving and leaving.

5. *Village Pizza.* It's located right behind Olaf's Creamery. You can order a pie and take it right over to one of the picnic tables outside. The pizza is delicious. Eating pizza outside in the sunshine in February in the Florida sun? Priceless.

Scenes from Pinecraft

Photographs courtesy of Katie Troyer, Sarasota, Florida

The Pioneer Trails bus arrives in Pinecraft.

Siblings and friends at Big Olaf in Pinecraft.

Enjoying a Song Fest at Pinecraft Park.

Playing bocce in Pinecraft Park.

A Sneak Peek from the Final Book in the Amish Brides of Pinecraft Series, *A Christmas Bride in Pinecraft*

Coming Fall 2015 from Avon Inspire

BEVERLY OVERHOLT froze in shock the moment she turned the corner onto her street and spotted the pulsing red and blue lights in front of the Orange Blossom Inn. Lights that looked at first like the Christmas decor that lit some of her English neighbors' houses, trees, and shrubs.

Then reality set in. The lights weren't Christmas decorations. They were coming from the three police cars that were parked at the curb in front of the inn.

Immediately, instinctually, Beverly started praying.

The prayers continued as she started forward on the sidewalk, asking the Lord to give her strength to handle whatever had just happened at the lovely three-story Victorian that was not only her place of business but had also become her home.

And though those prayers were undoubtedly giving her some strength, one thing was becoming very apparent. Even the Lord's help wasn't going to make her calm, cool, or collected. No. She was on the verge of turning into a nervous wreck.

Unable to tear her gaze from the large crowd gathered in front of the inn, she picked up her pace, racing past all of her neighbors' houses without a scant look at their merry decorations.

She was quickly winded, and even the canvas bag on her shoulder had started to feel like it weighed a hundred pounds. All the Christmas gifts she'd bought that morning now felt like heavy burdens. To make matters worse, the tote kept painfully thumping against her hip with each step.

And when it wasn't clashing with her hip, it felt as if it was attempting to pull her arm from her shoulder. She was tempted to drop it on the ground and simply pick it up later.

Just as she stopped, prepared to divest herself from that bag, her best friend snatched it from her hands.

"I've got this, Beverly," Sadie said in that forthright way of hers. "You go on ahead."

"*Danke*," she murmured, reverting to Pennsylvania Dutch, as was her way when she was anxious. "Do you know what's happened?"

"*Nee.* I just noticed the police lights a moment ago. You go on ahead. I'll bring this bag inside and meet up with you." She reached out and grabbed Beverly's arm as she started forward. "Oh, and do try not to panic, dear. Just because you see a couple of police cars parked in front of the inn, it don't necessarily mean that there's something wrong."

If her heart didn't feel like it had permanently lodged itself in her windpipe, Beverly would have stopped and given her best friend a look of pure disbelief.

Of course something was wrong! She felt it as surely as if there were loudspeakers lining the street, proclaiming the truth of it.

Something mighty terrible had happened at the inn.

In the three years that she'd lived in Pinecraft, Beverly had never seen such police presence. This was a safe community. Peaceful.

Well, until now.

Luckily, her friend's words of wisdom enabled her to refocus. Falling apart now wouldn't help anything and would serve only to make things worse. She had to be strong.

Picking up her stride, she walked into the gathered crowd, then abruptly drew to a stop when the inn finally came into full view.

What a sight it was!

One of the windows was broken, the front door was wide open, uniformed officers were scattered around the lot, and yellow police tape kept the onlookers at bay.

As she looked from one officer to another, panic set in. She couldn't determine who to approach.

She continued to scan the crowd for familiar faces, for anyone to give her some indication about what had happened. Most folks, unfortunately, merely looked shocked.

Then she spied Zack Kaufmann. She'd gotten to know him and his family well a couple of months ago when he'd been courting one of her guests. "Zack?" she called out as she made her way over to him.

He stepped forward. "There you are! The police have been waiting for you." ▶

A Sneak Peek from the Final Book in Shelley's Amish Brides of Pinecraft Series, *A Christmas Bride in Pinecraft* (continued)

She pressed her lips together to keep them from trembling, drew in a shaky breath, then said, "Zack, what happened? Do you know anything?"

"As far as I can tell, it looks like you've had a break-in."

"A break-in?" It didn't even make sense. She'd never heard of any sort of crime happening in Pinecraft. Why, some people always left their doors and windows unlocked!

Zack looked as if he was attempting to figure out a way to reassure her, when he spied someone approaching from behind her. "Oh, *gut*," he murmured. "Officer Roberts, this here is Beverly Overholt. She owns the inn."

"Runs," Beverly absently corrected. Until recently, she'd believed she'd owned the inn. Now she knew that Eric Wagler was the actual owner. She just managed it for him.

Immediately, a new dread coursed through her. Oh, how was she going to tell Eric what had happened? And when she did, what was he going to say? Would he blame her for being careless?

"Miss Overholt, are you all right?" Officer Roberts asked. "You're looking a bit pale."

With a shake of her head, Beverly made herself focus back on the scene in front of her. Pulling her shoulders back, she strengthened her resolve. "I'm all right."

"Sure?" he held out a hand, as if he feared she was about to collapse at his feet.

"Positive. However, I will admit to feeling mighty confused. What in the world has happened?"

"You had a break-in, ma'am."

"I see." She'd been hoping Zack was wrong, but as the officer confirmed it, she felt slightly ill as visions of what that meant settled in her brain. Someone uninvited had entered her home. Most likely had stolen from her. Had obviously damaged the place if the window was any indication.

Zack grabbed ahold of her arm. "Easy now, Miss Beverly."

"Yes. Let's go sit down," Officer Roberts said. Snapping his fingers, he called out, "Hey, Morris? Is the front room clear?"

"Yep, we're good."

The policeman lightly rested a hand on her shoulder. "Come with me, Miss Overholt. We'll go sit inside and I'll fill you in on what we know." Looking at Zack, he said, "Do you want to join her?"

Zack nodded. "For sure. Give me a minute and I'll bring over my fiancée, Leona, as well."

Beverly sighed with gratitude as Zack trotted off. She didn't particularly want to sit with the policeman by herself. And though Zack and Leona were both only in their early twenties, she considered them both to be good friends.

Zack paused. "Bev, want me to bring Miss Sadie in, too?"

Noticing that Sadie was now crying uncontrollably, Beverly shook her head. "*Nee.* She has my tote bag, but I, um, would rather it just be the four of us for now."

"Gotcha. I'll grab the bag from Sadie, then Leona and I will be right there."

"*Danke,* Zack."

Beverly followed Officer Roberts up the front stairs of the inn. For the first time in memory, she wasn't looking at the pretty flower beds she'd spent hours tending or the colorful welcome mat directly in front of the door. She wasn't feeling pride about the neat and attractive way she kept the inn. Instead, she was noticing the broken glass littering the porch and the scratches surrounding the frame of the front door.

But then, as she crossed the threshold, Beverly couldn't refrain from gasping. The main gathering room was in complete disarray. Furniture had been knocked over; her pretty framed prints were off the walls and lying in pieces on the floor. One of her prized hurricane lamps had been shattered.

"Ack! Oh, but this is terrible." Tears pricked her eyes. "Who would do such a thing?"

Officer Roberts looked just as dismayed as she felt. "I'm sorry, Miss Overholt, but I have no idea."

"Beverly. Please call me Beverly."

"Oh, my goodness," Leona whispered as she came in with Zack. After a brief pause, she reached for Beverly's hand. "Let's sit down."

Beverly did as Leona suggested and squeezed her friend's hand as Officer Roberts perched on the edge of the chair across from her and fidgeted, as if he was extremely uncomfortable.

"Beverly, I've learned that in cases like this, it's best to be blunt. Two hours ago, we got a call from a neighbor that she'd noticed one of your front windows was broken and that things didn't look right. We drove by to check things out, and saw that the front door was cracked open. We entered, but whoever did this was long gone. Do you have any current guests?"

"*Nee.* I don't have any guests right now." At Eric's urging, she'd given herself a week's vacation. Why had she done that? If she hadn't left the inn, no one would have dared to come inside.

Or had someone been watching the inn? Had they known it was empty? It was such a disconcerting thought that she couldn't bear to dwell on it.

"Good to know." He punched something in his phone, then continued. "I'm sorry to tell you that the majority of the inn looks like this room. Whoever was here spent a lot of time causing extensive damage."

"I wonder why." The destruction all seemed so unnecessary.

"We'll do our best to find out, ma'am. But in the meantime, when ▶

**A Sneak Peek from the Final Book in
Shelley's Amish Brides of Pinecraft Series,
*A Christmas Bride in Pinecraft*** (continued)

you're ready, we need you to walk through the inn and tell me what you notice missing." He continued talking about fingerprints and motives, police reports and pawnshops.

But Beverly was done listening. She really couldn't take any more. Someone had ruined her livelihood, stolen her belongings. She felt as betrayed and dismayed as she had when she'd discovered her fiancé had fallen in love with her best friend all those years ago. And angry. She was so angry.

Taking a deep breath, she tried to push those thoughts away. This wasn't the time to examine those painful wounds.

"Are you going to be all right?" Zack asked. "Do you want me to get you a glass of water or something?"

"I'm fine," she said at last, and tried to mean it.

Because she had no choice.

"Your insurance should cover the damage," Zack said quickly, as though thinking that not having to worry about financial repercussions would ease her mind. It didn't, though.

Insurance could never replace the most valuable thing the burglar had stolen today— her sense of security.

"Do you want me to call Eric for ya?" Leona offered. "I don't mind."

She looked at Leona and shook her head. "*Nee.* I'll do it."

"Who's Eric?" the officer asked.

Beverly said, "He's the owner of the inn." During the last few months, he'd also somehow become the best friend she'd ever had. ⮌

D iscover great authors, exclusive offers, and more at hc.com.